*Caroline Nesbitt*

# RIDE ON THE CURL'D CLOUDS

**Epona Books**
*North Sandwich, NH*

*Ride On The Curl'd Clouds* is entirely a work of fiction. Any resemblance to any person living or dead is entirely coincidental, accidental, and without basis in fact.

If you enjoy this book and would like more copies, please enclose $19.00 per copy (includes shipping and handling) to the Author:

Caroline Nesbitt
P.O. Box 52
North Sandwich, NH 03259

Discounts are available on multiple copies. Thanks for reading!

ISBN 978-0-578-02384-7

# ONE

*Vouchsafe, thou wonder, to alight thy steed*
*And rein his proud head to the saddle-bow,*
*If thou wilt deign this favour, for thy meed*
*A thousand honey secrets shalt thou know.*
- William Shakespeare, ***Venus and Adonis***

Tension shimmered like vapor over the collecting ring. Some riders chewed lips and mentally rode every fence for the thousandth time. Some walked gleaming, muscular horses in figure eights and focused on an elusive inner well of calm. The crowd buzzed and rippled in the vast blackness beyond the brilliant lights that drenched the jumping arena. Under the lights the arena was an emerald billiard table littered with fences made of candy-striped rails, evergreen bushes, walls painted to look like Roman aquifers or stone or brick, or plastered with the giant logos of luxury cars and watchmakers, rimmed with flowers, all carnival colors and designs. Horses and riders galloped at them like thunder, sailed over them like giant birds of prey, chuffed hot breath like dragons. There were combinations set only one or two strides apart, fences set off corners or aimed frighteningly straight at the throbbing crowd, a last narrow gate just begging to be overshot if the rider's control failed for one split fraction of a second. When hooves hit the rails they tumbled like checkered matchsticks on the turf and the crowd's groan was enough to make me faint.

*Unforgiving*, the word came back from tired riders trotting out of the gate on steaming horses; warriors defeated by the jumps, the turns, the clock. *Rewards the adjustable horse.*

And the courageous; maybe the courageous most of all.

There were seven of us left to go. Scores lit the board like a pinball machine and I perspired nausea while Harry Daly went clean and very fast amid shrieks and thunderous applause but then a splintering crash and gasps followed as Hilary Knowlton fell. Hilary, walking out nursing an arm, rippling applause acknowledging her nerve, Harry Daly's brave young grey Holsteiner horse stalking beside her and thank God not discernibly lame, lucky because Harry was looking for major cash for that horse. My best friend Ivory Gardner next, clear though slow with big brown Memphis who flew over fences like a raptor, like an eagle, the crowd wild with delight because they always loved Ivory and Memphis...

...And then my turn.

'Breathe', hissed Ivory as we passed at the gate. *Slow and careful*, I whispered like a mantra. *Please God let the rails stay up.*

The crowd muttered and shimmered like the sea. Jake fidgeted underneath me and pulled hard against hand and leg, the fences as big as himself. As open horses go, he's a midget, not enough size or stride to do this stuff, but nobody ever thought to tell him that. His muscles bunched and ready, we cruised the edge of the arena at a balanced canter, picked up the pace through the center, shot through the timers to the first fence, the powerful jolt as he surged forward then launched himself up and over, *steady, Jake* sharp left to the big square oxer *punched* for a big ground-eating stride and powerful leap, I stretched from the waist out of the saddle balanced in heels in straining calf and stomach muscles chin to his neck as he soared and underneath an ocean of rails redwhitegreen halfway over he kicked for that extra inch, rattled the rail and I heard the crowd gasp but it stayed up. Sharp *turn right* to the triple combination that looked like a vibrating maze of impenetrable color, *stea-ady* for the first, up and over, pushed hard for that long stride and soared *over* the second *Git, JAKE!* for two strides even longer, flung himself into the air with a grunt and we were airborne for days, landed heavy, shock of concussion through my ankles and knees, galloped deep into the corner for the giant liverpool, Jake blasted off, folded his legs like Pegasus, soared again, landed hard *umphh*, our breath coming heavy in time with his gallop *chuffchuffchuff* and here too fast was the last narrow white vertical gate that kept falling, I sat back, checked, *ba-alance, ste-e-ady*, galloped down to it and leaped *big* and *easy* and *round* like a hunter and *ohmyfuckinchrist we were clean*. I laughed like a loon and crowd cheered and clapped and whistled and Jake spooked and bucked while I thumped his neck and punched the air and hyperventilated. I got him out of the ring fast and jogged to the furthest corner of the warm-up ring.

That's where I threw up.

I heard Harry laughing his ass off behind me. 'Shit, 'Chelle, whyn't you try *breathing* once in a while,' he suggested.

And Ivory next to him, all Southern honey, 'It's a disease, didn't you know? A jumping disorder. I keep *telling* her to breathe, but what do I know? It's pathological.'

'Thanks, Ive,' I mumbled thickly while I wiped my mouth on a handful of grass, 'You're a real pal.'

She thought this hilarious. But when she stopped laughing she told me what a pretty round it was.

No other horses went clear. Harry's time stood like it usually does – *'God for Harry England and Saint George!'* I shouted from Shakespeare's *Henry V* because I adore Harry, but everybody ignored me - and then came Diane Gambarini, no surprise.

But to my utter shock Jake's and my time stood over the great Olympian Michael Draper's, and after Michael came Ivory and Memphis.

On our lap of honor, with the giant yellow-streamered rosette fluttering from his bridle, little Jake tried to buck me off. The crowd loved him, cheered for him. They wouldn't know that the bucking was nerves and overexcitement.

They wouldn't know how far the winnings from this week would take us. Or how much I needed that money.

After cooling and rubbing Jake in the striped shadow and light of the stable aisle I put him away to eat some hay and called Camille at school, a deal we have after every important class at every show. Her squeal of excitement blasted the earpiece away from my head and made my ears ring.

'Was he just too cool, Ma? Was he just like totally awesome?' she shrieked.

'Wicked awesome. Like an eagle. Like a jet plane.'

'Oh *Gawd! I wish* I was *there*!'

'Vacation week's coming.'

'No, Ma. *Now*. Please *please* can I come down this semester. I'd work for you. I'd work hard.'

'School...'

'I'll home school. GranEllen would do it, we've talked.'

'Your Dad...'

'Oh, *fuck* Dad.'

'Camille...' I warned her, though I heartily agreed.

'Yeah, yeah. Okay. But this is like just such a *total* waste of *time*. I just want to do *horses* all my life, Ma. It's like all this boring *history* shit is so totally *irrelevant*, you know? I mean, who *cares* about Louis-the-fucking...'

'Camille…'

'…*freaking*… Sun King?'

'You might, later. You could learn from his example.'

'Yeah? Like what?'

'Well hell, *I* don't know. Like how not to treat your dependent citizens next time you get to be an enlightened despot.

'Like that'll ever happen.'

'"Who doesn't learn from history is doomed to repeat it",' I quoted inaccurately.

'*Ma…*'

'Aw, c'mon, Camille. It'll give you something to think about while you're shoveling shit in some big barn. You'll never be bored.'

'I'm *not* shoveling shit, Ma. I'm *riding*.'

'Yeah, you try telling that to Harry Daly, see how hard he laughs.' I could feel the rising tide of temper through 500 miles of fiber optics. 'Camille,' I implored. 'Don't get snarky, okay? School first. That's the deal.'

'It's *blackmail!* It's *heinous!* I'll never *survive!*'

'You'll survive. You want proof, I'm proof. So just hang in there and do the work so your Dad thinks he's getting his money's worth, yeah? Then when it's party time, we can party. You know, *if* you keep yourself together there's some classes you could do with Jennie when you're down in February. You want to? Maybe show her around the Juniors?'

'*Su-weet*. You promise, right?'

'I promise.'

'I mean, like *really* promise.'

'If you hold up your end.'

'It's like a *disease*, Ma. I've got it *bad*.'

'Yeah,' I laughed. 'It's better than…' I caught myself before I said *crystal meth* and settled for a more neutral '…drugs.'

And oh, it's true: riding beautiful horses over big fences is all rush. The height, the speed, the surge of bone and muscle and pumping blood, the spectacular falls and breathless leaps into space. No drug can match it. No thrill can compete with the sensation of galloping and hurtling and veering across the ground. Winning, if you can. Feeling a good horse grow bolder and stronger and more forward with every ride, every exacting course.

Because the horses have to love it, too. The ones that don't, won't make it. And contrary to what some believe, we don't try to change them. We let them find their niche while we go on looking, and pray each talented prospect we find will have that extra spark that makes it want to jump high and fast and clean.

Jake is one of those extraordinary horses. But now, the effort of his heavy workout behind him, he was empty of adrenaline and tired. Back at his stall, I straightened the wool sheet that warmed his weary body, snapped a shank to his halter, and walked him out into the chill dark air away from the bright chaos of the tents for a few bites of dried-up grass. Most other riders have grooms to do this for them, stables full of expensive horses owned by somebody else. I'm always on a shoestring, and I guess I've gotten used to it. I like the contact, the quiet rhythms that follow big efforts, the in-and-out of my horses' breath, the pattern of their thoughts.

Leaning against Jake's solid ribs, I laughed out loud at what we'd done tonight, and whispered to him because Shakespeare always says it best, *'by heaven methinks it were an easy leap, to pluck bright honor from the pale faced moon.'* Success is such a simple pleasure, really.

It wasn't long before Jake's grey half-sister Jennie broke our reverie with insistent whinnying and banging on her stall door, wanting company. We dawdled back along the aisles and I traded congratulations and commiserations with the other riders, trainers, and grooms as they worked by their stalls, re-riding fences that with 20-20 hindsight would have won the class. I soaked up the friendly night-time sounds of horses munching hay and sneezing, buckets clanking, bedding rustling, radios tuned quietly to rock-lite. Michael Draper grinned as he saw me coming. 'You in for the Grand Prix? Go for the real money, y'know.'

'You're joking, right? I'd need an airsick bag. Jake'd need a springboard.'

'He might surprise you. There've been other little horses that were amazing over a big fence. Remember Stroller, when we were kids? Jake's like that. All you can see's his ears pointed over the top rail and then *zoom* – he's in the air.'

'I dunno. It seems way out of my league, somehow.'

'That's just because he's the only horse you've kept long enough to get *into* the league. It's just another step on the ladder, 'Chelle. He's a gutsy little dude.'

'Yeah. But I'm not.'

Diane Gambarini walked by with George Andros in time to hear this and giggled. 'You've been saying that for years, 'Chelle. Jake's totally awesome right now. Why not give it a whirl?'

'What's my insurance agent say?'

'Since only your horses are covered, you can break your neck however you want,' said George. He's a talented amateur rider who pays for his horses by keeping track of all the stuff his clients can't legally avoid protecting themselves from. 'I keep offering you this great policy...'

'George, I can barely afford the one I've got. But if I *could*...'

'Hey, Michael, how's Hilary?' interrupted George. 'That was a nasty spill.'

'Ah, she'll live. Pretty pissed off, though. She hates to lose.'

'Not to mention what Harry probably had to say about it,' I grinned.

'Yeah, that too. She's trying to stay out of his way 'til he cools down some. He's looking at serious money for that big grey sucker. Won't do to have it dented before it's sold.'

'But it wasn't her fault,' argued George.

'Well...' started Michael.

'Tell that to Harry,' giggled Diane.

In the aisle behind us angry voices swelled like a wave above the rhythmic sounds of a nighttime barn. Startled, we all looked around.

'What the hell...!' started George, and took two steps down the aisle. Michael caught him by the arm.

'Leave it,' he advised. 'Probably just a pissing contest. Somebody thinks somebody else's horse robbed them of their Amateur Owner Championship or something.' But he looked tense himself, and listened intently.

Diane rolled her eyes in disgust. 'I wish,' she said. 'It's Ivory and Winston. Again. They've been at it all day, on and off. What's the deal with them, anyhow, 'Chelle? I said something about poor Ice Cream the other day – you know, trying to tell Ivory how bad we all felt - and she about chewed my lips off my face.'

I shrugged neutrally. 'Ive walks in where angels fear to tread.'

'And how did she ever hook up with Winston Desmarchais?' pursued Diane. 'He is, like, totally creepy.'

'Hey,' reproved Michael. 'He's a good owner.'

'You can have him.'

'I already did, honey.'

'*Mi*-chael!' shrieked Diane, and whacked him on the arm.

'I think they met on the rifle range,' I offered, as if that might explain everything.

'The... *what*?'

'You remember that weirdo, Jan, she was hanging out with a few years back?'

'Oh, yeah,' said Michael. 'Danish guy. Hell of a rider.'

'Hell of a temper, too. After she gave him his walking papers Ive thought maybe some defense lessons would be a good idea.'

'Came in handy, too, the way I hear it,' added George.

'Really?' breathed Diane, eyes eager.

'Yeah. He busted down her door one night – this was after she had that restraining order clapped on him, I think – and she creased his arm. I heard.'

'Holy shit!' said Diane, titillated. 'Is that *true*, 'Chelle?'

'Um… Yeah. Something like that.'

Michael relaxed a little and shook his head. 'Most people would be content with, I don't know, karate or something.'

'Has she *always* been like that?' asked Diane.

'Like what?' I asked.

'So *tough*. You know. Like, you wouldn't want to run into her in a dark alley.'

The voices on the other side quieted, replacing volume with intensity. Still nothing I wanted to walk into. 'I guess it's a lot like horses,' I said. 'They're all born sweet and beautiful. Then life happens.'

'But *Winston*... That guy's *connected*.'

'Now that is just one big nasty rumor, Di,' chided Michael.

'Hey, I didn't start it. What are you, his fan club all of a sudden?'

'Unh-unh, honey. But just because…'

'Well. You can understand why she sticks it out with him,' George pointed out pacifically. 'Those horses are to die for.'

'*Yeah-hh*. She's got the eye and he's willing to back it up, for sure,' Diane agreed grudgingly.

'The eye's not all she has to offer,' sniped Michael.

'*O*-kay, guys,' I said. 'Enough. We're all in glass houses in that department, huh?'

Diane giggled and shot a look at George, who blushed; then at Michael, who'd not so many years ago left his wife to take up with his new 'business partner' Craig Oppenheim. After two crazy years of erratic performances and trouble with the IRS, he went back to his wife. There was a drug bust in there, too, I remembered. Something about Craig, Customs, and a stash. Anyway, the wife had the money to keep Michael in horses and out of trouble. But I sure don't know why she took him back. I know love is blind. In her case, it must have been deaf and dumb, too.

'Ivory's Dream Team', intoned Michael. He grimaced. 'You knew it was almost Draper's Dream Team?'

'I thought I'd heard that,' said George.

'Oh, well. That's the jumpers.'

'They just got written up by *Sports Illustrated*,' said George. Did y'all see that?'

'Shit, everybody *knows* that's the kiss of death,' laughed Diane. 'Those horses'll be in your barn next week, Michael.'

'And that's the jumpers, too,' I said. 'Sometimes you're the bear, sometimes you're the salmon.'

'I like the Bear part,' said Diane. Her career was starting to take off nicely. George was currently her best owner. He was also pursuing her ardently for reasons that had more to do with her great body and sparkling personality than it did with horses. Nasty mouths maintained George was using horses to buy a fancy woman. Good old green-eyed envy, if you ask me. We're all scrambling for the good rides. Human as well as equine.

'I heard Janna's walking out because of Ivory,' said George.

'Where'd you hear that?'

'Well... from Di, actually.'

'Honest to God, Di,' said Michael. 'Janna's not leaving. She knows where her bread's buttered.'

'Then maybe it's his... y'know... *sinus* problem. Cuz *I* heard she's leaving,' insisted Diane.

'That's all behind him.'

'Hah,' she snorted.

'People *change*, Janna is *not* walking out, and Winston's *clean*,' insisted Michael, looking nettled. 'You are just *the worst* little viper, Di.'

'Well, ex-*cuse* me, Michael.' Diane's eyes flashed. 'I was just...'

'Digging up shit that's none of your business.'

Time to cut out of this conversation, I thought.

'*Done to death with slanderous tongues*', I intoned, and made a theatrical stabbing-myself-in-the-heart motion. 'I'm going to bed. See you all in Florida?'

'I'll be along a little later,' muttered Michael.

Diane glared at him sullenly.

'With a brief pit stop in Europe on the way?' jibed George lightly. Always the peacemaker, that George.

'Well, yeah. I leave right after the Grand Prix, in fact. Meet the rest of my people and the big horses over there.'

'*The rest of my people and the big horse*. What a life,' I sighed. 'You bringing anything back with you?'

'If I see it and I can get somebody to buy it, sure.'

'I thought you were the American-Thoroughbred-Is-The-Best-

Sporthorse-In-The-World guy', chided George.

'I am. But you know, it never hurts to look down the road. Good horses come from everywhere. Right, 'Chelle?'

'Sure. I look down that road all the time. *Buying*, now...' I sighed again. 'I need a rich owner. How 'bout it, George? You got any friends with big dreams and deep pockets? Preferably of the single straight male persuasion? No offense, Michael...'

'Well, as a matter of fact...' George began in his thoughtful way, but Diane cut him off.

'Maybe they'd start by buying you a new rig', she suggested.

'You're not driving that old crate to Florida?' asked Michael incredulously. 'I'll tell Richard to pick up the pieces, he finds you dead on the road.'

'You will not. I got a mechanic who's a wizard. I always owe him money so he's careful to keep me alive.'

We laughed some more, and I walked on, making a detour so I didn't have to interrupt whatever was going on by Ivory's stalls.

In retrospect it seemed like a poor decision.


The old crate my so-called friends love to dump on is an elderly bus that my brother the magician just happened to know about at exactly the right moment. I greased his palm and made rash promises about firstborn sons and so forth and he overhauled the engine, beefed up the underpinnings, and stripped the interior. Then he started turning it into a home on wheels for myself and four horses. It's a slant-load, so they ride comfortably on a diagonal and it saves some space.

I wanted to have horses in the midsection, living quarters in the rear. I figured this arrangement would let me talk to them on long, boring, solitary rides when my corgi Spring is asleep. Jimmy said no, flatly. Living quarters in the middle, horses in the rear, so their weight is over an axle. He'd put a window in the wall so I could still see them. He'd even put my bed on that wall so I could sleep next to them. He added that I was twisted, but what does he know? He likes engines.

We got the interior all fixed up like those fancy motor homes that us regular folks couldn't afford in our wildest dreams – fold-up table, couple of captain's chairs that make me feel like Jean-Luc Picard on the bridge of *The Enterprise*, little sofa that turns into a littler bed, slightly larger cab-over bed, miniature fridge, drawers and cabinets, sink and water storage, even a miniscule toilet and shower for emergencies. A small sliding door to get to the horse section. And on the exterior wall, panels of pipe fence I can set up to make a pen the size of a couple of box stalls for the horses with the van as one side. It's not big enough for more than a little leg-stretch, but when we're on the road it's better than nothing and safe to boot. *'Poor and content is rich, and rich enough'*, as Othello said before his life went south.

I spend about equal parts of the year on the road and at home. I like to leave New England when the year gets old - after the last orange and red leaves have fallen, after the last geese have flown overhead honking sweet goodbyes, after Camille has returned to school from her Thanksgiving break. Because the sleeping-earth season always means new beginnings to me - new black roads slick with rain, new russet hills folding into new blue distances, new sinuous rivers sheeting through new landscapes. Maybe new love, tough and bittersweet.

And while I love the leaving, the delicious limbo of the road, I love coming home to New England even more. For apple blossom, for lilac, for Camille's summer break... and for The Auld Sow's foaling date.

Because most of all besides my daughter, I love my horses.


Jake and Jennie, the heart and soul of my little stable, are offspring of an Irish Connemara pony who has been known as The Auld Sow for so long that hardly anyone remembers her real name. Which is, by the way, Epona. She is beautiful. Her behavior throughout her long life has been anything but. She earned her nickname by being imperious, opinionated, and wild.

I met her in Galway, when she kept appearing in my grandda's yard, hairy and covered in mud and burrs, to tease his coddled racehorses. Grumbling massively and uttering dire threats, Grandda would call the filly's owner to come and get her, which he would, sometime later, on a bicycle. He'd tie a piece of string around her neck and off they'd go, the pony trotting jauntily alongside of himself on the bike. I couldn't share my relative's grouchiness. I loved the unkempt pony's antics, independent soul, and trusting nature. And I coveted the light, airy way of going she demonstrated while trotting merrily down the road back home.

There were a couple of other considerations, as well. First, I knew to the inch the size and scope of the stone walls and ditches bordering the fields she'd jumped just for the pleasure of partying in our yard.

Second, I knew she was carrying a foal by the best three-year-old Grandda had ever had in training, because I'd been early to the barn on the morning she'd somehow freed him from his stall to respond to her invitation. With heart beating three extra strokes to the second, I got the happy pair separated, threw the filly into a paddock, and went over every inch of the colt's expensive body and legs, knowing that one knick would be enough to send my grandfather into a rage wherein he would shoot the mare, skin me, and only regret both actions after the funeral. Satisfied that he was unmarked, I took my brushes and groomed the colt until every glossy hair was back in place and no trace of the mare's mud and shedding coat remained as evidence of guilt. Then I swept the yard so it looked like nobody'd been careening around all night having wild and, as it were, unbridled sex.

I waited on tenterhooks for Grandda's eagle-eyed judgment that morning, but he merely commented on the colt's unusual tractability during the day's work. In my strung-up state I thought this hysterically funny and laughed far louder and longer than the statement merited. When my grandfather gave me a funny look, I shut up quick and found some really pressing piece of tack to readjust. And the germ of an idea took form in my head.

Some weeks later, when Padraig Kenney came to collect The Auld Sow in a vile rather than his usual sunny temper, I bought her off him with my whole season's wages to date.

People gave me unlimited chaff for my folly in taking on a wild little Connemara pony, but I just smiled smugly and kept currying, pulling, trimming, and pushing decent feed to her until nature unveiled the very pretty animal underneath the rough. I broke her and rode her bareback in spare moments after long days of taut, hair-trigger Thoroughbreds and my grandda's frequent tongue-lashings. I poured all my troubles into her dark dappled ears and rode as far into the barren hills as I could ride on her broad back. And later I made passionate love to Josie Lyons, a graduate student I'd met at University, who came down from Galway City to meet me between terms in the dark of my pony's stall.

The following spring, my Connemara pony produced a beautiful filly. And when my bemused ancestor commented on the similarity of its color and markings to those of his prized stakes winner Leopard's Choice, I took a deep breath and told him the story.

By this time, the bay horse had covered himself with the kind of glory that included Group wins in Ireland, England, and the

Continent, and he was slated to retire to stud the following season, property of an immensely wealthy syndicate of which Grandda as trainer had a piece. Having heard my story in stunned disbelief, he tried to speak, spluttered out a variety of incomprehensible Irish phrases, then finally gave it all up and laughed until he had to sit down. Success and financial stability had mellowed him to an extraordinary degree, I saw to my relief. Funny thing, money.

I brazenly suggested that my mare would be a great selection as a test breeding for Leopard's Choice, since they'd already met, so to speak. My grandfather gave me a five-minute lecture on crooked dealings during which I could tell his respect for me had risen stratospherically, and then he agreed to think about it.

Well before that happened, I discovered myself pregnant with Josie Lyons' child. We were married in a flurry of anger mixed with a certain amount of relief (on the part of my family) and bewilderment (on the part of Josie and myself). I didn't care; I was young and consumed with passion. I knew love would conquer all.

But the strain was too much for a big dreamer like Josie, and I was never easy to get along with at the best of times. He wanted to move to New York City. I refused to budge. Things deteriorated pretty quickly. Josie left 'to continue his education' (which even then included some very educational women with better bank balances than mine), but came back when I had a bad crash on a crazy two-year-old and almost lost the baby. He managed to stick it out until I was back on my feet. Then he took off for good.

It felt like Hiroshima, to me. I cried day and night. I couldn't eat. I was getting too heavy to ride. My mother came to Galway. Ivory oversaw the packing of my stuff. I went home.

Camille was born, the most perfect and dauntingly demanding creature I had ever met. I could not conceive how I could be related to her, or how I would be her sole support and guide. The first long, lonely months almost tipped me over the edge, but Ivory and Grandda saved me. They sent news that my little mare was on her way home across the ocean, bankrolled by the sale of her accidental filly by Leopard's Choice. She was arriving bred back to the big horse – this time on purpose - and the result was my little jumper, Jake. I'll never know how Ivory managed to convince my grandfather to allow this, and she never said. The various scenarios I entertained - which featured an unlikely combination of sex, guilt, alcohol, blackmail, and trickery - gave me the best laugh I'd had in what seemed like eternity.

I pulled myself together, hung out a shingle, and went to work doing the only thing I knew how to do – ride and train horses. Camille was my constant companion in baby carriers, backpacks, and finally her own little fat legs. For once my timing was good - the area I lived in was growing, and suddenly there was a lot of interest in horses. People appeared to learn how to ride them, then paid me to find the right ones to buy.

My little Connemara presented me with a new foal almost every year from the best Thoroughbred stallions I could afford, and so far I'd sold all but Jennie and Jake. Although I'd named their dam after the Celtic goddess of horses and fertility and long life, it was The Auld Sow that stuck. I guess it's appropriate. In ancient Irish and Welsh stories, kingdoms often appear to future rulers in the form of a white sow, a metaphor for fortune. And that grey pony began mine.


I've no clue what time it was when Ivory banged on the door of my rig, but I hadn't been asleep long enough to wake easily. I let her in, groggy and none too gracious. Ivory looked rattled, and was wrapped in a horse blanket for warmth.

'Can I bunk in with you tonight, 'Chelle?' she asked. 'I need shelter from the storm.'

'What's the deal, Ive?'

'Nothin' more than Winston bein' his usual variety of asshole.'

'What's that mean? He beating on you? Blaming you for losing that class? Talking out of turn? What?'

She shot me a look. 'Honey, you just don't want to know.'

'Well, I do want to know. You guys have been really peculiar since you put Ice Cream in the ground. People notice.'

''Chelle honey, listen. I can't deal with this tonight, okay? Can I just stay? I'll sleep on the pullout. I'll tell you about it when I can, I promise. Okay?'

'Well sure, but…'

'*Just don't ask*, honey? Just don't ask. I'm too goddamn tired.' My tough friend was trying not to cry.

So I let her stay the night, and I didn't ask, and I even agreed to take her pride and joy, the Thoroughbred mare called Dancing Fool, in my own rig when I pulled out in the morning. She said something about Winston's trailer being full because of some horses they were going to pick up somewhere.

'You and Winston?' I asked in surprise. '*Winston's* driving the rig?'

'Well why shouldn't he? He owns the thing.'

'I know. I just thought Santé...' Ivory shot me a look full of threats about my personal bodily health.

'Santé's down in Florida setting up, if you just have to know. Winston's got that Elliot creep to do most of the driving, but he's busy this week so Winston and I are using the trip to do some deep-ass talking about '*thangs*'. Okay? You satisfied?'

'Sure. Fine,' I said hastily; and made sure I got Ivory out of my rig and the mare into it early the next morning, before Winston's unfocussed baby blues were doing more than blinking against the morning light. And I still didn't press for details. It's a problem I seem to have, this blind belief in the privacy of my friends' lives. I told myself it was bound to backfire, get me into trouble big-time one of these days. And that wasn't even accounting for Winston's nasty temper or Dancing Fool's ability to kick my old rig to kindling if she wanted. I tried to remember whether she was an easy shipper or a hussy, couldn't, and cursed myself roundly and uselessly.

'Where you going with that mare, babe?' asked the ever-present and ever-nosy Harry Daly, breaking my ruminations from the shadowed doorway of his tack stall. As usual at a multi-day show, it was festooned with drapes in his royal-and-gold stable colors and dripped with ribbons, many of them that delicious variety we all aspire to: multi-streamered blue-red-yellow hanging from a blue rosette with *Champion* emblazoned down the center. Inside, there was indoor/outdoor carpet, an oriental rug, and several comfortable chairs flanking monogrammed tack trunks, all paid for by his multitudinous clients. The saddles, bridles, blankets, and other assorted equine paraphernalia that hung spotlessly on portable racks looked like they were put there for atmosphere, like nobody ever used them for anything but conversation starters. I tell you, some people really know how to travel.

He was sipping a cup of coffee that smelled fresh, strong, and delicious. I hoped fervently that he'd offer me some, but he didn't, the swine. Typical.

'I'm stealing her, Harry', I said baldly. 'It's the only way I figure I can beat Ivory with any regularity at all.'

'I see. Of course, I suppose you wouldn't think of trading those two ponies for a real jumping horse.'

'You just happen to have one for me?'

'I have.'

'And a couple of kids in the wings who'd pay you big money for mine?'

'Well, of course I do, darlin'. Of course I do.'

'I'll tell you what. Maybe I'll just keep my ponies and whip your ass anyway, Harry.'

Harry laughed so hard he almost spilled his coffee and had to wipe his eyes. He's been in this game longer than most of us. In fact, he coached a lot of us. People love to snipe about Harry because he's getting too old and too heavy and his eye isn't what it used to be and so on and so forth and then he still beats all the young lions over the big fences and goes home to his fourth wife covered with glory and the attentions of adoring fans, purring like a cream-fed cat. So it's sheer bravado for me to thump my chest around Harry.

But there's an element of luck in jumping, and I'd had a very lucky week, so I was feeling feisty. And Harry can afford to be generous.

'Go ahead, steal the mare', he said grandly, when he recovered from his mirth. 'But I do have a horse for you, babe. And I do want you to ride it for me. So I'll see you down south and we'll talk.' He dawdled out of the tent beside me. 'You know, babe, seriously. You just aren't going to get much further in this game without some real horses to ride.'

'I do all right with the green stuff, Harry.'

'I know you do. But you could be doing a whole lot better than all right. And don't you tell me you don't know that, too.'

'Yeah, but my nerves... the money...'

'Hell with your nerves, 'Chelle. Hell with the money. Lots of people have the money. What they don't have is the feel. So don't you be playing that nerves and money bullshit with Harry Daly. You want to ride? You better get out and ride.

'Word to the wise, babe.' he added. He glanced around, judged we'd gotten away from any other ears, and said soberly, 'Look after that mare, 'Chelle. She's the best thing Ivory ever put a leg acrost.'

'Of course I will, Harry. What do you think?'

'I *think* a lot of things. But I *know* you'll be good to that mare.' He clapped my shoulder, turned, and went back inside before I could ask him what he meant by that.

# TWO

What with one thing and another, it was midmorning by the time I left Virginia behind me. I had *The Tempest* on tape – *Why, there's my dainty Ariel! I shall miss thee, yet thou shalt have freedom* - tasting the incredible rhythm and lusciousness of the words, the world-weary Prospero, *We are such stuff as dreams are made on; and our little life is rounded with a sleep*; rumbling peacefully through the twice-a-year familiarity of countryside seen like transparencies laid on top of one another, season after season. Each an experience, a flavor, a color, a song sung to growling engine and whiffling tires *this field full of yearling Thoroughbreds, that development used to be a dairy farm, this was where I bought that nice roan mare, that's where I stopped over with Rick - remember him, Spring? Yeah, you hated him - Camille and I read* A Midsummer Night's Dream *by that river, she was so little, so loving then* until what exists in overlay along the winding road is a luminous window of my own life, richer and more deeply textured for movement and miles and seasons. Sadder and more joyful for it. No wonder people have been nomads for thousands of years. Time and distance intensify everything; remind us to laugh, cry, grieve, celebrate every new turn of the spiral dance of life. *There stand, for you are spell-stopp'd...*

It was nearly suppertime when I arrived in Southern Pines. Which could be called good planning, because my friends the Morgans are gourmet cooks and I love to eat stuff I haven't had to do anything about. Paul and Ginny had a potential jumper I might want, if its head could be straightened out. The nice gelding I'd picked up in Vermont for resale seemed like it might prefer Combined Training to the Hunter ring. If I played my cards right I'd leave in a few days with my stomach full of good food, my head ringing with good gossip, a new horse to school and sell, and maybe even some money. The bargaining process would be a leisurely affair that involved truth-telling when absolutely necessary, grand innuendo when it seemed appropriate, promises that nobody had any intention of making good on, and a good measure of hilarity.

Horse-trading helps bankroll my months on the road. I learned early from my grandfather that talent, scope, and heart aren't confined to horses of a certain size, color, age, shape, or breed. Since I can't afford to be a snob I'll yank an odd-looking prospect out of somebody's back yard if it has some talent, or take a flyer on something that smarter people have passed by.

Sometimes it works. Like the time I bought a horse everybody said was wacko, and it turned out he just hated anything in his mouth. The stronger the bit, the wilder he got. I tried him in a hackamore and got him going quietly and had a nice horse, all of a sudden. Graduated him to a soft rubber snaffle, cleaned up for a season at some big shows, sold him for more money than I'd ever seen to a little girl with guts up the wazoo and about the weight of a feather, and financed my farm.

Of course, sometimes it backfires. There was this chestnut mare I bought because I thought the people who had her were prejudiced by the old saw about chestnut mares being strange in the head. I figured I could turn her into a star.

While I was in the hospital waking up my brother Jimmy sent the hussy to a dealer in Massachusetts. I don't know what happened to her after that. I probably don't want to. I might have kept the mare because it breaks my heart to give up on a horse when I know it wasn't born bad. When I know what its life becomes when it gets passed from hand to hand to hand until it ends up in the sad herds that feed the summer camps, or at the killers. Horses deserve better than that from the people who control their lives. But I have no bankroll and no magic wand. And the truth is that horses can kill us, whether they mean to or not. Whether they were born sweet or not. Those who argue a ruined horse is better off dead aren't always entirely wrong.

I still pick up strays. I still try to prove it's not so.

As for Jake and Jennie, they were born on my place, and if the gods smile they'll die there. Maybe, like Harry said once when he was pissed off that I wouldn't sell Jake to him, I get them confused with the hordes of children he thinks I ought to have had. All I know is that the rest is only possible if I can take my favorites home.

So far, none of the horses I'd gotten from the Morgans had tried to turn my body into a badly made pretzel, which was another good reason to call them friends. They didn't disappoint me this time, either. After a great meal during which (as usual) I'd eaten, laughed, and drunk far too much, we got down to the business of horse-trading. Strolling to the barn in the soft dusk, opening preliminary sallies about the relative merits of the great horses we had to offer each other and politely listening to one another's lies, I gulped the mild southern air and hoped Paul's assessment of my current state was wrong and I wasn't really drunk enough to miss minor details like congenital attitude problems or feet whose internal structures resembled Swiss cheese.

But the horse he had to offer me was 'way more than nice: push-button on the flat, adjustable, and with a big, raking stride that took him to the jumps in a way that left me a little breathless. He could get off the ground, too, and didn't want to touch anything. I rode him around, grinning from ear to ear, power in the beast like under the hood of a Jaguar and just as smooth. I could have ridden him all night long.

Even so, I found myself reluctant to buy. He had a funny look in his eye that made me think I'd never turn my back on him, and a temper bump - a sort of dome between the eyes - which I've never liked. Old horsemen say it points to an erratic nature, a horse who'll be fine 99% of the time and then do something really stupid when you're least expecting it. Which could mean anything from refusing to jump a single fence after winning everything the week before, to actually hurting you.

Paul and Ginny admitted the animal could be a pain to deal with. I wondered how long Paul had worked him today to get him in a co-operative mood before I arrived, and tried to balance these drawbacks against the kind of obvious talent that made me drool with the anticipation of winning big classes and making big money.

I didn't risk blowing a deal by stating my reservations. I started price negotiations on my chestnut, which I'd intuited was just what Ginny needed for a certain client even though she was acting very casual about it. I mentally added a bit to the asking price, sensing they were going to make a quick profit on this horse.

Reluctantly, I handed the big gelding back to his groom with a pat, and strolled to the edge of the ring. It was dark now; lights blinked on and somewhere an automatic sprinkler system started its work damping down the dust.

'What have you got in there?' I asked Paul, indicating a chubby brown thing in a turnout paddock.

'That? Achh. That's just an old campaigner I bought off DiPrizio Brothers. He's taken a bunch of juniors to the Medal Finals and just done a lot of years of solid work. Not the soundest thing in the world. They were jumping the legs off him, keeping him on Bute, you know, special shoeing, 'til he was a complete cripple and then they'd throw him on the junk heap. I thought he deserved better.' He shook his head. 'I must be going soft. God knows what I'll do with him, he's too young to turn out for the rest of his life  and eats too much to keep.'

'Navicular?'

'Nah. Some changes, nothing big. Mostly I'd say it's arthritis. He won't pass a flex in his stifles or hocks. But I reckon he's got a bunch of real easy low-level miles left, if a body was careful of him. Lots of TLC and turnout, you know. A couple of months to rest. Hell of a packer, but not for jumping every day.'

I grunted, watched the horse move around, and did some fast calculations.

'I'm saving the best for last, though', Paul continued. 'Come on in here and look at this.'

We went back into the Morgans' well-lit, cool, commodious barn, a place that always makes me sigh with desire. Ginny was waiting for us in the aisle with one of the nicest grey mares I ever hoped to see; I guessed a Thoroughbred crossed with some kind of warmblood, a Hanoverian, maybe. Big boned, gracious, broad, and lovely no matter what angle you looked at her from. I paid homage as I was expected to, drinking in her perfection and lusting after her glossy hide with the intensity of a ten year old child looking at the toy of her dreams through the department store window.

'Nice, huh?' prompted Ginny.

'*Nice!*' I moaned. 'Who is she? Where'd you get her?'

Paul and Ginny grinned with pleasure. 'She's Ice Cream's sister.'

'*Ice Cream.* Wow. Ivory'll be here on the run when she hears about this.'

'Well now, maybe that's true', acknowledged Paul. 'But she's not for sale to Ivory. Not while Winston's buying.'

I was startled. 'Well, Winston's a problem, I know, but he's a good owner...'

'A *problem*!' exploded Ginny. 'Is that what you call that slime bag? I wouldn't sell him a lame dog, not to have it killed.'

'What?' I took a step back, blinked, mouth open in total bafflement, looking from one to the other. 'What are you guys talking about?'

'You don't think he killed Ice Cream?'

'Killed... Now just wait a minute, guys. You don't believe Winston was after the insurance money, the guy's fuckin' loaded.'

"Chelle, we hear Winston's in serious trouble. *And* we heard the reason has something to do with a certain plane that landed somewhere it oughtn't carrying something nobody wants to talk about and got looked at by the Feds. 'Course, nobody can trace it back to old Winston. *His* ass is covered, all right. But he needs to recoup some major losses, is what we understand. *And* he has some pretty angry clients down Miami who'll...'

'Ginny,' Paul warned.

'Well, it's true, Paul,' she insisted.

My mind went numb. 'But that's slander! You should know better than that, that's the kind of rumor that can... and Ivory... she would *never* ...'

'Honey, I know how close you and Ivory are. *And* I know Ivory would rather shoot herself than hurt a horse in her care. But you and I both know she has shit for brains when it comes to men. And she can't do anything about stuff she isn't in control of. We don't know anything for sure, you're right. But Winston's bad news. We won't deal with him. I don't think you would either, isn't that right?'

I looked at them in mute misery.

'Right?' Ginny prompted.

'Right', I agreed finally, feeling ill. 'The guy's an asshole. I always thought so. I just never...' I turned away and walked out of the barn.

'Hey!' Paul came after me and took my arm. "Chelle, come on, doll, we weren't gonna to say any of this to you. I *know* you and Ivory have been through fire together. It was just the mare, okay? Just the mare.'

'It's okay, Paul. But... shit, guys, you know I have Ivory's Dancing Fool with me right now. *Now* what am I supposed to make of that?'

'You can't make anything of it, 'Chelle. No more than we can, and for all the same reasons.'

'You mean like hard evidence, like Winston's a prominent guy with clout, like all that other stuff that makes me not want to believe bad things about the people I live around half my life? This is pretty hard to swallow, Paul.'

Paul sighed. 'You're a good friend, 'Chelle. I wouldn't want a better, if I was in a pinch. I guess you just better look after that mare, that's all. If Ivory wanted you to keep her. Had to be a reason, you know.'

'Oh, right. And act casual, or something really simple like that.'

'Yeah. Sure.'

'What about Ivory? What do I say to her?'

'Ivory's a grown-up. She's going to have to look after herself.'

'Yeah, well she's going to have to do some talking, too.'

'Don't push it, 'Chelle. I wouldn't', said Ginny, catching up to us. 'Just take a warning when you hear it, okay?'

'But if she knows what's up, she should blow the whistle. And if she's involved...'

'Right. *If*. That's the problem, isn't it. Meanwhile, there's not much the rest of us can do. Except keep our nice horses away from sleaze buckets like Winston.'

I nodded. We went back to the house in a subdued frame of mind, agreeing to a nightcap to try to put the evening back on track. But Ginny's and Paul's accusations weighed too heavily on me to respond to forced conviviality. The horse show world had been rocked badly in the past by insurance fraud; people killing horses for money. Nice horses, no more wrong with them than a failure to live up to some over-inflated idea of their worth as athletes. People we'd admired, watched, known, even called friends were now doing time in prison or ratting on other people to avoid it. People who'd professed to love horses. Who'd professed to love the business of riding horses, a business so old and so long ennobled that it is etched on every cell of our bodies from the ancientest days of pre-history.

I couldn't bear the thought of Winston opening another chapter in an ugly book. I could hardly keep my supper in place thinking Ivory might be a part of it. I'd intended to do some dickering with Paul and Ginny, but my heart wasn't in it anymore. I thought of calling Ivory, but didn't know where she was. I tried to track Harry down and demand to know more about his parting comment and got nothing but his voicemail. So I checked on my horses, and twice on Dancing Fool, and made some excuses about exhaustion, and went to bed.

I guess you can't keep a born trader down for long. I woke up in the Morgans' cheery back bedroom feeling like the previous evening's grand finale had been a bad dream built on nothing but the half-truths and rumors that fuel gossip around every prominent owner or trainer on the show circuit nationwide.

I bought the brown horse I'd seen in the paddock. I had the perfect owner for him, an empty-nester I knew would treat him like a pasha and use him with the care due bone china. With luck, he'd see out his days with her. I think I took Paul by surprise, although for all I know he'd planted the damn horse there for me to 'discover' in the first place. Anyway, I got him for a song, or so I thought, and Paul grumbled ferociously that I was sending him to the poorhouse while he forked over a hefty hunk of cash for the difference between it and my chestnut. Ginny still wouldn't admit to having a client for my horse anxiously chewing her fingernails in the wings, but I'd heard the phone ring all morning and drew my own conclusions.

The next days were sheer pleasure, time for my hardworking horses to eat grass and hack out and jump the jumps of an unfrozen country before engaging in the stress of the winter circuit. A chance to cruise the by-ways with Paul and Ginny, hearing the gossip and checking out the horseflesh. We parted, as always, in good spirits and as good friends.

I sang my way down the highway into the bright morning. Windows open to the air, tape deck resonating to old Crosby, Stills, and Nash tunes, Spring only moaning a little when I cracked the high notes. I had money in my pockets, money to look forward to, and an empty stall to fill if the right horse came along. Life looked pretty good.

It looked even better when I hit Camden, South Carolina in the pouring rain to teach a successful and reasonably lucrative clinic arranged months earlier to coincide with my trip. I left my three passengers behind there while I took a quick run to Columbia to get a new gas tank for my rig; I'd only been able to fill it halfway for weeks without losing fuel all over the road. Driving back through light drizzle, brand new gas tank filled to the brim, I whistled cheerfully. Yessir, life was looking better than it had for months.

But it flamed out half an hour from the city when traffic suddenly slowed and brought me to the twisted wreck of a six-horse van turned on its side by the edge of the interstate, still smoking, cab crumpled, crashes emanating from the back, a few cars with dents scattered here and there, dazed and fearful people milling around, blankets, somebody sitting by the side of the road crying, hysterical people on cell phones, no sirens or flashing lights seen yet, all of this I took in as I slowed to a halt in horror it *must have just happened* and my heart went from thumping hard to stopping with a sickening jolt as I realized that *I knew that van. Omigod*, I could hear myself whispering thickly, *ohmyfuckingchristalmighty*, Winston's rig. Ivory with Winston, going south.

Shaking, I pulled past the wreck, past the cars, and parked by the side of the road. Hauled myself out of the cab, legs rubber, *come on, goddammit!* running back, struggling to get through, *I know these people, let me through* and calling her name out, *Ivory, Ivory, oh holyfuckman, Ive*! Crawled up to the splintered window, blood everywhere, behind me in the distance I heard sirens coming closer, Winston all twisted in the driver's seat, head all red, and beyond him moaning gently eyes closed Ivory *'Ivory!'* I cried out to her but her eyelids didn't even flutter, she just kept moaning while she turned her head slowly side to side, side to side, and I realized dimly that she was mumbling over and over again, *The fucking asshole. The fucking asshole.*

Hands pulling me back. Police, ambulance people, I didn't know, pulling me back and me resisting until I realized that this man was shaking me, demanding I look at him, demanding I concentrate on what he was saying. *'Horses!'* He repeated urgently, sternly. 'There-are-horse-in-the-back. Can-you-help!'

I looked at him in alarm, suddenly returning to myself. 'Oh my God! The horses!' I went to tear myself away from the man's grasp and run to the back of the van, but he pulled me so roughly I almost cried out in pain.

'Drugs! Banamine, Ace, Rompun, anything. *Anything you've got. Please hurry.'*

I nodded speechlessly and sprinted to my rig, wrenched open the back door, dug into my vet kit, dragged everything out that looked like it might be useful, bottles, needles, syringes, the stuff we all carry for the disasters we hope will never happen. Ran back to the van on shaking legs, through the throng of people, of sirens, of crackling walkie-talkies, of onlookers and uniforms trying to keep them away.

He was already there, wrenching away at one of the twisted escape doors until he ripped it off its hinges so he could crawl in. When I caught up he turned to me, grim. 'It's bad', he said. 'Are you up to it?' I nodded and crawled in after him to unspeakable carnage; four horses, flung on their sides in the buckled, crazily tilted wreck, nearest me the one underneath had stopped struggling and lay groaning, glassy-eyed, the one thrown on top of it still trying to scramble to find a foothold where the floor had once been. Across from them another had flipped and struggled wildly against the chains that held it, the stall that confined it. The fourth, in the stall now beneath, utterly still, neck twisted grotesquely. 'Oh my god,' I breathed, taking this in in the time it takes to blink. 'Rougère.'

'You know these horses?' the stranger looked back at me incredulously and I nodded dumbly. He returned me a look of deep pity, but his voice was tough. 'He's done, but we've got to get some tranq into the others before they kill themselves. It's their only chance.'

I nodded again. 'Better do Morning Glory first. You want the head or the needle?'

'I'll take the head, I'm heavier,' he said. 'Have a care, watch its feet.' I nodded. We drew up syringes of tranquilizer and analgesic and crawled carefully around the wracked interior until we got into a position where we could unhook the horse's head. It took both of us to hold it steady, watch the flailing hooves, warn each other, help the horse with chirps and exhortations 'til she struggled onto her side then quickly and with all our weight pin her head down so that the man could sit on it and hold the animal still while I struggled to find the vein, get the needle into it, draw back to make sure I got blood, push the tranquilizer into its system, wait for it to work while we spoke soothingly, follow it with painkiller. I left the man on the mare's head and crawled back to where the horse that had been across struggled more weakly. *Heavensent, ah, Heavensent, sweet boy, shhh,* all the idiocies we whisper to horses, all the things we say to calm, to ease, even when there is no comfort to be had, even while they look at us in pain and trust and wait for us to fix the unfixable. And under Heavensent still groaning slightly, Memphis, *Oh, Memphis, you're the one, Memphis my buddy*, I stroked him and held his ear the way he liked, the man cautioned me to wait but I signaled I was okay and patted Heavensent's sweat-soaked neck, stroked around his fear-ringed eye with my hand, shushed him, put my knee on his cheek and leaned on it to keep him still while I found the jugular and filled him with the fluids that relieve distress, then did the same for Memphis.

The noise was now all outside; the horses breathed deep and moved their legs like dreamers, disconnectedly, and there were rescue squad and policemen's heads at the broken door offering help and asking how on earth we'd get these animals off. Somebody suggested we put them out of their misery, he'd get a gun. '*No!*' I said in alarm. 'Call a friggin' vet, will you!' and my helper behind me saying, 'We can't get them out the side, d'you have a way to get the back open so we can slide them?'

A conference outside brought a new face to the door. 'Jaws of life,' he said. 'We're done with 'em up front.'

'Good. Use them quick. These horses are dying.' British accent, some distant part of my brain registered.

The head disappeared and soon the noise of metal ripping, squealing, unwillingly torn from its tortured seating while the horses renewed their struggles and we held on like sailors in a tempest, calling encouragement and peace until daylight showed through the back and people arrived with ropes, blankets, hands, and in the back a vet yelled that he was here.

We worked like people in a nightmare, feverishly operating through what seemed like a morass of mud and blood and a haze that must have been induced by shock. We got Morning Glory out, several strong men lending a hand to slide her as gently as possible with ropes and blankets, muttered orders and the occasional shout until she lay in a heap, panting and dazed. We pulled and yelled and kicked her to her feet and finally she staggered up and stood unsteadily, lovely head drooping in the middle of the chaotic noise and movement that surrounded us. I got a spare rug out of my van to replace the remnant that hung in festoons around the shivering mare's sides and buckled it on. I galvanized my crew and we half carried, half dragged the mare up the ramp and into a stall.

When we had her secured, we went back out just in time to see my partner and another bunch hauling the great, broken form of Memphis from the wreckage. I ran over and knelt by his still form. He still moaned slightly, his breathing labored. I put my hands on him, *oh Memphis, Memphis, oh god*. There was blood coming from his nostrils. I looked up at the Brit and he shook his head, eyes full of pain. 'He flies,' I found myself saying idiotically, 'He has wings…' I was crying.

'We can't save him,' the man said. 'Internal damage is too great. He won't make it to a clinic.' I nodded dumbly, and kept stroking the noble head, the powerful neck, whispering nonsense to him, crooning to him, until the Brit came back with the vet and a syringe full of the stuff we call Death Juice. We put him down on the spot. The tranq in his system helped him go easy, kept him from convulsing too much. I held his heavy, noble head, tears rolling unchecked and barely heeded down my cheeks until the last breath came out of him in a long, whooshing sigh and the last electric twitches of his limbs and face had died away.

When I got numbly to my feet I was shocked to see TV cameras grinding away in my face. I turned blindly away, back to the trailer, back to where Heavensent had gotten to his feet with a little encouragement, dead lame, staggering from tranquilizers and shock, but more or less in one piece. We got him into the stall next to Morning Glory and the vet gave them more stuff for shock, stuff for pain, rigged them up with i.v. drips and fluids in three gallon bags to keep them hydrated, give them the chance to live, while I adjusted blankets for warmth and replaced their tattered shipping boots with the clean cottons and soft leg wraps I always carry for emergencies and had never until this moment needed.

We closed the ramp and I climbed into the cab. I pulled Spring onto my lap and hugged her while my partner got into the other seat. 'Okay to drive?' he asked, concerned.

I nodded. 'You sure you want to come?'

'I've got the directions.'

'Oh.' I looked at him stupidly, nearly cross-eyed with weariness. 'I never thought of that.' Then, completely unreasonably, I began to shake, clutching my dog until she squeaked in protest, sure I'd never be able to sit up straight again.

'Here,' he said, sliding over to me, removing the bewildered Spring from my arms, and gripping my shoulders 'til they hurt. 'Here. Don't fall apart yet. We've got two horses back there that need immediate attention.' He held me at arm's length, eyes boring into mine. 'Right? Drive. Now. Or move over and let me.'

I nodded. Gulped. Wiped my face on my filthy, bloodstained sleeve and started the bus. Pulled out onto the road and looked through the windshield, astonished at the incongruity of daylight when all of this activity had seemed to take place in swirling, nightmare dark.

But it was dark by the time the horses had been unloaded and properly attended to, by the time I'd called the hospital to find that Ivory would be moved out of the I.C.U. in a few days but that Winston was in a coma; by the time the police had tracked us down for statements and had informed my already overloaded self that there had been cocaine worth ten times my last year's total income found in a broken bale of bedding in the back of the trailer and did I know anything about Ms. Gardner and Mr. Desmarchais' business dealings, as I appeared to be a friend of Ms. Gardner's. My new friend took one look at the raw fear and disbelief on my face and stood in the way of me and the uniforms, stating that I had received a terrible shock and wasn't in any state to talk to them tonight, and while they hassled him I pulled myself together enough to say I wanted a lawyer and burst into floods of overwrought tears. One of the vets entered the fracas then as well, and finally the clinic cleared out, me promising not to leave town and the director offering both a parking space for my portable home and an extra person to go back to the scene, pick up anything we'd left behind, and bring my companion's car back.

With gratitude we accepted this, the use of the clinic's shower, and a sandwich I was too tired and sick to eat, and wandered wearily into the night and the blessedly normal little home space of my rig, the blessedly normal greeting of a loving dog. We stood on the threshold, sagging with exhaustion. 'Where do we sleep?' my partner asked without preamble. I pointed at the cubby above the cab. 'Very neat', he said. And next thing I knew we had turned slowly to one another and were kissing first tentatively, then like starving people at a banquet, getting out of our destroyed clothes any graceless way we could and falling into each other's bodies, each other's living, breathing arms-mouths-forms, and making ferocious love as if our very existence hung on the outcome. Which maybe it did.

Much later, he paused, took a long, deep breath from somewhere in my neck, mumbled inconsequentially, 'Where'd you get this beautiful hair?'

'Grandmère was French and Penobscot. How 'bout the swell accent?'

'Welsh borders.'

My phone began to ring. And again, and again, 'til I groped around, found it, and turned it off. And then my beautiful stranger and I were all entangled again, all consumed in each other. And by the time I'd reached the point of converting forever to whatever religion might be spent worshipping his wiry body we collapsed beside one another in blessed oblivion and slept like... well... like the dead.


I prayed to wake up to an empty bed and the knowledge that I'd hallucinated the entirety of the previous twenty-four hours. I wasn't expecting the exquisite aromas and dulcet sounds of bacon and eggs frying and coffee dripping. I didn't dare open my eyes. I just lay still for another lovely few minutes of unreality, smiled, inhaled, and listened to the quiet rustle of one person trying not to awaken another. Given the size of the space we shared, this wasn't easy. When he hit his toe on something and cursed, I laughed. I opened my eyes to take in the sight of a half dressed, slender man of middle height and probably a few less years than mine. Curly brown hair tousled, hazel eyes rueful, mouth working from irritation to humor and back again. Humor won.

'Breakfast', he said triumphantly. 'I've already fed the dog. She lived.'

I sat up and held my hands out expansively. '*I am amazed, and know not what to say,*' I said.

He pointed a spatula at me. 'You can't fool me, that's *A Midsummer Night's Dream.*'

'You recognized it? I *am* amazed.'

'My wife was on the stage before the children were born.'

'How many kids?'

'Two boys.' He indicated the photo I always keep on the wall of Camille and me laughing, to remind me that we are capable of being happy in each other's company. 'Yours?'

'Yeah.'

'Her father?'

'Left before Camille was born.'

'Sorry. That's rough.'

'He got his green card, I got Camille. It was an okay deal, really.'

'Still...'

'So you know Shakespeare by default,' I said, bringing the subject back to one I cherish far beyond the actions of my ex.

'No, I actually enjoy the stuff. '*O, that this too too solid flesh would melt/ Thaw, and resolve itself into a dew...* '' he stopped, blinked, busied himself turning eggs onto plates. 'Not a very good choice, that. Sorry.' Then, more brightly, 'I bet you didn't know that line is always used by Shakespearean actors to tell their friends they've gone up.'

'*O that this too too solid flesh?*'

'No, the other one. '*I am amazed...*' and so forth.' I laughed in delight. 'Quite true!' he insisted. 'You listen, next time you see Shakespeare. Dead giveaway. Um... I hope you like your eggs scrambled.'

'I like 'em any way you cook 'em.' I got up and fumbled through my clothes until I found something clean enough to wear. I was stiff and bruised in all sorts of strange places from the previous day's work. So was my companion, judging by the careful way he moved. But we ate as if everything were normal and we the oldest of friends, living in that odd place known to survivors of wars, shipwrecks, and earthquakes, that exists completely out of any time continuum known to ordinary life. Which is a form of healing, though some might call it shock. Or denial.

We couldn't stay there long. By the time we'd eaten and gotten the place cleaned up it was time to come back to the real world. He went with me into the clinic to see the vets in charge of Heavensent and Morning Glory. Of the two, Morning Glory was the worst off, with broken withers that would be career-ending. Heavensent, though lame, cut, and badly bruised, had a greater chance of returning to work. I gave the vets my number and said I'd be back with some sort of decision on what should be done with the horses long-term. For the meantime, at least they were safe, filled with i.v. fluids, antibiotics, painkillers, and hay, and their conditions were stable.

My partner and I lingered by the stalls. 'Lovely animals, they must have been,' he remarked. 'Jumpers, were they?'

'Very good jumpers. You've heard of Ivory Gardner?'

'Ivory Gardner! No, these weren't hers?' he looked doubly shocked.

'Ivory's Dream Team. What's left of it.'

'That was… In the van…'

I nodded. 'Ivory Gardner and Winston Desmarchais.'

'Dear God in heaven. What's to become of them now?'

'I don't know, really. Especially… well, especially with what they found in the shavings bags.'

'Likely to be a hell of a mess.'

'Yeah.' I looked at him, and wanted nothing more than to take him back to the van and get lost in his body again, forever and ever. 'Look, you've been great to stay so long, but you really don't have to. I can take over here, I know everybody involved. No sense you getting wrapped up in it.'

He thought for awhile, eyes on Heavensent's bandaged legs as if they were a map that might tell him where he was.

'I hate to leave you in the lurch.'

'You aren't. You've done plenty. More than plenty.'

'Look,' he said, pulling out his wallet and fishing a card out of it. 'If you need anything, call, will you? Anything I can do…'

I nodded my thanks. Thought of all the trite things I could say about help and ships in the night and troupers and all that, but it sounded pretty stupid, even in my head. So I didn't say anything.

'Nothing at all? Give you a lift to hospital? Anything?' Stalling for time. People at an airport, unwilling to say goodbye; becoming more awkward by the moment. I shook my head again and we stood and looked at one another for a moment, then hugged and kissed lingeringly and not without regret. And he left me there.

On my way out, I tossed his card into a garbage can without reading it. I knew I'd never call him.


Half way to the hospital the last vestiges of shock wore off. Niggling flashes of yesterday's horror became recurring images of magnified hyper-reality, details I'd not been aware of absorbing. Brave Rougère's twisted neck and death mask grimace, Morning Glory's thrashing legs and moans of agony. Memphis, flying over Grand Prix fences like a soaring bird of prey. Memphis lying broken on his side, shuddering out his last breath, never to walk again, never to fly. I started to tremble, then to shudder so hard I couldn't drive anymore and had to pull over to the side of the road. Beside me, Spring whined. I pulled her soft furry body to me and with my arms around her tightly I sobbed uncontrollably and inconsolably.

They say that horses will always break your heart. Those of us who love them learn early how to grieve. But it never gets easier.

I got into the ICU by swearing I was Ivory's only living relative and gave the people there a stare that begged them to differ. They didn't. My friend looked small and crumpled under the stark hospital bed sheets. Suspended over her were smaller versions of the bags I'd last seen delivering the same combination of fluids, antibiotics, and painkillers to the two horses we'd rescued from the wreck. I sat wearily by the bed and whispered to her that I was there and stroked her hand lightly in case she could hear me through her narcotic sleep. I brushed a strand of hair back from her damp forehead; still beautifully blonde but colored now, Ivory too vain to let even the smallest sprinkle of grey give her away. Her hands were thickened with work, the joints swollen despite the creams she rubbed into them with religious fervor. Replacing the peaches-and-cream complexion of twenty years past were a dark tan and deeply etched lines which gave her expression a harsh and uncompromising look. All courtesy of years of hard living, too much sun, and the unrelenting physical labor that go with life in the service of horses.

I wondered if I would see the same things in myself if I looked in the mirror. I fondly felt I hadn't changed much in twenty years, but knew it wasn't true. There were the grey hairs that stole in, the worries printed deeply around the eyes, the bearing and arthritic joints that spoke of old injuries no longer repairable by the rare and simple bliss of a good night's sleep.

'Maybe we're getting too old for this kind of life, Ive', I said to the air. 'Maybe we should be thinking about something else.' I didn't know what, exactly. The time I used to think I'd have to change my mind and investigate new options seemed to be sliding by me like a river, inexorable, as I grew mummified by the mounting evidence of seasons lived and horses cared for. I flexed my fingers, feeling them gnarled and sore. I wanted to crawl into a hole like a woodchuck in December and sleep forever. I wanted to shed my skin like a snake and be new again. I wanted to revisit whatever crossroad had brought me here and make a different choice.

Or maybe the same again. Maybe this had been the right - the only - choice for me.

It was a profoundly frightening thought.

Because no matter how much I might struggle against my daughter, no matter how much I might preach the gospel of a different kind of life, I was no different than Camille. I had never wanted to do anything but ride beautiful horses.

# THREE

*Think, when we talk of horses, that you see them*
*Printing their proud hoofs I' th' receiving earth...*
- William Shakespeare, ***Henry V, I.1***

*Come, let me taste my horse,*
*Who is to bear me like a thunderbolt...*
-   William Shakespeare, ***Henry IV pt. 1; IV.1***

Ivory and I met in college, unlikely roommates. She was sleek and
golden as a greyhound, beautiful in the opalescent manner of
groomed and wealthy young women who end up as celebrated movie
stars or the wives of royalty or the owners of famous race horses and
show jumpers. But even then she'd been a rogue, thrown out of at
least one prep school for sneaking out at night with boys and
smoking and drinking and all that stuff people do when young and
stupid. I was merely lean, with an attitude and a mean sense of
humor. I thought her a rich, spoiled snob who didn't have any idea
what life was really about. She thought me an uptight small-town
bitch. We were both right. Eighteen is such a graceless age.

We discovered early on that we had horses in common. We also
discovered drugs and sex at approximately the same moment and
there was no looking back, although in an era of wild abandon we
were certainly no wilder than the norm. I don't honestly remember a
lot of what we got up to, except that it involved ingesting a
chromosome-bending array of illegal substances while an equally
staggering number of men - some shared - passed through our beds. I
cringe to think of it now, in an era of HIV, but that was what people -
or certain people, anyway - did then. We weren't even very original.

When after two years of living this fast and loose I announced my
intention to bag school and embrace horses as a profession to my
mother, all hell broke loose. I - strung out, fed up, rebelling against

The System And Its Ills, yearning for the escape my obsession with horseflesh offered - thought this a reasonable concept. She, good educator that she is, freaked. Home was a war zone. She shipped me off to my father, a racetrack vet in New York, in despair. I thought I'd died and gone to heaven. I went to Saratoga in August, rubbed horses, cleaned up after horses, did drugs, galloped horses, breathed horses, did more drugs, and had an affair with one of Dad's clients. I figured I was made in the shade. My da didn't agree.

Next thing I knew I was getting off a bus in a tiny town near Moyard in County Galway, Ireland. I was to apprentice and straighten myself out under the iron fist of my grandfather, a man of legendary temper and a magic touch with Thoroughbreds, in one of the rockiest, poorest, greenest, mistiest and most isolated landscapes I have ever seen. And I was not happy about the arrangement.

Now you'd call us dysfunctional and slap us into family therapy, but in those days who knew? Parents did what they had to do, and kids either flouted them or knuckled under.

I fought my grandda for every inch even though I was scared to death of him. Fortunately an acute mind and a great sense of humor matched his violent nature. He simply stuck me on every personality-disordered young Thoroughbred he had in his yard and let me work out my issues on them. Since horses don't respond well to anger, inconsistency, or laziness, this proved to be a brilliant tactical move. After I'd taken any number of spectacular falls in the process of losing arguments with half-ton racing machines at the peak of their condition, I gradually learned heretofore non-existent qualities of tact, inner strength, and a disciplined mind in order to survive.

Ivory, meanwhile, created a scandal at school by having an affair with a married professor three times her age. Somehow he didn't get fired and she didn't get the boot - maybe her folks endowed a psychology chair or something - but it didn't make her mend her ways. I knew she'd been dealing by this time and getting in with some characters who were fringy even by our loose standards. She moved in with one of them, a real scumbag she was completely in love with. Sure she could be with him forever in a rosy glow of unreality. They were going to do one more really big deal - buy acid cheap, sell it in Amsterdam, and retire on the proceeds. It was the kind of thing we all talked about doing, but Ivory had the money and her boyfriend had access to the stuff.

He was a narc. He busted her and broke her mind in two, all at once. Her parents paid for the best lawyer money could buy and got her through the trial with less time in prison than she'd have had if she'd been a poor girl. Then they disowned her.

She did six months of whatever it was she ended up with, and got out with nowhere to go, not much to live for, and feeling suicidal. I begged grandda to let her come over and work for him. He was vehemently opposed. 'One of youse is about all I can stand', he vowed. I told him Ivory was the best rider he'd ever seen with hands like silk and an incredible gift for bringing out the best in any horse, which was no exaggeration. He relented. The condition was that 'you keep your arses straight, work harder than any of the lads - and hands off them, mind' - and use the time off he intended to give us to go to University and 'by-Christ do something with those useless fockin' brains besides tourn them into porridge'. I think Gran had something to do with that part. Or else my rough edges and his were working each other like fine-grained sandpaper until all the ridges were being turned into something of a smoother texture.

''Chelle.'

I woke up with a start. Ivory was looking at me blurrily, blue eyes clouded with hurt and loss and fear and painkillers.

'Right here, sweetie.'

'Tell me...'

'Not now, okay? You need to rest.'

'I won't be able to. You know that. I gotta know. Is Winston...'

'In a coma. They won't say anything, but it doesn't look great.'

She turned to look at the ceiling. Closed her eyes. Opened them again. 'The horses...'

'Ive...'

'*C'mon,* 'Chelle. Give it to me straight.'

I took a deep breath. Cleared my throat and tried to speak. Couldn't. Cleared my throat again. 'Rougère died instantly. Memphis... We got Memphis out but we couldn't save him. He was too... he'd been...' I stopped and struggled for control. Of my shaking voice, of the lump in my throat, of my burning mind. *Breathe in,* I told myself. *Breathe out. Breathe in.* 'Morning Glory and Heavensent are at a good clinic. Glory crushed her withers. Heavensent might go sound again, but at least they'll both be okay and you'll have a nice broodmare in Glory. If you want one. If nothing else...' I choked. I couldn't make my voice say the words.

'They'll probably have to be sold, once the insurance gets straightened out,' said Ivory. 'They were - are - all Winston's. All but Dancing Fool. I got half of her, pay off the rest... I was afraid...' she stopped. Tears ran from the corners of her eyes unchecked. 'The fucking asshole,' she said.

'Ive? Sweetie? I'm so sorry. So sorry.' I was crying again, too. Ms. Big help. I took Ivory's hand and she squeezed mine and we just wept silently for a long while.

When we'd run out of grief she took a long, shaky breath. 'So. Okay. That's that part. Give me the rest, now.'

I hesitated. 'The rest?'

'I found out what we were carrying back there, 'Chelley. How deep is the shit I'm in?'

'Looks pretty deep, Ive.'

'I wasn't in it, you know.'

'I couldn't believe you were. But will Winston try to take you down with him? Would he do that?'

'I don't know. He might. If he wakes up.'

I digested this carefully while silence grew between us, filled with the kinds of things that are better not said. Better not thought.

'Yeah,' I said finally.

'You want to know the biggest irony of all? The accident wasn't even our fault. Some yo-yo trying to pass on a double yellow line in the rain. We tried to get off the road but the rig skidded and jackknifed and the asshole hit us. And then... we'd been arguing about... we weren't paying close enough... If we had, we'd... it might never have...'

Ivory was crying again, the rough, desolate sound of despair wracking her broken voice. 'Oh my God, 'Chelley, all my beautiful horses. And now... I'm not going back there, 'Chelle. I'm not. I'm not getting set up again.'

'I don't think it's hopeless.'

'With my record? Hah.'

'That was a long, long time ago.'

'They won't care. They'll just love getting their hands on my bony ass.'

'We'll just have to keep 'em off it, that's all.'

'Yeah? You got any bright ideas?'

'A couple. Not for this minute, though, okay? You have to rest.'

'What do I do when they come around asking questions? You know how soon that's gonna be.'

'You don't have to say anything 'til we get you a great lawyer. All you have to be is too emotionally traumatized to speak.'

'That shouldn't be hard.'

A nurse took that moment to pitch me out, but Ivory's voice stopped me at the door. 'You won't leave?' Her eyes like a child's, imploring and frightened. A long distance from my hardboiled friend the steel magnolia.

'Promise. I'm just going to call my mom in Florida. Tell her what's up, see if she can recommend a lawyer. And check on the horses, but I'll come by to see you again in a bit.'

Ivory managed a smile and nodded. The nurse was adjusting the i.v. and my old friend looked ready to drop back into the kind of sleep I wished I could find.

Back in my rig in the hospital parking lot I turned my phone on and found about ten thousand urgent messages, none of which I felt capable of answering. I deleted them and prepared to leave, but was stopped by a visitation of police officers. I invited them into my tiny space and told the whole truth and nothing but the truth about my part in the whole accident and that was it. They already knew from witnesses how the whole mess had happened, that the accident hadn't been Winston and Ivory's fault. But the unfortunate bonanza of a drug tie-in made them officious, like a pack of hounds with a 'coon up a tree. When they pumped me about Ivory I painted her as a hardworking professional (true), totally at the mercy of an unscrupulous owner and his whims (not entirely false). And mentioned their fucked up relationship because they'd find out about it from his wife and all our mutual acquaintances, anyway. And swore to the fact that Ivory was a dupe, which wasn't so much an untruth as it was prevailing opinion around the barns.

When they asked me who Winston's friends were I said I had no idea, not being a part of his crowd, and that they should ask his wife. They told me not to be a wiseass. I said I was only telling them the truth like they'd asked, and that all I was was a person at the scene of a tragic accident, that happened to be a friend of Ivory's and a fellow professional. They said they'd check into all that, which they'd probably already done without finding anything to hang a drug charge on. Maybe that was why they were so pissy, I don't know. It's been over twenty years since I've thought of the police as anything but regular guys trying to do a tough job right. But when this pair finally left, I had to take a shower to get them off me.

I called my mother, who'd seen the news and was worried.

'I guess you'll be needing a terrific lawyer for Ivory, will you?' she said.

'Looks like it.'

She sighed into the phone line. 'I get this sense of déjà vù. You're sure she's innocent?'

'Poz, ma. She's just...'

'Stupid.'

'Well… I was going to say she lacks judgment.'

'You know my dog, Chloé?'

'Sure. What's that…'

'She has an insatiable passion for porcupine meat, but she always forgets about the quills. Seems I have her off to the vet at least once a year to have them pulled out by the fistful and it's always a hideous, painful, bloody mess. I never stop hoping she'll learn, but she doesn't.'

She left me to make the obvious connection. Subtle woman, my ma.

She had me call a lawyer friend who had me call another friend who turned me on to a guy everybody swore was the best in the business for this kind of screwed-up case. Not that I knew what kind of screwed-up case it really was. Turned out he kept a couple of Quarter Horses, so at least he'd know something about our life and its ramifications.

I called Camille at school, who'd also seen the news and was also worried, but who thought my appearing on TV was way cool (*I what?* I asked dumbly, *On what?*) and seemed to think that knowing somebody involved in a live action drug scandal lent her life a certain seedy rock star glamour.

I figured it wasn't a great time to be making stuffy speeches about reality, but wondered if I should have gone ahead when I intercepted a call from my ex-husband Joe-Don't-Call-Me-Josie, demanding to know how I'd gotten mixed up in this kind of situation and what the hell did I intend to do about it and he was having serious thoughts about forbidding Camille to see me over February break. His voice was filled with pomposity and self-importance, as if a big-deal business title and a wealthy society-type wife gave him a leg-up on moral righteousness. In a funny way these made him much easier for me to ignore. I just looked out the window of my van and said *uh-huh* at various intervals while he thundered on until he ran out of gas, accused me of not listening to a word, and hung up. I wasn't too worried about losing Camille. I knew his wife had had more than enough of contending with her over Thanksgiving. In the cold light of day Josie (*'that's* Joe, *Michelle'*) would be more than delighted to have her with me in Florida rather than get stuck between them for another nine rounds.

I called my friends in Camden to check up on my horses – and especially on Dancing Fool. I cried some more when I found them safe and their caregivers concerned.

'Have you watched the news?' my friends asked, when they'd managed to get me off the worn-out subject of the safety of my horses and Dancing Fool. 'You're a hero, 'Chelle.'

'No, I'm not.'

'It's in all the papers, too. God, 'Chelle. How did you do it?'

'I didn't do anything,' I said. 'Not enough.'

'And that British guy. Incredible that he was there. What was his name? He's somebody famous, I think. If I can just remember...'

'I never asked,' I said. 'Just tell me again, okay?'

'Jake and Jenny are safe. Dancing Fool is safe.'

'Really safe?'

'Safe as we can make them. It's okay, 'Chelle. You just do what you have to do and trust us here. Okay?'

'So they're okay.'

'Yes.'

'Jake and Jenny.'

'Safe.'

'And Dancing Fool.'

'Safe.'

I breathed. 'Okay. I'm sorry. Thanks. It's just...'

'They're safe, 'Chelle. Goodbye.'

Finally I called Santé, the Puerto Rican jockey-turned stable manager who'd seen to Ivory's horses ever since the combined forces of injury and a drug problem (now controlled) ended his racing career. Santé loved his horses like family. He wept openly and blamed himself, as I knew he would. He wanted to come and look after the others, as I expected him to. I said no, sit tight, he'd be needed later, take a break. And for God's sake, don't fall off the straight-and-narrow.

I turned my phone off again and lay down for a few minutes before going back to the Equine clinic. I was too spun to sleep, but exhaustion rolled over me like a wave. I would probably have lain there in a semi-conscious stupor for the rest of the day, but Spring, ever helpful, stood on my chest, licked my face, and smiled her best doggy smile while her little stumpy tail wiggled. I galvanized myself, took her for a walk, then drove out to see Ivory's horses. Morning Glory and Heavensent were stable - that was the good news - but battling infection - that was the bad. I conferred with the vets, made more calls, ate something tasteless out of a can, fell into bed, and dreamed of broken horses all night long.

When I got back to the hospital next morning, the first person I met in the lobby was Winston's wife, Janna. With Winston still in a coma, she looked about as badly off as you might expect. I'd never known her all that well, but my heart went out to her. In spite of myself, I gave her a hug. In spite of herself, she seemed grateful. She was even more grateful when I offered to make all the necessary arrangements and decisions about her remaining horses. Janna liked the cachet that went with being a big time owner, but she wasn't a horseman by any stretch of the imagination. So it was a good trade - her belief in my magnanimity for my enlightened self-interest.

Which is to say that I wanted those horses alive. 'They shouldn't be put down before they've had a chance to prove they can pull through,' I insisted.

'Oh, no no, of course. Of course. But... um... how do we, I mean the insurance people, you know... decide...'

'Do you know what kind of insurance you had on them? Mortality? Loss of use?'

'Loss of use, I think that was it.'

I breathed a sigh of relief. 'That's okay, then. You should get whatever value you had on them. It'll take care of a lot of the bills they're running up.' Then, out of politeness, I asked about Winston's condition.

'There's no change yet,' she said, gazing around her in a puzzled way. Her eyes looked funny, and I wondered if she was drugged. 'It's so... strange. We were just going to... everything was so much better, we were going to... you know, take a vacation. Buy a little place in the Keys...' her hands fluttered in her lap, butterflies on a windowpane. She clasped them together, frowning at them. She looked about twelve years old without the pounds of make-up she usually hid behind; orphaned.

'Then... all those officers. Agents. All those questions. Oh, 'Chelle, it's so horrible, I just don't know what to do, they made me feel like a *criminal*, as if I would...' she stopped and shudder. 'I still can't believe... that my Winston...'

'Did you have any idea about Winston's business? I mean, what it really was?'

She shook her head. 'Never. I never knew. Just that... it was, you know, international trade...'

I almost laughed out loud. I couldn't think how anybody could be this seriously naïve. I wondered if Janna was in fact a world class actress, but the pain and fear reflected in her eyes persuaded me that she was not.

'I'm sorry, Janna,' I said, suddenly overcome with guilt. 'It must be awful.'

She looked up at me, nodded, tried to smile, and started to cry. I sat down next to her and put my arm around her so she'd have a shoulder to sob against and cursed myself for ever having derided her shallowness, for ever having thought unkindnesses of her. Being alone and friendless is scary. Being abandoned is worse. Facing a life without something you've come to rely on…

I asked if she needed me to stay with her, but as she was sweetly saying no, a thick-set man in an power suit that exuded influence and expensive aftershave arrived to take her away, full of condolences and a strong arm for her, barely more than a dismissive glance toward me. Which was a good thing. The man was scary enough to make me want to run in the opposite direction as fast as I could go.

But I still gave Janna my number and told her to call me. At that moment, I even hoped she would.


Ivory was out of her room, something about arcane medical tests. I sat in the waiting area and opened a magazine intending to read about raising emotionally healthy teenagers in a fucked-up world, which seemed like it might help me with Camille. But before I got to the article I was arrested in the Entertainment section by photos of Lou Reed and Johnny Depp. I paused to sigh deeply over their deliciously weird minds and artistic mastery and, well, okay, yeah. Lou Reed's arms, Johnny Depp's mouth… I found myself thinking again about the Brit who'd been my briefest of lovers. *You bonehead. You didn't even find out his name.* Shit. Shit, shit, shit. I wanted to jump up, run to the vet clinic, rifle their trash to find his card, call him, find some way to bring him back.

I closed the magazine, threw it on the table, and buried my face in my hands with a groan. Raising emotionally well-adjusted teenagers was probably way out of my league, anyway.

When Ivory came back she was looking almost chipper and demonstrated her dubious prowess with a wheelchair by nearly wiping out an elderly man in a walker and totally entangling herself in the wires and tubes that still dangled from her like the appendages of a sea anemone. 'The good news is, I'm out of here in a week or so,' she said. 'The other good news is I'll walk again.'

'Will you ride?'

'Well, of *course* I'll ride.' She looked mulish. 'These doctors don't know from nothing about that shit. Yeah, 'Chelle, I'll ride. But not yet awhile. So I'm gonna need somebody to take Dancing Fool around for me. I was hoping you might…'

I winced and my stomach started churning. This was like winning Publisher's Clearinghouse, like getting the Olympic gold, the stuff we dream of without ever considering it seriously. I raised my hands to try to ward it off. 'Oh, God, Ive, don't even *say* it. I can't stand it.'

'Don't you want the ride?'

'Of *course* I want the ride. But there are so many better riders you could get. You don't have to offer her to me because I'm your friend. I'll gladly get whoever you think would be best. Michael, for instance. It should be Michael.' I could barely breathe at the thought of riding this talented animal over big fences. It made me moan with lust.

'I don't want Michael Draper within 100 yards of my horse.'

'But why? He's...'

'Honest to Christ, 'Chelle, you are your own worst enemy, you know something? It's a wonder you get any rides at all, the way you keep trying to give them away. I'm asking you to ride my horse because I want you to ride my horse. I'd turn over *all* my rides to you, if they were mine to give.'

'Okay! Okay, you talked me into it. I'll ride your horse. Thank-you thank-you thank-you. A million times, Ivory. I mean it.'

'Yeah, well I'm not doing you any big favors. She's a whore. She needs a certain kind of rider. I happen to think you're it.'

'I wish you were it.'

'Me too. But...' she trailed off and gazed out the waiting room window until I thought she'd forgotten I was there. Then she said, 'I'm getting a lot of thinking done these long dark lonely nights, 'Chelle. It's not all pretty, but I guess it's necessary.'

'Yeah? Like what? You make me nervous when you get philosophical. It usually means you're about to get into major trouble.'

'Oh, don't you worry. This is about staying *out* of it. Life stuff. '*Thangs*', you know? There's gonna be lots of time to talk to you about it when I get out of here. But first I guess I need to talk about this lawyer guy, and all that shit. Fuckin' Christ, what a mess.' She shook her head, but didn't look as down as she had before. The old tough gleam was returning to her eyes. She looked up at me with an intensity that could have blown me out the window. 'And I by-God am certainly going to ride that mare again. So don't you get too awful cozy with her.'

Guy Carmouche met us that afternoon. He was tall, broad, black, and looked pretty straight and extremely arrogant. We'd been told he was tough and smart, which we needed. We also figured he couldn't be a complete dweeb because of the Quarter Horses. I mean, if horse ownership is any measure of character, which as we knew from Winston it wasn't. But it helped.

The mess was a big one. It was several messes, in fact. The accident was the most straightforward of the lot, even though it involved bringing in a second lawyer from Guy Carmouche's firm. Then there was the drug rap, that was something completely different and - worse - a problem for the Feds. There was Winston in a coma, which was really different. And there was Ivory, which somehow seemed even more different. At the end of a meeting that took all afternoon my head was spinning.

I walked out of the hospital with my mind in a blur of legalese and was stunned to see a bunch of news vehicles and people with mics and cameras clustered around my van while Spring did her most aggressive growling, barking, and bouncing around the furniture routine from inside it. While I stood there blinking and working my mouth like a hooked bass, somebody turned and saw me and they all descended on me and asked questions and wanted information that I didn't have and asked me to relive moments that I wanted to forget and generally pestered me until finally a cop came and told them all to go away. I thanked the officer, staggered into the rig, locked the door, sat down, and shook. The horrifying work of one afternoon was looking like spinning into an unending nightmare. I cried some more, surprised I still had tears left to spill. I wondered how on earth I would carry on under all the shit that kept hitting me and my friend.

And I still had to get back to Camden to resume the care of my own horses. I still had to get myself down to Florida for the first show of the winter series before I ran out of money again.

I offered to cancel everything and stay with Ivory, but she turned me down. 'Standing around in Camden won't do those horses any good,' she pointed out. 'They'll lose condition fast, you don't get them back in work pronto. I'll be okay here yet awhile.' I looked into her eyes and knew damn well what lay behind her words. Like cold fear, and a sense of horrible inevitability. We made arrangements to talk daily until the first legal batch of stuff was over, court hearings were set, and she could travel south. If they'd let her travel south. There was some doubt about this, which neither of us was ready to dwell on.

And it was true about the horses. Like children, their demands are constant. If you're exhausted, they must be exercised. If you have influenza, they must be cleaned and cared for. If you're too broke to eat, they must be fed. And if you've been in a horrible accident and might end up in jail, you still have to address their needs on schedule. This is the price we pay for unswerving loyalty, unquestioning service, and unparalleled companionship. The price we pay for taking an animal whose nature it is to roam vast miles over grass-covered plains in close family groupings, and cloistering it away from its world and its herd in stalls or paddocks, dependent on us for life and wellbeing.

What makes us God? Why did we make ourselves utterly responsible for the existence of an autonomous creature? How marvelous is the generous nature of that animal, accepting us without comment? Our survival has so often hung on the milk, the flesh, the speed, the warmth, the endurance, the loyalty of horses. Worshipped as a god; companion in war; partner in conquest; vehicle for geographical expansion; tiller of soil; nourisher of body and soul alike. A mysterious blend of servant and savior without whom humankind could not have traveled so far or accomplished so much.

People may say that the dog is man's best friend. But the horse is his soul mate.


When I'd done everything I could for Ivory I left her languishing at the hospital and the two horses languishing at the clinic, and went back to Camden to pick up the pieces of my life. I stayed overnight and rode Jake and Jennie early in the morning before heading south. They were high as kites from several days of relative inactivity and even sensible Jennie tried to pitch me when a rabbit bolted across the trail I'd taken to give her a relaxed outing.

I didn't dare sit on Dancing Fool outside a ring, but walk-trot-cantered the temperamental mare in big loopy circles for an hour and a half while I tried to figure out how to ride her. I found her as slippery as an eel and twice as fast. One ounce too much hand and she'd jump in the air and go on a bucking spree that was anything but light hearted. One fraction of an inch out of balance and she spooked violently and tried to run away. Every time we got around the ring twice without mishap and I thought I finally had the knack, she'd leap straight in the air or sideways and try to bolt and we'd have to start all over again. I never so much as hopped her over a cross rail. I felt like a total novice.

I gave up on her in despair, finally. I cooled her out, rubbed her down, administered fresh hay and water all around, and staggered back to the rig for a brief lie-down.

Four hours later, I woke up. In a daze I wrapped all three horses' legs with special care, loaded all the gear I needed, settled my charges in their traveling stalls, thanked my friends another dozen or so times for their friendship and help until they practically threw me off the place, and pointed the rig south.

Within moments of leaving I fielded a call from Harry Daly, who wanted to know a) whether we ought to be starting an Ivory Gardner defense fund (*yes*) and b) if I could pick up a horse for him from a neighboring farm and bring it to Florida *(anything for you, Harry)*.

'Big bay thing. Only six. I figure he might make a nice Junior or Amateur Jumper, with some mileage.'

'What is he?' I asked.

'Oh... some kinda warmblood, I guess,' he said vaguely. 'That's what I'll call him, anyway.'

Maybe a little side trip was just what I needed. Maybe if I said yes Harry would finally offer me some of his wonderful goddamn coffee. I agreed to get the horse.

When I met the beast I found that 'big' just barely described him. At over 17.0 hands, or nearly 70" at the withers, he looked like an equine mountain. It was clear that he was about half Clydesdale; he had that bright bay coat, the blaze, and four - count them - long white stockings. Feet the size of a kid's swimming pool. He kept stepping on himself and everybody else who came within yards of him, too. I couldn't see how the creature would ever get out of his own way, let alone over a big fence. I called Harry back to make sure he knew exactly what it was he was going to take delivery of.

'Look,' he said in exasperation, 'don't gimme any lip, willya? Just bring me the horse. I got some ideas about him.'

'Like what? Hook him to a beer wagon and do the lunchtime entertainment? Teach him to sit up and beg? I mean honest to Christ, Harry...'

''Chelle babe,' he said, choking back laughter, 'you are just one big pain in the ass, you know that? Now are you going to bring me the goddamn horse, or do I have to...'

'Yeah, Harry. Yeah, I'll bring you the horse. But don't say you weren't warned. I pity the soul who has to ride the sucker, that's all.'

'Yeah, well not yet you don't,' he said elliptically, and hung up.

It was nice to laugh. Nice to be back on the road. I sat with Spring next to me and the countryside rolling by outside the windows and sang along with Mary Chapin Carpenter about there being a whole lot of ground to gain. I started to cry again when it got to the part about flying, but it didn't feel quite so desolate this time, and Spring comforted me by crawling into my lap so I could hug her with one arm.

That afternoon my best friend Ivory Gardner was arrested in her hospital bed and read charges that included possession with intent to sell, interstate drug trafficking, and a whole lot of other stuff I couldn't even remember.

'*Ivory,*' I wailed. 'Did you know this was going to happen? Why didn't you tell me? I would've…'

''Chelley, yeah, I knew. I didn't want to upset you. I knew if I told you you'd still be here, and there's nothin' you can do but chew your tail. C'mon, honey, it'll be okay. I got me a cute guard posted outside my room whose ass is not such bad scenery. I got Guy Carmouche who's a good guy, he thinks it'll be all right and I gotta trust him. All I can do, huh? Just trust the man.'

'What about Winston?'

'Still in a coma, doll.' There was steel in her voice. 'Can't say anymore than that. 'Bye now. They're cutting me off.'

'*Ive…*' but she was gone.

I dropped my phone on the grassy verge of the rest stop where I sat with Spring and flopped onto my back to stare at the sky, my mind as blank as the blue heaven above. I kept segueing into a time warp, a scene twenty-five years old. Only I'd been lying on a hill in Galway then, with seagulls wheeling and crying above me and a fine mist soaking my face. *Plus ca change; plus c'est le meme chose:* the more things change, the more they stay the same. Grandmère's favorite line. I'd never liked it much.

In the back of the van, the horses were getting restive. I got up, adjusted their sheets, offered them another chance at water, refilled the hay nets, and spoke to them all in the soft language of touch and word that is shared between horses and their people. By these small ceremonies we define ourselves. By these unthinking occupations we reinforce the rhythm and necessity of daily life, and find comfort.

If I drove all night I figured I'd make Florida by dawn.

# FOUR

*Sometimes he trots, as if he told the steps,*
*With gentle majesty and modest pride;*
*Anon he rears upright, curvets, and leaps,*
*As who should say 'Lo, thus my strength is tried...*
*-William Shakespeare, **Venus and Adonis***

When I arrived at the show grounds dew clung to the live oaks and palmettos that dotted the landscape, glistened on the stabling tent roofs, and shimmered from grass to sky. The morning air resonated with the drum of hooves thumping down the ramps of just-arrived vans, whinnying horses wondering where the hell they were, people yelling greetings, laughing at really bad jokes, and swearing good naturedly at spooky horses and the inevitable horde of yapping terriers. Outside the main gate, a gaggle of animal rights activists marched and chanted, brandishing placards denouncing the cruel use of horses for human recreation. Somewhere a speaker churned out canned Christmas carols. Inside the big tent-barns that made up the temporary stabling on the grounds horses rolled, napped, sneezed, pawed, and kicked walls, people shouted orders, buckets clanked, hoses spouted water, electric clippers buzzed, radios competed like battles of the bands, hammers clattered a staccato counterpoint, deck chairs, saddles, bridles, and rakes appeared, and fancy draperies went up around tack stalls until the grounds reverberated with carnival energy.

The first close acquaintance I ran into after I parked and headed off to find the show secretary's office was Craig Oppenheim, who didn't introduce me to the young man accompanying him but instantly dubbed me Our Lady of the Van Wreck and pumped me for information about Ivory and Winston, the horses, the gossip, and the legal stuff - none of which I wanted to talk about. When I'd insisted about fifty times that I wasn't a heroine, that Ivory and two of the horses were doing okay, and that other than that I knew zilch in the line of either gossip or hard fact, he rolled his eyes in exasperation and told me I was useless.

'But how 'bout that Colin Rutherford, Huh? What a hottie.'

'Who?' I asked, mystified.

'Colin Rutherford. The guy you worked the wreck with.'

'Colin Rutherford?' Gradually the cogs fell into place. 'You mean... *Colin Rutherford?* As in the won-Badminton-three-times-Colin Rutherford?'

'You didn't *know*?'

'Fuck no, I didn't know. *Jesus.*' The world suddenly tilted about 30 degrees. I almost had to sit down.

Craig laughed. 'Don't you read your own *press*? Didn't you even *recognize* the guy?'

'It was not exactly the moment for social introductions, Craig.'

'Shit, 'Chelley, you are just about as dumb as a post!' He laughed some more. 'There you were, middle of a crisis, hauling...'

'Craig. Don't,' I said tightly.

'Yeah, Craig.' The young man standing with him touched his arm warningly. 'Not the time for this stuff.'

Craig sobered up. 'Sorry. Bummer about Rougère and Memphis. Ivory deserves a whole lot better than that. Not like some people we could mention.' He shot a meaningful look at his friend, then remembered his manners and introduced us. 'Bye the bye, Tommy Essex, this is 'Chelle Martin, our very own Heroine Du Jour. 'Chelle, if you're an observant girl you might remember Tommy from the Juniors awhile back.'

'Oh, yeah. Sure,' I said, trying and failing to recall either the name or the face.

'I used to ride a horse called Radical Right,' Tommy offered helpfully. 'Been off at college, the last couple years.'

Horse people might forget each other. They will never forget a nice horse. I grinned as light dawned. 'Radical Right! He was a character-and-a-half. I *loved* that horse. Johnny Halloran's, wasn't he?'

'Yeah.' Tommy looked delighted. 'Still is. Nicest thing I ever rode. He's gotta be over twenty...' he hesitated for a moment, then blurted, 'It was great, you know. What you did for those horses. For Ivory.'

His simplicity caught me by surprise; my throat lumped up suddenly and I blinked away tears. The loudspeaker blatted out *Ding Dong Merrily On High* in what seemed like complete incongruity.

'It could have been any of us,' I managed.

'Horrible.'

'Yeah.'

'Anything we can do for her? For the horses?'

'I dunno, yet. I think Harry's taking up a collection. There'll be a lot of legal fees.'

'Let me know, okay? If there's… I mean, she shouldn't take…'

'Oh, by the way,' Craig broke in, 'Sara Wychoff is looking high and low for you.'

'Sara Wychoff? What for?'

'Probably something to do with your heroic acts and how to turn it into a media feast, if I know Sara. I don't know whether to congratulate you or pity you. Gotta go, Tommy, gotta go. See you around, 'Chelle.' He took Tommy by the arm and hustled him away, Tommy's face mirroring surprise. I wondered idly if Tommy Essex had supplanted Michael Draper, who'd been tight as a married couple with Craig for more years than… well, most married couples. Until Michael went back to his wife and daughter, that is. I guessed Craig must finally have moved on. Nobody likes the yank-around of always playing second fiddle - mistress, lover, or what-all.

In the show office I found not one but several messages waiting for me from Sara Wychoff, each more urgent than the last. I left a vague note, picked up my stabling assignments, numbers for the upcoming week, and other various bits of information, then left to find a place to unload my horses and park my home on wheels for the duration.

Sara was hot on my heels. I'd just let Spring out, opened the windows so the horses could hang their heads out, and started setting up their pen when I heard the piercing trumpet of a voice that could only be hers calling my name. It caught me wrestling sweatily with a section of pipe that for some infuriating reason refused to go together properly and was requiring more four-letter words, hammerings, and well-placed kicks than seemed decent, all to the tune of the loudspeaker's relentless rendition of *We Three Kings*. I didn't dare risk having the whole damn section fall on me by letting go long enough to get a cotter pin out of my mouth. I hazarded the briefest backward nod and *mmph* in Sara's direction and kept working.

''Chelle,' she boomed as she hove-to behind me. 'I've been looking all *over* for you. What rock do you hide under, lady? Got somebody here I want you to meet. Or re-meet. Colin Rutherford, this is Michelle Martin, your fellow hero of the hour. Or it's her back, anyway. 'Chelle, turn around for God's sake and say something civil to Colin. He's here from England to compete and he's going to be doing the Jumpers here before he moves house to North Carolina.'

My innards froze as if somebody had mainlined ice into my veins. I gave the fence section one last bang to get it in place, grabbed the cotter pin, rammed it home, and stood up.

Two panels immediately fell over, in a cloud of dust.

'Fuck', I said in despair.

I wiped my greasy hands on my jeans and gulped a deep breath that almost choked me. 'That wasn't directed at you,' I said helplessly as I turned. 'It was...' I gestured toward the half-built pen and then looked at the man I had shared some of the worst - and best - moments of my adult life with.

Even with an iota of preparation, the shock of seeing him hit me like a blow to the solar plexus. My throat dried, my stomach churned, and I could feel my face flush red, then drain - like his was doing - and I self-consciously stuffed my hands in my pockets - like he was doing. We lamely said, 'Um... hi...' in each other's direction while Sara looked at us quizzically.

'Oh. I mean... You *do* know each other, don't you? You were both in the *news*, and we understood...'

He said, 'Er... sort of...' and I said, 'Um... kinda...' more or less simultaneously and then I mumbled something incomprehensible about good Samaritans and scenes of disaster which sailed right past Sara's grey matter while she drew inaccurate conclusions and breathed, 'Ohhhh, I *see*. Ye-e-s, what an *awful* experience to share.' The intently sympathetic expression on her face said she thought it anything but. She reminded me of a raptor looking at a fresh carcass.

'Yeh', agreed Colin Rutherford. Then he caught my wince and quickly added, 'I mean... it was... the... er...' his voice tailed off and he looked at me helplessly.

'Shock,' I supplied.

'Shock. So we hadn't the chance to be... um...'

'Properly acquainted.'

'Properly... um,' he agreed.

'Yeah,' I stumbled. 'So...'

'Oh, gosh, I can just *imagine*,' said Sara brightly. 'But, you know, I started thinking the other day that, well, aren't we *fortunate* to have two committed people like yourselves - *strangers*, appearing on the scene of this *dreadful* crash, and, well, *saving* two of the horses. And here you both are, ready to get on with your jobs. *The show must go on*. You know? So-o-o, I was thinking, given that the industry has had such a *lot* of mud slung at it over the last several years, it would be *so terrific* if you two would be willing to do an *interview* for us.'

'An interview?' I said suspiciously. 'What kind of interview?'

'Well, TV, probably, one of the statewide talk shows. Linda Lerner's interested. Maybe some radio or print tie-ins. It would be so *helpful*. Good for the industry. And for the shows here, too, of course.'

'Of course,' agreed Colin Rutherford blandly.

'But... what for?' I looked at the Brit to see his reaction to all this and found him studiously examining the red dirt of the parking area. The corners of his mouth twitched suspiciously.

'Well, to tell us what it was *like*. People love hearing about courage and bravery in the face of catastrophe. How you *felt*. What was going through your *mind*. How you rose to the occasion and did what had to be *done*.'

'Well, I don't know about Mr. Rutherford...'

'Colin...'

'...Colin here, but I can already tell you I didn't feel brave *or* courageous. It was disgusting and sad and horrible and I was scared to death.'

'Ex*actly*!' said Sara triumphantly. 'And that's why it's so important that people *hear* from you. So that the public *knows* how much you care, how much most horsemen *care*, about their animals.'

'Yeah, but TV. I wouldn't know... I mean, jeez, Sara, I might pick my nose or fart or something...' Even with his back partly turned I could hear Colin Rutherford choke, but Sara seemed oblivious.

'Oh, 'Chelle *darling*, don't *worry*. You looked *fabulous* on the news accounts. You looked *brave*...'

'Brave?' I wrinkled my forehead in total bewilderment.

'and... *concerned*... and... *beautiful*...'

'Wait a minute,' I said, 'you're going too fast for me here. Who are you talking about?'

She looked at me earnestly. ''Chelle, didn't you watch the *news*? Didn't you read the *papers*? Didn't you *see* yourself?'

'No', I said baldly. And as I spoke I could feel one of those untamable absurdity-of-it-all laugh attacks welling up from deep inside my belly and I knew I was going to start giggling and spluttering uncontrollably at any moment and couldn't think how to get out of this horrible situation when I was rescued by Harry's youngster, who picked that moment to try to climb through the window of the bus. I excused myself in a hurry, turned down offers of help, swore to Sara I'd get back to her, and raced up the ramp yelling insults at the animal.

This kept me pretty busy for awhile. The horse was bored with his confinement, and I couldn't blame him. Every time I thought I had him quieted down and tried to leave to find Harry he'd start thrashing around again and Jake and Jennie and Dancing Fool were starting to look at him like they'd maybe join the fun and games and eat him for breakfast having first destroyed the rig. So I offloaded him and took him with me, all 17 plus hands of the sucker dancing around on his huge platter feet with head and tail in the air like a giant dog, snorting loudly at everything. By the time I found Harry's stalls my toes were bruised, my arm about ripped from its socket, and my elbow sore from shoving the oaf away from my body. Harry thought all this was hilarious, and asked if the horsie had taken me for a nice walk and whether I'd had enough exercise yet.

'Because if you haven't, I'd like you to get on him for me.'

'You want me to ride *this*?'

'Yes, darlin', I do.'

'Huh,' I said, with immense originality. 'Okay, I'll be back when I've got the rest of the gang settled.' Then I limped away with whatever shred of dignity I had left to tend to my bruises and my own horses, cursing Harry roundly because I could *still* smell his wonderful coffee and the asshole *still* hadn't offered me any.

When I got back, my horse pen was fully constructed and stabilized and The Brit - who, now that I knew his name, I knew to be one of the best Three Day riders in the world - was sitting on the step of my 'house', waiting. My stomach did a few thumps and revolutions. Why do people talk about hearts doing somersaults? Mine *was* beating a few extra strokes to the minute, but it's always my stomach that behaves like a crazy thing. And my legs, which at the moment resembled Jell-O.

Colin Rutherford, looking cool and collected - though he was sitting down - smiled like a normal human being and said hello. I said *Hi* back, and *thanks for putting my pen up* and then dried up completely, like that was the sum total of my grasp of English. He said I was welcome, and blushed. In this completely tongue-tied fashion we looked sheepishly in turns at the landscape and each other for awhile.

'Interesting dirt you have down here,' he said finally. 'Very... um... red.'

'Yeah.' I started to chuckle in spite of myself. 'Studied it pretty closely for the last half hour, have you?'

'Have done, yeh.' He hazarded a twinkle in my direction. 'Odd way to meet, that. Wunnit?'

'*Yeah*. Why didn't you *tell* me who the hell you were, back there?'

'I gave you my card.'

'Ahhh… right. You did. I… uh… threw it away. I never looked at it. I didn't think… y'know.'

'I see. Well… Um. There wasn't much *time*, was there. For introductions. We… er… couldn't know whether it might be necessary. Under the circs.'

'Ships passing in the night, that shit. Right.' I must have blushed, because he laughed. A nice laugh, I remembered.

'Something like that, yeh.' He pronounced 'something' like 'summing', which I found unreasonably sexy. 'Of course,' he grinned evilly, '*Some* of us stay abreast of the news. I made a point of finding you out. Just in case. And the press were very helpful in that regard, too.'

'The *press*! Oh, God. I ran into them at the hospital. Fucking bunch of sensation-seekers.'

'Well, yeh. Nasty piece of work. We should have expected it, I suppose. As soon as I arrived here I had to… Look, um… 'Chelle. Why don't you invite me in? Will you? This music is driving me mad.'

The loudspeaker cranked out its version of *Joy To The World*. Every third note was flat. I grimaced. 'I think I picked a really stupid place to park. I should have figured it out when I saw this big empty space.'

'So does that mean we can go in?'

'I have a few things to set up here, first,' I said defensively, suave to the end. 'Get these guys into their stalls and all that. It could take awhile.'

I turned down his offer of help, but he looked at me as if I were mentally deficient and helped anyway. He liked my van side paddock-ette. He loved Dancing Fool. He admired Jake and Jennie without being suspiciously effusive about them. He refrained from commenting on their size and cuteness, earned extra points by guessing they were half-bred Connemaras, and got a gold star by saying he'd grown up riding them himself and had even taken one to tenth place at Badminton; the biggest, toughest Three Day Event in the world.

'He handled the size and the distance beautifully; it was only the speed that was difficult,' he said enthusiastically. 'Now, if I could find one three-quarter-bred for size and speed - and keep the quarter

Connemara blood for good Native soundness and durability - I reckon I'd have an upper level horse worth feeding.'

Okay, I was melting.

When I let him in after all the chores were done he stood inside the door for a moment as if looking for something he'd misplaced. *'This castle hath a pleasant seat,'* he said with a smile. *'The air nimbly and sweetly recommends itself unto our gentle senses.'*

'Yeah. Well, it's home sweet home', I said, cringing at my banality. I was too tense to remember what came next; something pretty about birds nesting in favorable places. Which should have been reassuring except that the play was *Macbeth* and the speakers were all about to be murdered.

The Brit smiled lopsidedly at me and my stomach did a few more gymnastic exercises. I offered him drinks, snacks, anything to keep myself from sitting down. But since there wasn't a lot to offer or much space to pace in I ran out of stalling techniques almost instantly and had to sit.

'I don't know what to do here', I said, with a deep breath. 'I'm having some trouble getting my head straight about you-the-thing-that-happened-one-strange-night and you Colin-Rutherford-the-international-Three-Day-star that I've read all about and never met. What are you doing here, anyway?'

'It's rather a long story. But in general - taking a year to ride for a client who just moved back from the U.K. See if I might relocate.'

'Jumpers?'

'Mmm. Possible change of career focus.'

'So... we're going to be running into each other. Like... Around.'

'Yeh.'

'Well... don't *you* find this a little awkward? I mean, we don't know...'

'Yeh, yeh. Whether I'm still married, whether you're involved, whether we've given each other horrible diseases, whether we both like Newcastle Ale or *The Tempest*, whether we have anything besides... um... well... *anything* in common, whether anybody knows or will guess... am I warm?'

'Hot. You're very hot. I mean...' I blushed furiously and blurted, 'I don't mean hot like... *hot*, I mean like *temperature* hot, like *Fahrenheit* or *centigrade* or whatever, I didn't... mean... oh, *shit.'*

'Right,' he said solemnly. And then he started to laugh and I started to laugh and we just rolled around in uncontrollable hilarity for awhile.

'So,' I said, when we'd regained our senses and wiped our eyes.

'*Doesn't* it strike you as odd?'

'It was like combat, 'Chelle. Like a natural disaster or 9-11 or something. Most people don't go through that much in a lifetime together.'

'You think that makes a difference?'

'Must do. Make a weird bond. Don't you think?'

'Yeah,' I sighed. 'Yeah, I guess I do.'

'How've you been, then?'

'Shaky. You?'

'After we parted I drove for an hour or so. Then I had to pull over and weep.'

'Yeah, me too.' Without conscious effort, our hands met and clasped. Life rafts. Life. And death so near.

'Your friend... Ivory?'

'She's in serious trouble. We found a great lawyer.'

'I met that character Harry Daly. Thinks the world of you both. He's begun a defense fund for her. We're all pitching in.'

'Even you? Who've never met her?'

'It could have been any one of us.'

We sat in silence for awhile and looked out the window at Jake and Jennie. Jennie was looking back at us from the pen, steaming up the glass with her nostrils, hoping I'd open up and feed her something.

I shrugged unhappily. 'So what now? We can't just... I mean I suppose we should forget about it. Act like it never happened. Start all over like strangers. I mean we are, really. Strangers.' Reluctantly drew my hand away from his.

'Yeh,' he agreed. 'Seems a shame, dunnit?'

'Might make life easier, though. Under the... um... *circs*.' I stole a sly glance at him and he laughed. I wondered how the guy could sit there looking so fucking *rational* when all I wanted to do was jump his irresistible bones and claim him for my very own, stranger or not.

'I suppose we should,' he said, finally. 'Take a step back. Let a new slant on the whole experience take hold. Go from there.'

'It was awful heavy to...'

'Too heavy to...'

'And we're so adult and *civilized* that we can just...'

'Yeh?' His smile was inviting. Hopeful, even.

'Sure. Yeah. Whatever.'

'Right.' He got up, offered me a hand, and pulled me to my feet. 'Thanks for the drink, Ms. Martin. I'm awfully glad to have met you at last.'

'And *clap hands on the bargain.*'

'*Me understand well.* Henry V and Katherine.'

'No flies on you.' I shook his hand solemnly, assured him that the pleasure had been mine, and added, 'Oh, by the way, since it looks like we're going to be media stars, could you give me your autograph? For my elderly mother?'

He threw back his head and guffawed. 'You're a *menace*, you are.' For one blinding moment I was sure he was going to reach out and grab me and hug me and kiss me, but then he flinched and said something totally neutral instead and left.

*Angels We Have Heard On High,* chimed the loudspeaker.

'Oh, shut *up*', I told it irritably.

And watched Colin Rutherford's beautiful narrow backside going away from me. I still didn't know whether he liked Newcastle Ale or *The Tempest*. But lurking in the back of my mind was the memory that he was indeed still married, and that there were sons, and that he adored his family. I sat down miserably. Spring poked her nose under my arm and whined. 'Oh, Spring,' I said. '*Think you there was or might be such a man as this I dreamed of?*'

Fuck. Fuck, fuck, fuck. I jumped up, stalked around in a small circle, and didn't know whether to laugh, cry, throw a plate, or eat something. Bad signs, all. So I put on my chaps, took Jake and Jennie to their stalls next to Dancing Fool, refilled water buckets, and threw them all more hay. Then I went to commit lunacy on Harry's new horse. And cursed a Fate that had taken a nice fantasy from me and turned it into yet another nasty reality dedicated to making porridge out of my already addled life.

There are times when I just want to sit down and howl at the moon like a dog.


Harry's horse, which was called Clyde for reasons too obvious to elaborate on, wasn't as bad to ride as he was to lead. By the time I'd worked him on the flat for awhile and gotten used to his long, galumphing stride I'd decided he was pretty cute. After he'd lumbered willingly through a few simple gymnastics with his long ears pricked up happily I was giggling. And when I tried him through a simple bending line and some vertical-oxer-vertical combinations with varied striding, I fell in love. The horse could really get off the ground. It would take some work to get him balanced, and he needed help in the steering and adjustability department, but the ability was there. Better yet, the horse was all desire. He actively wanted to jump the jumps.

'This is a wonderful horse, Harry,' I enthused. 'A *wonderful* horse.'

'I'm glad you agree, darlin'', Harry answered, looking at us reflectively. 'Since I want you to start him Schooling next week.'

'I'd love to have the ride', I admitted, 'but how come? I'd have thought Hilary would take him around. What's the deal?'

Harry shrugged noncommittally. 'Maybe I think you suit the horse. Maybe I think you deserve the break. What do you care?'

'Just curious, I guess.'

'You want the ride?'

'Yeah! I do want the ride.'

'So take the ride and don't ask stupid questions.'

I decided not to look into Harry's motives. I took the ride.

'I hear from Ivory you're gonna be taking Dancing Fool around, too.'

'Yeah,' I said ruefully. 'I ought to be dancing on a cloud over it, but I'll tell you, Harry, I can't ride one side of the hussy. I could sure use some help, if you're willing.'

'We'll work it out, babe, don't worry about that.'

'I just keep thinking Michael might be a better choice...'

''Chelle, darlin', that's fear talking. The mare's not easy. You know it and Ivory knows it and so do all the rest of us know it. Now you may never be the kind of rider Ivory is over a big fence, but you've got a way with awkward horses.' He pointed his finger at me sternly. 'Now shut up and listen to me, 'cuz I believe it's time you got some recognition for what you do best. Dancing Fool's not gonna trouble you for long, you just give her a few days to make the transition. She'll come around, you'll see. What's she doing? The Preliminaries?'

'Yeah, that's where I'll start with her, anyway. She's still pretty green.'

'Well it's perfect, see? Time Ivory's back on board she'll have all the mileage in the world and be ready for the big-time. And if things don't go right for Ivory, you'll have earned your first ticket for a ride in the clouds.'

'Jesus, Harry, don't talk like that. It gives me a stomach-ache just thinking about it.'

Harry laughed and shook his head. ''Chelle, you are the damnedest woman. Every kid that ever trotted a cross rail down here thinks she's ready to do the Grand Prix. You're the only Grand Prix rider I know that can't get your head beyond Intermediate.'

'It's stupid, I know. I just have this thing about jumping fences held up by killer whales and giant beer bottles and effigies of Clyde, here.'

'You do not. You're just scared of making a mistake and dying.'

'Yeah, well, it's not much of a life, but I *like* it, you know? I don't want my daughter to be an orphan. And... I guess it doesn't seem right, prospering from somebody else's misfortune.'

'Nobody ever prospered any other way that I know of.'

'Doesn't make it good.'

'Doesn't make it bad, either. So you might's well use it when it comes your way. We'll work on it, darlin'. I'm gonna see you in that ring smiling if it's all I do this winter.'

'Deal,' I laughed, and got off of the now-cool Clyde to hand him over to his groom.

But in my soul there was a knot, and in that knot a question that wanted to know if I really had the ability to ride fences that topped five feet and were wider than I am tall. Or the guts. Or even, if I dared look this one in the face, that undying flame that made riders like Harry Daly and Ivory Gardner what they were. That defined horses like Clyde and Dancing Fool even from the beginnings of their careers.

We look so hard for horses with desire. What happens when we look inside our selves and find it lacking?

I wasn't sure, when it came right down to it, that I wanted – had ever wanted – to dance on the roof of the world. I really had been pretty content where I was, several layers of atmosphere further down, where the oxygen was easier to breathe. Where nobody expected me to be any better than a little above average.

And now, suddenly, my life was on a track that seemed too fast. Too new. Too heady. And really, really uncomfortable. Because when you're in the public eye, when you're going up that ladder, people start expecting you to be something. And while it's one thing to be a popular rising star, it's quite another to be falling down the other side. To have people find out you weren't really sitting on the right hand of God or anything. Because then they get mean and nasty and start taking you down.

Ohhh, maan.

All I wanted to do was ride horses and live my life. That's all.

On the other hand... I wasn't saying no to anything, either. *So what's that about?* I asked myself. *Maybe you want it all, after all. Maybe you really can do it.*

*Oh Time, thou must unravel this, not I. 'Tis too hard a knot for me t'untie.*

But for once, Shakespeare didn't make me feel any better.


With Christmas only days away, the grounds took on a festival air that not even I was immune to. I bought a wreath to hang on my home's front door and hung the interior with tinsel. I even made Spring a collar of it, which embarrassed her so much that she wriggled out of it at the first opportunity and buried it decently under the rig. Some people had neon Christmas trees lit up inside their motor homes. One or two jokers had rigged their horses' bridles with stuffed cotton antlers and rode around the grounds that way.

I had another loud and useless go-round with Josie-It's-Joe-Michelle and had to admit that it was in fact his turn to have Camille for Christmas. I only argued the point because I knew his real reason was to keep her away from my bad influence. And, well, because I was lonely. I missed my daughter. I missed Ivory. I needed some tidings of joy.

But all I got were interviewers, and the dubious pleasure of cameras in my face, quotes taken out of context, and the discomfort of being in Colin's presence at least once a day in an official capacity, shepherded by Sara Wychoff, surrounded by so many people that we never dared speak anything but banalities. I suppose the good part of having Sara in charge was that at least she kept most outsiders at bay, so we could work.

Meanwhile the grounds filled like a giant tribal encampment, tractor-trailers and huge vans emblazoned with the names and logos of every famous trainer and every known shipper in our world pulling in from all points of the eastern seaboard and beyond. Everybody coming south to be warm, to gain experience, to get a leg-up on the long season of chasing points toward the big national year-end awards, be seen in the right company, earn some money and spend even more.

By Christmas Eve I had to exercise Dancing Fool at dawn, before the crowd in the schooling rings got too bad. She was only marginally improved from our first encounter, but I knew Harry was right. Horses are sensitive souls, easily upset by changes in rider. Some learn to truck around stolidly no matter who they carry, and these are the ones we call 'packers'. Clyde was going to fit that bill, in time. Some, like Dancing Fool, never settle and can be ridden successfully by only one very special person at a time. And their tastes are all different - one hot horse might prefer a featherweight who lets it make its own decisions. Another might only gain confidence from a rider who takes control of every step. Some handle pressure; others go to pieces at the slightest breath. The thing that makes riding an art - that takes it out of the realm of a mechanical exercise - is learning to feel what each horse needs. Then giving it to them.

Watch riders at a show, sometime. Come to that, watch jockeys at the track. After a few hours you'll start to notice that some of them make every horse they get on look easy. These are the artists. The mechanics are the ones who make a big show of riding out the spooks and bucks and resistances. It might look impressive if you don't understand what you're seeing, but in reality it's an ego show disguising a failure to adjust to the needs of every individual horse as it comes.

The great horsemen may not always be the constant blue ribbon winners, which is as often as not a matter of luck, money, readiness, and opportunity. But they always leave a horse better than they found it. They can often achieve levels neither the horse nor its owners believed possible. They can often take that difficult temperament and turn it into something special, something successful for the next person waiting in line to ride it to the top. And they do this over and over again, on horse after horse, year after year. They earn the undying respect of the equestrian community and the unquestioning loyalty of every horse they ride. And that's about the highest compliment a rider can have.

So I took a deep breath and listened to Dancing Fool, giving up on any notion of getting a real performance out of her and just trying to open some kind of conversation. We trotted and cantered and walked and cantered and trotted and walked and cantered some more, big loopy circles and bends and curves and changes of direction on loose reins, asking nothing more than quietness. After about an hour she started showing me moments of what she could do. Those were enough to make me sing, those moments; balanced, forward, powerful. A horse to hang a dream on: light, sensitive, and unbelievably flexible.

Then she'd leap in the air and bolt. She was the dancer; I was her fool.

By the time I'd gotten around to Jake, the grounds were jammed with horses and humanity - a noisy crush of trainers yelling at snotty juniors with no manners riding dark brown horses that looked sour, people yelling greetings at each other as if they'd returned from Siberia against all odds, horses schooling on the flat, horses jumping in every conceivable direction regardless of the laws of etiquette, gravity, or physics, horses sneezing and bouncing, horses standing, horses horses horses everywhere you looked. It was pandemonium. Later in the season I'd grow bad tempered and irritable about it, but not today. Today it was all new again. All filled with the promise of adventure. I cursed cheerfully every time some idiot cut me off in a corner, traded greetings and *Merry Christmas* with friends, acquaintances, and people who I normally didn't even like, and loved every minute of it.

The Accident was on every tongue, of course. I heard all manner of speculation, every second-guesser's theory, fielded every kind of question while I went about my work. What with one thing and another, it was later afternoon on Christmas Eve before I had my horses attended to and settled for the evening. I drove out of the show ground gates, waved and called 'Merry Christmas' to the glowering placard-carriers who scowled back at me (*I'd scowl too, if I'd had to spend Christmas Eve picketing something this stupid*, I thought), and escaped to my mother's house for Christmas dinner; and I was exhausted.

She met me at the door, gave me a long, silent hug, and ushered me into what seemed a pool of quiet and order after the chaos of the last weeks.

'It's been all over the papers and TV, naturally,' she said as I sat wearily in one of her divinely squishy armchairs. 'You and that Colin Rutherford looked very good as People Of The Week. How does it feel being a bona fide heroine?'

'If I hear that word again I'm going to blow lunch. The truth is I'm exhausted and strung out.'

'I can well believe it. But you're also a genuine...' she caught my warning look, smiled, and said '...Savior. And an eloquent spokesperson for your chosen profession, I might add. It's made me very proud. D'you want to see the papers? I saved them, in case.'

'No. It's all too clear every time I close my eyes.'

'Better to leave it, then.' She brought hot tea from the kitchen and we drank it and ate lemon squares to soak it up.

'Disavow yourself of any notion that I made these', she said as she passed the plate. 'I got them from a great new bakery downtown.'

I grinned. 'I'm honored.'

'You should be.'

I don't know where people get this idea about the ideal generic Mother. In the ads on TV and in magazines, Mom is always over seventy, grey haired, and double-chinned, with a cozy round figure and children who look a biologically impossible twenty or so. And she always serves a great meal.

My mom is small and wiry, with short, dark, glossy hair only lightly peppered by grey, and intellectual to the roots of her being. When she moved to Florida to console her recently widowed father and get a job teaching at a big University, my brother and I joked that they'd have to live on words. Both were prone to forgetting to eat when thinking about something esoteric, which was most of the time. But they did okay. The fortunate part of being spaced-out about food was that, once one of them remembered to cook a meal, they didn't much notice if the flavor was a little strange or if it was burnt around the edges.

'Where's The Rev?' I asked, after we'd gotten through all the nasty details of the accident, Ivory's health, wellbeing, and legal status, my own next move, and all the tea and lemon squares. 'Hanging out at the library?'

Ma shook her head. 'He's on a date with his new lady friend', she said, with nary a twitch of the mouth. 'They've gone to a matinee to see a Molière play.'

'No shit!' I said, astonished into forgetting the strict edict on four-letter words in her house. 'Is this serious?'

'Well, I'd have to say it appears to be. They've been... ah... keeping company... almost since the last time you were here. They met at somebody's 80th birthday bash, I forget whose, and they've been together ever since. But here's the punch line. She was not one of the old biddies. She is the daughter of the guest of honor, and she's younger than me.'

I whistled. '*Cradle* robber! That's scandalous!'

'Well', said Ma drily, 'In this family, would you have it any other way?'

'Does she know he hasn't got any money?'

'Oh, yes. She has more than enough for them both, as I understand it.'

'Wow. And here I thought he'd forsworn women altogether. I thought he vowed eternal devotion and undying love on Grandmère's sainted grave. In fact, I know he did. I saw him.'

'Well, he couldn't help that, dear. He's Irish. They're supposed to. Anyway, be nice to him. He was lonely, and this is really bucking him up.'

'Oh, I will', I promised. 'But I'm dying of curiosity. When do I get to meet this paragon?'

'They'll be back for supper. Oh, yes, I should add - she's a *terrific* cook.' She grinned wickedly, and I doubled over in hilarity. It was the first real belly laugh I'd had in days.


A little background may be in order.

'The Rev' is my grandfather, James Roche. About a million years ago he left Donegal as an idealistic young priest and ended up in Halifax. There he met a sweet wild thing named Nettie Poulin and found himself, as he put it, 'entangled in the tresses of her Raven's-wing hair'. Nettie was half Penobscot and half French and I guess the combination was too much for The Rev, because the next thing you know all priestly thoughts had flown from his head and Nettie was obviously pregnant. So there was a big scandal and The Rev left the Church under a cloud and married Nettie Poulin and consoled himself in his spiritual loss by joining her in the rapid production of four other little Roches, of which my mother was the third.

Grandmère ruled the roost with fire and her own brand of tough-as-nails wisdom while The Rev taught his and the other area kids how to sing and dance and play poker and love the words of Shakespeare. But he missed the Churchly life, so he converted to Anglicanism, which created another scandal in the very Catholic community, moved to Boston, entered the Episcopal seminary, and became a minister.

He really did swear on her grave to be eternally true to Grandmère's memory. I nursed a little resentment at his betrayal, even though he's just as human as any of us. Or given his history, maybe more so. But he was still so handsome and active at eighty-four that women were always throwing themselves at him, so it was no surprise that he'd fallen under the spell of a sweet young thing of 60.

And Beverly really was a good cook. A festive dinner at my mom's was – had always been – the sort of thing that was prone to culinary surprises of the sort that ended with everybody going out for dinner while the house aired out. But with Beverly in the kitchen creating extraordinary feats with a ham that smelled like heaven, and *The Nutcracker* playing quietly in the background while The Rev and my mom kept up a flow of great conversation, and a lot of really nice wine... well, I felt positively civilized. And pampered. And not even Camille's desperate call to tell me that her father was a prick and his wife a controlling bitch and that we were all ruining her life could change my all-too-rare sense of ease.

'Merry Christmas, love,' I crooned to her. 'I miss you, too.'

'And *don't treat me like a toddler!*'

'Okay. But I still miss you.'

She relented, then. 'I miss you, too, Ma. I wish I was with you and GranEllen and The Rev.'

'Me, too.' I regaled her with the story of The Rev's love interest and her ability in the kitchen. Camille laughed long and hard, and we parted friends.


'Now don't worry about me,' said Ivory through the phone lines when I called on Christmas day. 'I am having me a wild Christmas dinner surrounded by my guards and my nurses and Guy Carmouche who is just a very cool man. And I hear you are becoming a regular media star down there, you and that cute Colin Rutherford.'

'I feel like a trained seal, Ive. Sara Wychoff even has us all set to appear on some TV show next week. Um... Linda Lerner? I don't know what I was on when I said yes.'

'Linda Lerner? Isn't she that Nazi that's always shooting her mouth off about animal rights?'

'Oh my God, Ive,' I groaned. 'Don't tell me things like that. It's bad enough *thinking* about it. I'm afraid I'm going to do something totally embarrassing like throw up all over her nice taupe suit in the middle of the show.'

Ivory cackled her ass off and wheezed, all at once. ''Chelle, honey, don't make me laugh, it still hurts,' she begged. 'Honest to Christ, if you threw up half as much as you always think you're gonna you'd be bulimic. Anyway, she never wears taupe. More likely to be red.'

'This is serious, Ive. Can't you try to get your hearing moved so I can beg off this thing and come help you instead?'

'C'mon, have a heart, 'Chelle, I need some laughs up here.'

'Yeah, I knew you'd be sympathetic.'

'I am. I happen to think y'all'll be great. You got that old gift of gab, you know. Shit, throw some Shakespeare at her, that oughta impress the local audience. They all think riders are complete illiterates anyhow.'

'Yeah, yeah. Okay. So anyway, about this hearing...'

She sighed. 'Yeah. Well. First thing, see, is they have this preliminary deal to see if they want to post some ludicrous bail that I can't pay and let me come on down to Florida, or whether they want to throw me in the can pending trial.'

'Jesus, Ive. No way out?'

'No. Appears not. It's a federal case, you dig. And that fuck Winston is still deep-sixed. I swear, 'Chelle, there's part of me thinks he's staying there on purpose.'

'But do you... I mean you don't...'

'No. I'm probably not goin' inside. 'Cause of my condition. Guy figures he can prove I'm not a flight risk and keep me out. Then they'll do a Grand Jury hearing within another month.'

'Whazzat? You want me there?'

'No. I won't even be there. The judge and the Grand Jury just sit around listening to the prosecution rant and rave and decide whether there's enough evidence to screw me. If they decide there isn't, I get to come on home. If they decide there is, the whole thing goes to trial and...' The silence between us grew longer.

'You could get fucked.'

'That's it in a nutshell, honey. But. There's some options that could save my ass.'

'Like?'

'Like maybe if they're feeling real kindly and Guy's ultra sharp the Grand Jury'll drop charges because of the van and the horses being Winston's property and me being an employee. Or if they aren't feeling quite so kindly they might postpone everything 'til Winston does whatever he's gonna do while they investigate.'

'How likely is that? Since we're talking South Carolina, I mean.'

'Hard to say, 'Chelley. Best thing would be if we can dig up someone - *anyone* - who saw Winston and Elliot loading up that van with shavings...'

'Where were you when they did it?'

'Probably with you, but I can't prove the timing. I didn't see it happen, so it had to have been late that night.'

'I imagine old Elliot is out of the country by now.'

'Bank on it.'

'How about Janna?'

'She was in New York. Swears she didn't know anything about Winston's business except that it was some kind of import/export thing.'

'Yeah. That's what she told me, too.'

'It's probably true. She was always off shopping somewhere or going to parties. Not exactly a rocket scientist. And Winston, well, he's just a wild card. Who knows what he'll do, he wakes up.'

'I don't see him finding God in a blinding flash of light.'

'Me neither. More likely to take as many people South with him as he can grab on the way down. Especially me.'

'You sure you don't want me to can this next show? Come stay with you?'

'No. Not yet, honey, thanks. Best you stay where you are and maybe keep your ears open, huh? And cheer me up by keeping my mare safe. Speaking of which, how is the hussy?'

My turn to sigh. 'We're making progress. Harry's helping. But I have to admit, she's one of the toughest mares I've ever ridden, and I even like mares.'

Ivory chuckled. 'Well, I'm glad you said that. If you told me everything was hunky dory I'd know you were a lying bitch and I'd be worried. What's she doing?'

'Jumping in the air and bolting, mostly.'

'Ah, shit, that's *nothin'*. You're almost there.'

'I'm glad you think so.'

'You wait 'til you get her over a fence, honey. You'll be singing arias.'

'Yeah, I'm sure I will, but I'll be really glad to turn her back over to you.'

'That might take awhile yet, honey. Longer than I thought.'

'Why? Are there complications or something? I thought you'd be out of a wheelchair...'

'No, no, I'm gonna walk, all right. I'm coming along real fast in that department. But there is a little bitty complication. I just didn't mention it before 'cuz I didn't think it survived the crash and all. I'm pregnant. That's part of what Winston and I were fighting about.'

This news numbed my brain to the point that I could not think of a single thing to do but ride Dancing Fool. I went out to the barn in a sort of trance, tacked the mare up, and got on. And as if she could feel Ivory's presence through my body, she came round and soft and obedient almost immediately. When I pointed her at a simple grid of three in-and-outs followed by a straightforward line of two fences she floated through them like a dreamboat. Harry raised the fences and made the lines more demanding, and she came down to them straight and true again. She didn't care where I put her or how I got her there - straight on, at an angle, off a turn, from a forward stride or a collected one, it was all the same. She met every fence with her ears forward and finding her own distances.

'Good thing, too,' said Harry, trying hard not to split his face grinning. 'Since her first class is day after tomorrow.'

My stomach went a little funny at that, but this time it was excitement, not fear. I couldn't wait to ride Dancing Fool over a nice big course. Not just for myself. I was carrying a big romantic 'one for the gypper' type sentiment about doing it for Ivory and - whoever it was, growing in her belly. I could see the big home run sailing past The Green Monster and the miracle happening as the final credits rolled. Ivory walking, Ivory free, Ivory applauding me... I wanted it so badly I could even name the flavor: rich, dark, 70% cacao chocolate.

# FIVE

*Now by my art I find
My zenith doth depend upon a most
auspicious star, whose influence if now
I court not but omit, my fortunes will
Forever after droop.*
-William Shakespeare, **The Tempest; I.1**

Horses are the world's great levelers. In her first class of the whole winter circuit, with everybody I knew and a whole bunch of strangers watching, Dancing Fool jumped three fences like the world's most promising World Cup horse, then swerved out of a blue-and-white oxer so fast that she sent me through it without her. I could hear gasps from a titillated audience over the clattering of rails bonking around my head and wondered completely inconsequentially if it was the same response Roman audiences had to gladiators being eaten by lions. As falls go it was more visual thrill than death-defiant, but it was enough to hurt. Enough to eliminate us from the class.

Thanking the gods for the protection of my ugly regulation helmet with the brown chin harness on it, I picked myself gingerly out of the mess and walked stiffly to collect my horse, which one of Harry's minions had kindly dashed in and caught for me. Then I limped out ignominiously while the crowd fluttered its applause and the announcer reminded everybody about what a hero I was. I tried to sneak away fast before I had to wear my embarrassment in front of my friends and co-workers.

Not fast enough. 'You shoulda *known* better than that, you dumb bitch!' Harry greeted me at the out-gate. 'You were nothing but asleep at the switch up there, like you were out on a Sunday *drive*! What did you think, the mare came with autopilot? Like one of your *ponies*? *Je*-sus, 'Chelle!' Etc. etc. etc. while everybody nearby (many of whom had suffered the same treatment at one point or another) made a wide berth around us. All except Hilary, that is. She stood as close as she could without seeming too obvious, and smirked.

And I just stood there like a kid who'd lost the home game in the last inning, full of shame, letting it rain down on my head and mumbling, 'Yeah Harry, I know, Harry, you're right, Harry,' until I just wanted to crawl into a little hole and die. Because he was right. I had been asleep. The first three fences had felt so good I'd stopped riding every stride to the fourth, one of the dumbest and most basic mistakes a rider over fences can make. I vowed to be more together next day, and Harry swore that I'd better be, not (I groused to myself) that he was in control of the situation.

Ivory was, though, and I sure didn't want to tell her about this. I couldn't bear her disappointment. And I didn't want to lose the ride on Dancing Fool.

As I walked away with the bay mare I passed Hilary just in time to overhear her say to some one just out of my line of sight, 'I don't know *why* she's riding Dancing Fool and Clyde. I think Ivory and Harry just felt sorry for her...'

I pretended not to hear. I comforted myself that at least Dancing Fool hadn't fallen; unlike Harry's grey Holsteiner the day Hilary misjudged that fence up in Virginia, a lifetime ago.

Fortunately, my next classes were on Jake and Clyde. In my determination not to make the same mistake twice I overrode Clyde to a substantial oxer and he had the back rail down. But the crowd didn't faze him, being on course by himself didn't trouble him, Harry was pleased with his first competitive round, and it even turned out to be good enough for a low ribbon. 'Everybody else musta dropped dead,' Harry grumbled, which was pretty much the truth. But hey, it paid the entry fee and helped my self-esteem.

Being on Jake for the afternoon's featured Welcome Stake was like home sweet home, and together we zipped around a twisting course clean and fast to end up fourth. After that all I needed was a hot bath, a glass of wine, and a handful of ibuprofen to be content.


The following morning I awakened with a looming sense of doom worse than the one I get when contemplating leaping over very large fences on very small horses. It was the morning of the great Heroes-du-Jour television interview, an event about as exciting as a root canal. I considered any number of excuses to get out of it - the dog ate my homework? My lobotomy was scheduled for today? - but it was Colin Rutherford who suddenly came up with a pressing engagement. Being Colin, it even sounded plausible - something about a vet and a horse with a pulled suspensory ligament. I complained that this was why God made barn managers, but Sara just smiled brightly and shrugged and away we went.

Sara did the backstage intros to Linda Lerner (who did wear red) and her crew and showed me through to all the make-up people who did things to my face and hair that they hadn't seen in my whole life. Then somebody else took over and steered me through a cavernous sound stage onto the familiar cozy living room set that was in reality half a box with a couple of walls and no ceiling, surrounded by banks of cameras, lights, wires, booms, and other paraphernalia I could not possibly have named.

Linda told me approximately what to expect, how to tell which cameras were on (*don't stare into them, please*), said we might be using video clips of Michael Draper provided by Sara (*for color*), and exhorted me not to be nervous (*yeah, sure*). Then another guy clipped a little mike to my lapel, we said a few words, the sound guy said I sounded good, the make-up people said I looked good, and away we went into the inevitable audience-pleasing warm-ups about how it felt to be on the scene and what was going through my mind and all that horrible stuff. Then she cut to the chase.

'Gee', she said, 'A lot of our viewers - especially younger ones - probably think you have the best job in the world, riding horses all day. Tell us, just how much fun is it?'

'Ummm...' I said, hoping my bewilderment wasn't too evident, 'It's a business, like any other. I guess I'm not sure *fun* is exactly the word for what we do...'

'*Not fun*? Oh, come on. All that fresh air? All those horses? All that riding? We have thousands of little girls out there watching today who would sell their souls to do what you do.'

'Well...' I laughed. 'It *is* a great job, if you love horses. But you have to realize we only spend about 10% of our time actually riding. There's the feeding, the grooming, the cleaning, the lugging water and hay, the vetting, all that stuff. Then maybe you're up three nights in a row waiting for a mare to foal, or trying to save that foal when it's trying to come backwards. Or sometimes you're doing all that stuff when you've got pneumonia and ought to be in bed. There's no vacations and no days off. Anybody who thinks it's all rides through the fields with your hair blowing in the wind is hallucinating.'

'But then you get the pay-off, you get to rub shoulders with High Society...'

'We're more likely to rub shoulders with some lame horse. My latest wild night on the town was sitting in a freezing barn soaking a leg in a bucket of ice water while everybody else was eating Thanksgiving dinner in a nice, warm house. I was lucky to get dessert.'

'I bet most of our viewers have never thought of it like that. What *do* you do when you've got pneumonia?'

'Care for the horses, just like every day. It's part of the bargain. You know, we take a wild, free roaming animal away from its natural life and teach it to count on us for every piece of its existence. We'd better be there when it needs us. Sick or cold or whatever.'

'Wow. Hear that, all you horse-crazy girls? Sounds like hard work. Now tell us about the show jumping part of your life. What's that about?'

'Thrills, chills, and spills,' I quipped. Then Linda Lerner hit me between the eyes.

'There are those who say that show jumping is cruel and should be abolished. What do you think about that?'

'Cruel? What do you mean, cruel?'

'Well... Forcing those animals to jump giant fences out of sheer terror...'

I could feel heat rising to my scalp the way it always does when I am faced with unbelievable stupidity. 'First of all, let *me* ask *you* how you think anybody who weighs 120 pounds could force a 1000 pound animal to do anything that it doesn't want to do,' I suggested quietly.

'Well, you hear things. You know, electric prods...'

'*Cattle* prods? Are you even *suggesting...*' I bit my lip hard. 'Look here. Horses have survived for eons because they run *away* from things that scare them. They're prey animals, not aggressors. Anybody who thinks they can scare a horse into jumping is just asking to be killed. We *train* our horses, slowly, and carefully, to do a specific job, whether it's jumping or racing or cutting cattle or taking grandma for a ramble through the woods. If at any point a horse shows us it doesn't want to do that job, we'll find it one it likes better. A scared horse is a dangerous horse. A confident horse is a willing companion. They might be our servants. They are not our slaves.'

'So how *do* you train a horse to jump fences? Can you tell us in a few words?'

'The easiest way is to teach them right out on the trail. A young horse will usually play 'follow the leader' with an older one and learn to trot and canter over little - I mean we're talking no more than 24" - logs and streams and things like that. Just like they'd learn from their mamas in the wild. Then it's all play, they learn how to handle their feet, you can pretty much just encourage them to go forward and be brave and give them lots of praise when they do.

'When they get to be bold or eager over the little stuff - or even if they get bored by it and need more challenge - you start adding. Ditches, bigger logs, panels from one field to another, that sort of thing. But it's like kids - you don't send them to second grade 'til they know how the alphabet goes and what two-and-two make.'

'How long does it take?'

'It varies. Some horses love it immediately and catch on to the whole thing in a few weeks. Those are the ones you have to be careful of overfacing, like child prodigies. Some take months. Those might just need more confidence in their riders and their abilities. Or maybe they end up being dressage horses instead.'

'So how about the show jumpers? We're going to show our viewers this film clip while you tell us.'

'Sure, this is a good one, Michael Draper on a green horse. First you have poles on the ground, see, trot-trot-trot over the poles to give them the rhythm of a stride. Called cavaletti. Then you add a little hop - there it is, that's called a vertical, it's only one pole wide - and later add a fence with some width, called an oxer, shaped like a box, so the horse learns to be round over a fence and stay in the air longer. See how this horse just trots down to it with his ears up and how Michael isn't even putting any contact on the reins. The exercise is doing the work. Then you add a little course. Look how happy the horse is, cantering around with his ears up and his little knees snapped up over the jumps all pretty. Would you say that looks forced?'

'No-o-o... But when the jumps get so much higher... do you mean to tell me you never reprimand your horses? Never punish them? We all know that's not true. Let me show you another clip, one we received from an outside source.'

The next thing I saw on the screen was a clip a couple of years old, taken surreptitiously of a well known international rider who commonly used wire strung above the top rail of his schooling fences to trip his horses and force them to fold their legs more tightly. There had always been rumors. The video evidence had caused a scandal when it first surfaced.

'There are criminals in every walk of life, Linda', I said, trying to sound smooth through gritted teeth while my mind was saying *you fucking bitch*. 'That rider was using methods ruled illegal in every country that I know of. He's been banned forever from international competition. Behavior like that happens, but it is *not* the norm.'

'Yet it proves how *unnatural* it is to…'

'*Everything* we do in the modern world is unnatural. If we were being *natural*, you'd be in a cave grinding meal, picking berries, and trying to survive childbirth while your man was out hunting. Horses would be hanging around on the prairies eating grass and trying to outrun predators. Which, just by the way, means jumping ditches and ravines and rocks while galloping at high speeds. *And* your man the hunter would be trying to catch that horse so he could either eat it or figure out how to sit on it to be a better hunter. And while we're on the subject of what's unnatural, I'm surprised you haven't mentioned all those poor mares that are kept pregnant, locked up in stalls 24/7, wearing bags to collect their urine so that some menopausal woman can take estrogen replacement. Every year those mares produce foals that are considered total by-products. They are dispensable. You can't tell me those foals all find happy, useful homes, so you tell me what happens to them, okay? To my way of thinking this sort of treatment – in the name of human health - shows ignorance and exploitation of the worst kind, *and* it gets zero notice from the public, because it's not in our self-interest.'

Linda Lerner recoiled and the expression that flashed across her face was pure rage. Then she masked it again, and went on like a well-oiled machine.

'That is certainly a part of the equation,' she said, 'and a whole new conversation. It merely serves to illustrate the fact that horses are dying every day through some kind of abuse, exactly as we just saw on tape. What about the recent scandal that uncovered so many people killing horses for insurance money?'

'Those people are a very, very small minority,' I said. 'Most of us love our horses and do the best we possibly can for them. We consider it an honor and a responsibility to be working with horses every day of our lives.

'You know,' I added, really rolling now, '*domestic* abuse happens every day, too. But we don't say marriage and parenting are dangerous because of the acts of a sick minority. We just keep working to improve the odds.'

'Then how do we deal with that small minority?' she insisted.

'There is no punishment bad enough for them, if you ask me. To betray the trust of a creature that depends on us, that has offered nothing but its loyalty... just like people who molest children... nothing. Nothing bad enough.'

'So what do *you* do if your horse is having a bad day?' she pressed. 'Get off and take it back to the barn? Miss your big class?'

'Of course not. If the horse isn't lame or sick, I do what I have to to make it attend to its job.'

'So you *do* punish your horses. Hit them with whips? Kick them with spurs?'

'Sometimes. If it's called for.'

'And you don't call that cruelty?'

'No. I call it discipline, and I use it very carefully, like I would with a child.'

'What if the horse doesn't *want* to do what you say? Do you still force it to work?'

'Do *you* like going to work every day?'

'Of course not,' she said lightly. 'Who does?'

'But you do it anyway, right?'

'Well, yes. I have to pay the bills.'

'And you'll get fired if you don't turn up. Right. Horses have to earn their supper, too. And to do that, they have to be obedient. Disobedient horses aren't safe - not to me, not to you, not to those animal rights people hanging around the front gate of the show grounds, not to themselves. They're big animals that can hurt us. But they're also herd animals that like to do right. An obedient horse learns that when it listens to the boss, it's safe, fed, and cared for. That's not cruel, it's sane.'

'Okay, so let's watch our last clip. Tell our viewers how this relates to everything you've been saying.'

'Sure. This is Michael Draper again, same horse three years later, winning a $50,000 Grand Prix at Tampa last year. Qualified them for the World Cup. Can you say that horse is terrified? I think he looks pretty damn pleased with himself.' I stopped talking for a moment, overwhelmed by the beauty of the picture, the big chestnut horse galloping down to its fences, ears pricked, Michael sitting cool as iced lemonade, poetry, like Ariel in *The Tempest*, '*I come To answer thy best pleasure; be't to fly, To swim, to dive into the fire, to ride On the curl'd clouds*'... I hadn't realized I was saying it out loud, it just came out, but Linda Lerner was looking at me in a very unfriendly way. I smiled and shrugged. 'Happy horses are willing partners who love their jobs. In our horses' cases, that happens to be jumping fences.'

'Well, Michelle Martin,' Linda Lerner smiled blandly while her eyes said she wanted to stab me, 'we're fresh out of time. Thanks for joining us today. You have certainly opened our eyes about the whole world of Show Jumping. But one more question in closing... you've shown us that life with horses is not all erotic meetings and glamour and blue ribbons...'

'No! It's more like a terminal disease.'

'...So why do you do it?'

'Because I love horses. I can't imagine doing anything else.'


'Honestly, 'Chelle, I thought it was going to be a cozy little *chat*. Talk about your great *deeds*. Talk up the joys and beauties of *Show Jumping. That's* what we had all set up,' swore Sara, equal parts pale and elated as we strode away. 'But you were *awesome*. Truly. That horrible woman, I had *no idea* she was going to do that. *None*. To pull out that old clip of Franke Jurgen...'

'I sure feel like I got my ass scorched big-time. I was ready to *kill* the fucking bitch.'

'Oh, but that's where you're wrong. *She's* the one licking her wounds. Of course,' she added regretfully, 'you'll never be invited back. You aren't supposed to show up the talk-show host.'

'Well thank heaven for small favors!'

She looked at me assessingly. 'I had no idea you were so eloquent. How'd you learn to talk like that?'

'I come from a long line of teachers, preachers, and Irishmen. If you don't talk fast you can't get a word in edgewise.'

'You ever think of being a commentator yourself?'

'After that debacle? Be serious.'

'It wasn't a debacle, and I'm very serious. We've been looking *everywhere*... well, obviously not quite *everywhere*, but we've been trying out every well known rider we can *think* of to be a spokesperson for jumping. You know, to do the you-are-there commentary for viewers on TV. We could get so much more *coverage* than we are. Look at *figure skating*, or *tennis*, for God's sake. Jumping is *ten times* more exciting. But let's *face* it, sometimes the people who are in it every day can't *describe* it very well. It's like great riders who can't teach, it's all so *instinctual* for them.'

I was laughing. 'So you mean, now you're looking down a rung to the people who can't ride but can talk, huh? Like the old *those who can, do - those who can't, teach* thing?'

'Now, 'Chelle, that is *not* what I mean. You have no idea how powerful you are on camera. The camera *loves* you. Your whole facial structure, your voice...'

I was blushing bright red by this time. '*I am amazed, and know not what to say*', I said lamely. 'Thanks for the flattery, Sara, it's great. But I'm just a rider, okay? Just an old schooling rider with lots of bills and lumps and bumps that won't go away and a surly daughter. Nothing special. I'm glad I could help out today, if you think I did.'

'Oh, you did, believe me,' said Sara. 'But don't think you've heard the *end* of this. You aren't going to get off as easily as you *think.*'

At the barns, I got a standing ovation from everybody who'd taken time out to watch the show, which seemed to cover the entire population of the grounds. It was so embarrassing I wanted to scuttle into a hole like a sand crab, especially when somebody who'd taped it replayed the look on my face as I essentially recommended the death penalty for the crooks who kill horses for profit. I ran away to hide on the backs of my horses.

I got Dancing Fool around, that afternoon. Two rails in the jump-off kept her out of the ribbons and she was as wiggly as a trout, but it was a big improvement. Clyde bumbled his way cheerfully into third in his class, which made Harry happy, Jake had the day off, and then I got a catch-ride on another Thoroughbred whose owner had come off it and broken a collarbone. Squirrelly it definitely was, but nothing next to Dancing Fool. I booted it around, came out with a pink ribbon and some money, and Darcy Noriega was so tickled she asked me to stay on this horse and her Regular Hunter until she could ride again. So it looked like I was going to be busy.

But a return to my customary anonymity wasn't easy. All I had to do was poke my head out of a stall or ride once around the schooling ring and somebody would stop me. It seemed that somehow I had managed to voice the emotions and thoughts of about 90% of the people on the grounds and settle some scores, while I was at it. And every one of those 90% was bent on telling me about it. It made progress in any direction very slow.

Not that you can expect to please all the people all the time. As I was leading Dancing Fool out for a stroll and a bite of grass I was accosted by a woman from the latest batch of animal rights picketers who barged through the gate onto the grounds with her placard and accused me of whitewashing the cruel reality and covering up the sorry truth behind training jumpers. Just as she was really winding up and I was wondering how to escape, a little breeze sent the papers she clutched in her hand flapping across Dancing Fool's line of vision. True to her nature, the mare swerved violently, knocked my antagonist sideways, and stepped firmly on her sandaled foot. I tried to help her up, but she shook me off angrily. I could see how much her foot hurt, and I felt sorry for her in spite of my irritation.

'Look,' I said, 'this is silly. I'm truly sorry about your foot, but you should know better than to stand right in a horse's blind spot flapping papers. Or if you're going to keep doing it, don't for God's sake wear sandals. It's their instinct to spook. You're really welcome to hang around, you know. Learn what we do.'

'I wouldn't be a part of what you do!' she spat.

'You don't have a clue what we do!'

'I know enough to know it's unnatural and cruel! And I intend to do everything I can to stop it!' she vowed, and limped huffily away.

Craig Oppenheim happened along at that point, leading a nice bay horse. 'One of your fan club?' he drawled.

'Yeah', I said grouchily. 'Fuckin' ignorant twit. I even invited her to come watch me torture my horses, but she wouldn't have it.'

'Ah', he said, casting his eyes skyward, 'the price of fame, the fickleness of public opinion.'

'I never even *thought* of public opinion. I just want to ride my horses.'

'Then you'd best put tape across your mouth, sugar, 'cause from now on people are going to be listening when you talk.'

'I guess you speak from bitter experience, huh?' Craig had served his time wriggling on the slide of public notoriety, all right.

'That's the whole truth,' he said, 'so take my advice and watch your back. You don't want to end up like me.'

'Now what's *that* supposed to mean?'

'There's some nasty people around hereabouts, that's all, and they can make nasty trouble that maybe you haven't earned. Now, you've always been quiet, you just live your life and don't get too involved in the bullshit and do nice things with your horses and people respect you for it. Only since you're the Heroine du Jour... well, it could get interesting, what with the trial and all. It's like that insurance business. Everybody knew about it. It got hushed up as long as it did 'cause people didn't want to call it. Too much to lose. Nobody's *that* clean.'

'But that doesn't have anything to do...'

'Let me tell you something, 'Chelley. If Winston Desmarchais wakes up there's gonna be scared people doing weird stuff to stay out of the wallow. That's all I'm saying right now, but you ask Ivory, she'll back me up.'

'*Ivory?* '

'That's what I said, sugar. There's my crew coming. 'Bye now.' He smiled brilliantly and walked on to greet a group of young riders. I retreated to the barn bewildered. I reminded myself that Craig was a noted gossip. That all I'd done was be on the scene at an accident and go on a talk show. But the whole day had me upset and confused.

When I went to meet a few of our group at the local diner later, the sight of Colin Rutherford and Hilary Knowlton sitting amid my friends didn't improve my mood.

'So where were you when I needed you?' I sniped irritably, sliding into a space George made me on the bench across from Colin.

'Limelight doesn't suit you?'

'No, it by-god doesn't.'

He bowed his head and struck his breast lightly. '*Nymph, in thy orisons be all my sins remembered*', he said apologetically.

'Yeah, well you can count on that. *How does your honour for this many a day?*'

'*I humbly thank you; well.*'

I suddenly became aware that several pairs of eyes had swiveled to Colin and me as if we were apparitions; several mouths had stopped in the middle of chewing; several burgers were suspended between plate and mouth. '*What* are these people *talking* about?' asked Diane, the first to speak.

'*Hamlet*, actually,' I said sheepishly.

'*Ham*let? You mean like *Shake*speare? You guys are quoting *Shake*speare?' She rolled her eyes incredulously at George, who shrugged.

'Well, yeah,' I teased. 'See, Colin's an educated kinda guy. He knows this stuff is important.'

'Oh my God,' groaned George. 'Please don't get her started.'

'What do you mean, get her started?' said Diane. 'I mean this is like really weird, don't you think? *Shake*speare?'

'Why do you think it's weird?' I demanded.

'Not so much weird, 'Chelle,' said Tommy Essex placatingly. 'More like *foreign*.'

'But... these are beautiful words. Not foreign. These are the rhythms of the English language. Right, Colin?'

'Er...' said Colin.

'Yeah, right,' Hilary broke in. 'All those thee's and thy's and where-for-art-thou's. Like I talk that crap all the time.'

'Uh-oh,' said George.

'Well I'll tell you something, Hilary. You ought to try it sometime, because you might sound half intelligent if you did. I mean...' I could feel myself flushing... 'I didn't...'

She turned red. 'Well fuck-you very much, 'Chelle. You're a doll.'

'Surely that was a bit mean?' asked Colin mildly.

'I'm sorry, Hilary, I guess I'm feeling a little stressed out. People have been either fawning on me or yelling at me all day.'

'Fifteen minutes of fame, you know,' smiled Colin. 'And no one to share the trauma with, since I left her in the lurch. Thank God for well-timed lamenesses.'

Hilary didn't look convinced.

'All I meant was, speaking Shakespeare's a lot like galloping down to a fence and knowing how the strides are gonna work out. The rhythm *is* the rhythm of our language. It's what makes it beautiful to taste and listen to. It's natural.'

'Natural!' said Tommy Essex. 'How do you call all that Amber Penta-whatzit natural?'

'You asked for it,' said George.

'Iambic pentameter,' supplied Colin. 'Da-*dum*-da-*dum*-da-*dum*-da-*dum*-da-*dum*.'

'I had a horse walked like that once,' reflected Hilary. 'Lazy sucker.'

'See? The words are archaic, that's all. But if I say something simple, like... um... well, like "we're having turkey for our Christmas meal"... that's iambic pentameter.'

'Yeah, but we'd say 'dinner', and then it wouldn't fit,' George pointed out.

'Oh don't be so literal. You know what I mean. I mean it's graceful and probably less unnatural than jumping an oxer to a vertical in one stride.'

'And we still call it poetry when a person does it right,' pointed out Colin.

'The oxer-to-vertical or the Shakespeare?' joked Diane.

'Well... both!' They twinkled at each other in a way that made my spirits sink even further. I glanced at George, and he didn't look too happy, either.

'Okay, Perfesser,' said Hilary. 'Check it out. *I think I'd better go and ride my horse.*'

'*I think that's pretty good for your first try.*'

'*I think I'm gonna puke if this goes on,*' said Tommy.

Everybody laughed uproariously at that point. Everybody except

Sara Wychoff, that is. She just kept eating her burger and looking at me reflectively, which I should have known was a bad sign.

At the end of the meal I was just getting up my nerve to invite Colin back for a coffee or a drink when George leaned over to me.

"Chelle, if you can spare some time in the next couple of days, I have a friend I'd like you to meet. Looking for a couple of nice horses to add to his string, needs a partner-slash-rider. Divorced, plenty of money, attractive, and straight. I think I remember those being your criteria.' He smiled humorously as I stared at him with my mouth open, barely remembering the conversation.

'Uh... sure, that'd be great,' I stammered. We agreed on a time, then I turned to catch Colin and found him walking out the door with Diane, looking very cheerful. My lowered spirits hit the basement.

I glanced back at George, whose expression had gone taut. 'George,' I suggested, 'you look like a guy who could use a drink. You want to come over?'

He looked grateful. 'Yeah. Thanks, 'Chelle, I'd like that.'

As we rose to leave, Hilary grabbed my arm and pulled me aside. 'You owe me,' she said, looking angry.

'Hilary, I'm really sorry I came off like that...'

'I don't give a shit about that. I'm talking about that big bay horse.'

'Clyde?'

'Oughta be my ride, 'Chelle. Mine. I don't know what you've been saying to Harry...'

'What are you talking about?'

'Going behind my back...'

I pulled away. 'Hilary Knowlton, I can't believe this is coming out off your mouth. What kind of person do you think I am?'

'I thought I knew,' she said. 'Now I'm wondering.' She barged past me out the door.

'What was *that?*' asked George.

'I have no idea,' I said, nonplussed. 'God, what a day. C'mon, George. Let's get that drink. Shit, let's get two.'

When we got back to my place there was an express package from Ivory resting against the door of the van which, when opened, proved to be a large, red, heart-shaped box of chocolates. The note attached read, 'Thanks, sweetie, I haven't laughed so much for weeks. P.S. - you missed your calling.'

George and I ate about half the chocolates. They weren't bad - hardly stale at all.

# SIX

*I saw young Harry...*
*Rise from the ground like feathered Mercury,*
*And vaulted with such ease into his seat*
*As if an angel dropp'd down from the clouds*
*To turn and wind a fiery Pegasus,*
*And witch the world with noble horsemanship.*
-     William Shakespeare - ***Henry IV pt.1;IV.1.104***

I had Jennie in the First Year Green Hunter Division, 'green' meaning relatively inexperienced. This is where horses headed for bigger things get what you might call their training wheels. The jumps are 3'6", straight-forward, nothing wildly striped or bizarrely configured, a relatively simple figure-eight pattern over natural-looking chicken coops, slatted gates, rustic rails, and walls painted to look like stone or brick. The sides of the fences are flanked by wooden 'wings' adorned with potted shrubs and colorful banks of flowers. Easy galloping in between jumps encourages young horses to move forward, jump out of an even stride, learn about being adjustable between fences – which really means steering and brakes – and look for the next fence eagerly.

If they have the scope, temperament, and soundness, confident horses that have learned their jobs well move up to the Regular Hunters at 4' or to the Jumper divisions. The weird stuff is saved for the jumpers, which test horses and riders by asking difficult technical questions that demand split-second timing and the courage to make flying leaps into space – literal leaps of faith – with the confidence that there will be solid footing on the landing side.

Most horses don't go this far. They stay at 3'6" as steady, reliable rides for Junior or Amateur Owners, or maybe slide back to the less demanding 3' Children's and Adult divisions that attract the vast bulk of competitive riders now.

Time was, you didn't bother bringing a horse to a show if you and it couldn't jump a 3'6" course. Anything smaller barely qualified as a fence, in the minds of our competitive forbears. These were people who galloped around all sorts of wild countryside in all sorts of weather jumping whatever obstacle lay in their paths, just for fun. Their instructors and mentors were ex-cavalry men who had relied on the scope and courage of their horses in wartime, dusted the animals off to do things like compete in the Olympics when there were no pressing wars, and chased hounds and foxes on them all winter. Which is, after all, why they were called hunters in the first place.

From the very first time one of our ancient ancestors discovered that he could catch game faster on horseback than on foot, he began breeding horses specifically designed to have the guts, agility, and brains to be a safe partner in an endeavor that included spears and large, streamlined dogs. At that time, stags and boars were the main quarry in Europe and the British Isles. Wolves, if they were too numerous or too close for comfort. Bison, if you were a Native American on the plains anytime after 1600. Later, Europeans hunted for sport and social contact as well, and found the fox – a primary exterminator of poultry and general neighborhood hell-raiser – to be worthy of a good day's gallop. From the 18th century, women found their way into the ranks of those who loved an excuse to thunder across the countryside on a wonderfully fast and agile horse.

Hunters are a luxury item now; no longer a necessary part of survival. Show hunters are pampered, expensive, often flighty, and – according to their frequently inexperienced owners - generally unsuited to dashing about the hills risking damage to their pricey limbs. But galloping through a windblown landscape is natural to a horse. It's more accurate to say that it's the humans who are at issue, since most of us are not born knowing how to ride. The process of learning – which takes years – often results in trips to the ER to have bones set or teeth re-aligned. Many novice riders aren't willing to serve the necessary apprenticeship or take the risks involved in becoming horsemen. They sure want to ride in horse shows, though. They like winning ribbons, and they want to win them *right now* (*and what's not to love about that?* the child in all of us might well ask).

If they have plenty of money, they can. Show rings are teeming with people who have learned to be pretty good passengers, given the right trainer and a compliant horse. They can find their way around eight 3' fences well enough to collect a kaleidoscopic selection of fluttering rosettes, they get to be involved in a sport that nourishes both body and soul, they interact with a noble animal, and they come about as close to 'nature' as is possible in our suburban society. Which is a pretty nice way to spend a weekend.

But they aren't horsemen. They haven't developed the instincts, strength, sensitivity, or muscle memory to understand at any given moment precisely what is going on in the horse's mind and body, and either adjust to it, change it, or heal it. Some fortunate people are born with an innate understanding of a horse's thought processes, which increases with exposure and experience. The rest of us have to learn it. But everybody who aspires to being a true horseman has to put in the years, take the spills, make the mistakes, and get into the wide open spaces to interact with a hundred different animals in every kind of situation. And after that there is still more to learn.

The show ring standard for Hunters is accuracy, manners, and fluidity, sort of like a gymnast on the balance beam. The judge also looks for a horse that appears to be an uncomplicated pleasure to ride over fences. In other words, the most boring round wins. Horses that are fun to watch might demonstrate some enthusiasm for their job with a little snort or head-shake between fences. But they don't win. It's like riding isn't really supposed to be fun. Like 'getting to the jumps' in an exact, pre-ordained number of strides is what matters. Well, shit. You could just about do that on a moped. You can watch paint dry and have as much fun as you can watching a class of 45 bay hunters.

Even so, when I've finished pissing and moaning and carrying on, I still love riding and watching show hunters. There's poetry in a beautiful, balanced, graceful horse cantering down to a pretty construct of rails and greenery and sailing over it out of stride with its ears forward and its knees tucked up around its chin. There's extraordinary joy in riding a hunter that is happy, relaxed, and enjoying its job. There's music in trying to ride that horse with such precision that it seems to float from fence to fence all by itself, with never an awkward stride or missed step, in a syncopated waltz-time that is the epitome of dancing with a graceful partner.

The *sine qua non* of the American hunter is the American Thoroughbred - an animal bred for three hundred years to go very fast at a very early age with no consideration for minor details like brains, brakes, or self-preservation. This creates an interesting double standard. While the market demands superheated Thoroughbred beauty and athleticism, average riders need something quiet enough not to kill them and sound enough to jump the jumps year after leg-pounding year without breaking down. These attributes don't come readily to mind in speaking of the Thoroughbred horse, but the many breeds and crossbreds known for them generally don't have Dream Horse charisma.

So, given that the Thoroughbred - or, failing that, one of the more refined members of the European warmblood tribe - is the accepted physical pattern for a hunter that can win at the big shows, there are always people who'll give their horses 'just a little sniff of something' to keep them quiet or to unlock the stiffnesses that inevitably arise after weeks of competition. A little phenylbutazone – a non-steroidal anti-inflammatory that acts a lot like aspirin in humans - is generally accepted as okay, within strictly monitored dosage guidelines. After all, who *doesn't* pop a few hundred milligrams of 'vitamin I' after a long period of muscular self-abuse?

But most of the little sniffs that make a hot horse quiet enough for a relatively inexperienced amateur to ride, or those which disguise serious lamenesses, range from tranquilizers to OTC non-steroidal anti-inflammatories that exceed 'maintenance' dosages to a pharmacopeia of arcane substances that mask the presence of illegal chemicals in the horse's bloodstream. The United States Equestrian Federation – the national governing body of our horse show world - has a stringent random equine urine testing program designed to keep everybody honest, which has operated since about the 60's.

Sound familiar? It should. It's exactly like the programs used to keep our baseball and football players on the straight and narrow.

But imagine trying to get a horse to pee on command. Tradition dictates that sometimes you can make a horse urinate by whistling. It's never worked for me, but on every showground throughout the nation at any given time, you'll find some poor slob hunched in a stall, bored to death and whistling vainly in the hope of inducing his horse to present the stewards with a chemical-free specimen.

Of course, random testing doesn't catch all the offenders, so some escape notice for awhile. So the unrelenting race is on: people bent on finding ways to mask the drugs in their horses' systems are on one side; the organization determined to discover these and outlaw them on the other.

As is true of every form of sport we participate in, the problem permeates every branch of the equine industry – racing, showing, western events, even children's ponies. It's a function of money: made, spent, or lost. Of broken dreams. Of glory denied. It turns what might otherwise be a circular Keystone Cops scenario into tragedy. It's how horses end up dead, and how otherwise reasonably honorable trainers and riders end up illegally collecting the insurance on them.

These were the kind of thoughts that kept turning in my mind as I mucked stalls, fed, groomed, cared for my horses, and rode. Winston and Ivory. Ivory's exquisitely talented jumper Ice Cream, the one that was going to take her to the magical stars, the first one to die. Ivory's Dream Team, destroyed. And all for what? Human greed? Or something more specific, that involved my closest friend?

But I was talking about Jennie.

When she remembered her manners and didn't pop the odd good-natured buck after one thrilling oxer or another, she was getting good ribbons in big classes. She was a crowd pleaser, too. By the end of her first couple of shows up north, Jennie was trotting into the ring scanning the stands for her public, the hussy. Everybody would mumble and clap for 'the cute pony' and then she'd turn her focus on the jumps and just be the smuggest and most perfect little hunter that ever cantered a courtesy circle.

This week was even better. Sailing around the arena with her light, bouncy canter, marbled grey ears pointing straight forward in front of me, she came down to every fence bold and balanced. I'd cluck, she'd fly into the air and land moving straight into my hand, making little *prrr prrr prrr* noises as she arched her pretty neck and breathed in time with her step. She jumped as if she were born to do nothing else; as if heaven was a ring crowded with birch rails over brush, with green roll tops, with white coops. And I just laughed and watched the fences come up between those ears and remembered the same ears on her mother all those years ago in Galway, the green hills and stone walls framed between them as we galloped and jumped from field to stony field.

She got a call in one class, which means no ribbon but the judges were watching her. A fifth in the next, another call in the hack. She was third in the Handy Hunter. Then she won the Stake, the money class, the one that pays for all the rest.

'Now *that's* a horse to love', said Tommy Essex as I came out with a Cheshire-Cat grin plastered from ear to ear, a long, pretty, blue-streamered rosette pinned on sweet Jennie's bridle, a nice silver trophy, and a cash-filled envelope in my hand. 'She knows the class to save it all for, don't you, sweetheart? Bless your little soul.' Jennie rubbed her head all over him with the violence that passes for affection in horses and left his navy jacket plastered with grey hairs.

He shoved her away, laughing. 'I'd like to call on you sometime soon, 'Chelle, if I may. You be in your rig after next week, or are you headed for Wellington?'

'Not going anywhere. Come over for breakfast sometime. I'm great at toast with jelly.'

'That'd be just right,' he said. 'Uh-oh, that's my class they're calling. Later.'

I had a ride in the same class. With a sigh, I jogged Jennie back to her stall, quickly put her away with *mea culpas* and promises of a better future, grabbed my saddle, and dashed to the neighboring tent where Darcy danced nervously from foot to foot, horse bridled and ready. I tossed my saddle on, did up the martingale and girth, accepted a leg-up from her good hand, and trotted back to the ring where I had just time to loosen the horse up and give him a couple of quick fences before they called my number. It wasn't enough preparation by a long shot, even though I'd given him a good school on the flat in the predawn of what seemed to be an eon ago but was really only this morning.

Fortunately the horse was an old pro and knew his job, even though he had to negotiate fences that were a bit larger than he was used to in Darcy's Amateur Owner divisions. He didn't care. He galloped from fence to fence like a true southern gentleman, neither brilliant nor gorgeous but as consistent as a metronome - da-da-*da,* da-da-*da,* da-da-*da,* - all the way around. All I had to do was point him in the right direction, steady him a bit on the corners, and stay out of his way. I felt like I was on vacation. When we'd negotiated the last fence and trotted out of the ring steaming and happy we met an owner capering in delight. 'Oh, 'Chelley,' she squeaked, 'he just looked *so nice.* If he gets a good pin in this class he could be Reserve Champion of the division!'

I grinned back at her delight, and was tickled to hear our number called in second place. It was true - the horse had done well enough to be next-best out of the twenty-six he was competing against in this series of five classes. Which is the kind of result that makes owners smile, and keeps riders like me employed.

I jogged him out of the ring, stripped my saddle off his back, left an ecstatic Darcy kissing her honest old horse, and trotted off as best I could to the distant jumper ring, where Harry's working student had Clyde waiting for me. Diane zoomed by on her four-wheeler, a vehicle that is *de rigueur* for busy riders on these immense grounds and as ubiquitous now as Jack Russell terriers. I'd spent a lot of time cursing ATV's when they ran me off the path or scared my horses, but when Diane skidded to a halt and offered me a ride I was ready to start with the Hail Mary's. I was that tired from all the running.

Not as tired as I was after riding Clyde, though. He was getting cocky, the way horses do when they think they know their jobs better than you do, like teenagers a month after they get driver's licenses. He pulled me around the course like a fire engine and I battled to keep the sucker from taking off on me. It was a pretty rough-and-ready trip, but we made it to the jump-off. Then the big slob galloped through his bridle coming into the triple, took off at a very weird distance going way too fast, stuffed himself so badly against the base of the second element that he had to more or less crawl over it, and gutted out the last oxer in complete disarray with legs all over the place, which left a wild assortment of striped rails crashing around his legs.

There were several good things to say about this experience. First, his impulse was to jump rather than run out, so his heart was in the right place. Second, he stayed upright, being built roughly like a large ferry. Third, his legs were unharmed, and he galloped off sound. The near-crash backed him off a little, though, and I had to leg him pretty sturdily to the last several fences, but we finished more or less unscathed.

'Sorry about the expensive school,' I said ruefully to Harry when we came out.

'You ended good. Maybe he'll be more careful next time,' Harry said philosophically, which was as close as he ever gets to saying you did something right. 'What have you got coming up? You look beat.'

'Dancing Fool and Jake yet to go. I'll be glad when this week is over, I'll tell you. I'm cooked.'

'Hire some help.'

'All I can afford is addicts and lunatics.'

'Santé needs a job. He's eating his guts out over Ivory's horses.'

'I'd love to have Santé. I just can't pay him.'

'You keep holding it up all by yourself, you'll burn out for certain and lose your edge. That's how people get hurt, you know.'

I grimaced at him and set my aching doggies back to get Dancing Fool. I knew he was right, but I was too busy and tired to think about alternatives.

And fatigue has its benefits. Too worn to argue with Ivory's temperamental mare, I left her to jump the jumps her own way. She responded with the kind of round that makes you believe in God, and won it. Then my trusty Jake was in the top six in his last effort and brought in another nice check.

When we came out of the ring after his jump-off I realized that for the first time in my life after jumping big fences, I wanted to down a quart of water, not throw up behind a bush. Maybe it was another side effect of exhaustion. I chose to accept it as major progress, and was pleased.

Sometime after dark I finished all my chores, crawled back into my trailer, and blearily went over the week's accounts. Harry was right, I was doing pretty well. But success affects me oddly. It's never sunk in that it's a process like any other, that builds inertia and reaches a sustainable level. I'm always looking over my shoulder, waiting for the ax to fall. I went to bed wondering if I would hear the gods saying, 'Oops, wrong person', like the bank does when it discovers an error in your favor, or like my idol Shakespeare has Henry VIII advise when he says, *'Fling away ambition. By that sin fell the angels'*.

I dreamed that night of Memphis and Rougère in the wreck, of Jake and Jennie in their places twisted and dying, and jerked back to consciousness sweaty and shaking. My heart pounded, and I couldn't breathe. Panting, I got up in the pitch dark and thought I'd call Camille just to hear a human voice, but it was three a.m. Besides waking her up, I'd probably freak her out. Then there'd be two of us up all night being scared of the unseen. Instead I pulled on a bathrobe, snapped my fingers at Spring to follow, and weaved through the camper-city that had sprung up all week around my rig to the stabling tent.

My horses were alive, they were warm. As I entered their stalls they nickered breathily, soft eyes shining, pleased for the company and the promise of an extra flake of hay. I hugged them and crooned to them and drank in their solid presences, their warm breath. I told them how much I treasured them, *'where thou art, there is the world itself'*. Maybe they don't get the exact words. They certainly understand the vibe.

Most of us who rise or fall, eat or starve by horses, feel the same way. They are not our tools. Not vehicles to fame and fortune. We love them because they are colossally beautiful, inspiringly athletic, poetically faithful. It is we, not our horses, who are blessed by the connection.

Somewhere in the warm Florida night an orange grove bloomed and its sweet scent wafted over us on the soft air. We drank it in, and were content.

I had the next week 'off', if you can call it that, having decided to keep my horses *in situ* and give them a break rather than move to Tampa for a big show there. I spent my days working fulltime as a combination masseuse, maid, cook, and personal trainer to my charges. They all had tender muscles to be rubbed, there were endless stalls and pieces of tack to clean and repair, bodies to groom, feed times to adhere to, and exercise to dole out appropriately. Jake had an unexplained tendon swelling that didn't seem to affect him but might point to a brewing problem if not tended carefully. I hosed it, rubbed it, wrapped it, stretched it, and walked him out for hours every day to see if light exercise helped. It did. Both Jennie and Darcy's old boy needed some long hacks around the grounds to keep them interested in life. Youngsters like Clyde needed attention to problems of jumping style, approach, and attitude to improve them for the upcoming week's events. And the weird ones like Dancing Fool and Darcy's other wing nut needed to be bored to death - or, if you want to be politically correct about it, 'acclimated to their surroundings' - so they could accept the environment and focus on their jobs. Harry Daly bounced back from Tampa a few times to help out with their continuing education over the jumps.

'I hear Hilary Knowlton's been on your case,' he said casually after one of these sessions.

'Where'd you hear that?'

'I got ears.'

'I guess she feels like she oughta have the ride on Clyde. I guess I don't know why she doesn't, either.'

'Let's just say I'm not real fond of the company she keeps and leave it at that,' said Harry.

'Okay.'

'I had a word with her, anyway. You oughtn't to have any more trouble.'

'I can fight my own battles, Harry.'

'Not a question of that, doll. Just, I don't have room in my barn for attitude. I'm in the business of selling horses. And that means putting the best riders I can find on 'em.'

And with that remark, he went back to Tampa.

Hard work aside, there's still time to gossip and visit and generally goof off in Florida in January. Still a pretty good party. If the show circuit was nothing but work people wouldn't spend so much time looking forward to it every year.

Because of the Winston/Ivory Affair, this season was unusually fruitful in the gossip department. We constantly fell over members of the press sniffing around for dirt, or a scoop. Most of the larger papers had left off trying to sensationalize the story, having run out of both facts and interesting speculation. That left only the smaller journals, the gossip columnists, and the equine journalists.

The latter are not generally *Jaws* types like their tabloid brethren, but I guess the combination of drugs, sex, and wealthy upper level horse personalities was too good to pass up. Colin Rutherford and I inevitably found ourselves being interviewed with a supporting cast of anybody who wanted to go on record with a gripe. In the absence of new facts, these conversations had devolved into soliloquies on ethics in the elite world of show jumping, each delivered with a proper sense of righteous indignation. Colin and I merely provided background and color at these moments. The press had long run out of things to say about us. Being British, Colin had very early run out of things to say to them. And neither of us had anything to do with the whispers that inevitably dredged up old gossip about Craig Oppenheim, Michael Draper, their past relationships, dealings, and subsequent situations. I found this as unstoppable as it was unpalatable, denied all knowledge when the topic came up, and cringed whenever somebody brought another piece of dirt to light.

There were other strangers among us, too, who watched and asked the occasional question but otherwise didn't say much and were clearly not journalists. These we instinctively avoided unless they pressed a meeting. Feds? Friends of Winston's? There was no way of knowing, but their vibes were sure not cozy.

And in the background there hovered the omnipresent cadre of the animal rightists, who felt we should turn our horses loose to 'express their horse-ness' and get eaten by cougars or starve to death in the normal way Nature takes care of its own.

'If it wasn't so unnerving it'd be hilarious,' I said to Ivory on the phone. 'All this moral outrage, like nobody ever snorted a line or juiced a horse.'

'Yah, I'd *love* to be a fly on that wall,' Ivory agreed. 'Anything real?'

'Not much. Tommy Essex - you remember him? - he's very tight with Craig, these days. Seems to have something on his mind, but I don't know what. And Craig keeps dropping hints, you know.'

'Hints… like what?'

'Well, like the kind of shit that might happen if Winston wakes up.'

There was a long silence on the other end.

'He said you'd know something about that,' I offered suggestively.

More silence.

'Ive?' I prompted, finally.

'Yeah.' I heard a long sigh. 'I'm awful close to getting out of here, 'Chelle. Awful close. Will you trust me to hold my thoughts a while longer?'

'I don't have a lot of choice, do I? But I have to tell you, I'm feeling a lot like the Tarot Fool. I don't want to go walking off some cliff in the dark.'

'It's okay, doll, I'm not dragging you into anything dangerous. It's just that I still got a lot of ducks to get lined up.'

'So do it quick, Ivory, okay? This could get pretty old.'

'C'mon, sweetie, don't get huffy on me.'

'I'm not huffy. But if you want my help you're gonna have to be a little more forthcoming. Yeah?'

'Yeah. Promise.'

'Yeah. Sure.' I didn't believe her.

My unfortunate tendency when nervous and feeling cornered is to chatter inanely. When interviewed – an occurrence that was happening with fair frequency - I seemed incapable of doing anything but blathering on in my very own characteristic unedited style about horses and love and ignorance until either I ran out of gas or the interviewers' eyes glazed over. Colin, conversely, always sounded taciturn and heroic in these situations, like Gary Cooper in *High Noon*. Maybe it was because he'd had more practice, being a famous rider and all, I don't know. But I could almost hear the collective horse-crazed female hearts of our noble nation going *ka-thunk-ka-boom*. And it was wreaking havoc among the lady riders on the circuit, because in addition to being a bashful media star, Colin had 'that accent', was charming, a stupendously committed rider, and straight. Very clearly straight.

'That man is just a thing of beauty on a horse,' sighed Diane predictably as she and Hilary and I walked a fresh batch of equids into the ring. Colin, oblivious of our scrutiny, diligently schooled a big, rawboned bay thing with lots of white that could have been Clyde's brother.

'He's just a thing of beauty on the ground,' agreed Hilary. 'That cute little *ass…*'

'And he likes women. God, It's almost too good to be true.'

'Well, it is too good to be true, girls,' I said primly. 'He's married and has two kids, remember.'

'*Pfft.*' Hilary waved her hand dismissively. 'They're in England. It hardly counts.'

'I heard they're splitting up, anyway,' said Diane.

'That's just a rumor,' I said crabbily.

'Yah, but *where there's smoke*, you know,' said Diane archly. 'I mean, you don't see them hurrying over here and hanging on the rails, do you.'

'He probably told you all that himself, huh, Di?' teased Hilary. '*Nobody's* so married they don't want to have a good time when they're off by themselves. So-o-o... *c'mon*, girl, we got ears!'

'My lips are sealed,' Diane giggled.

'Jesus, Diane,' I complained. 'I thought you were hanging with George Andros.'

'Aw come on, honey,' said Hilary. 'The choice between an insurance tycoon and an honest-to-God hero of the world class British Three-Day variety? I mean like that is just *no choice*.'

'Yeah, but I might point out this extremely nice horse Diane is riding...'

'George'll live, honey. He'll live. Nobody with that kind of money ever lacks for love. Give it a shot while it's hot, is my theory. Who knows how long he's gonna be around. *Some*body better be snapping him up before it's too late.'

Diane, still pink, started to respond, but I couldn't stand any more. 'S'cuse me,' I said, quivering with the possessiveness and jealousy you usually associate with being oh, say about age thirteen. 'I have to get this animal tightened up or Harry'll have my hide.'

'Oh, c'mon, 'Chelley, you're so goddamn *straight*. We got the makings of a great little contest here,' chided Hilary. 'First one to stay in Colin Rutherford's bed for longer than...'

'Not me,' I called hastily back over my shoulder in what I hoped was a light tone. 'I'm too old for that shit.' And I purposefully trotted Clyde through a couple of serious-looking serpentines.

'Too old for what shit?' asked our subject himself, coming up beside me as Clyde and I rejoined the rail.

'Jesus!' I yelped. 'You scared me to death. I about fell off this horse.'

'Impossible. You might as well be sitting on a barge on the Danube.'

'That's true,' I admitted. 'I never felt so safe in my life. It's like riding around on a small mountain.'

'Especially after the sporty models you're used to. Now what shit are you too old for, Ms. Martin? Surely not riding very small horses over very large fences. Or are you considering a new line of work?'

I blushed to the peak of my helmet and hoped it looked like exertion. 'I'm... um... too old for a lot of things, if you really want to know. Which I'm sure you don't. But you know what? Sometimes I think I really would rather be on a barge on the Danube. It sounds so *restful*.'

'Ah,' he said.

'Well... you asked.'

'I did.'

'Look at these two,' he added, after our horses had trotted another length of the ring in perfect harmony. 'We should be riding them in Pairs of Hunters. They're perfect.'

'Yeah. They are. Perfect,' I agreed. 'They'd make a great coaching team, all that chrome on bay.'

'Rather that than ride this beast at a triple. But for God's sake don't tell its owner I said so.' He circled away with a grin.

I schooled on, the endless circles, serpentines, and counter-bending we use to warm, balance, and limber our horses before trying anything that involves getting off the ground. Clyde was learning how to move without depending on my arms and legs to keep him from falling flat on his long white face. He was so naturally laid back I figured I could warm him up in rush hour traffic. I loved cruising along on his broad brown back, watching his big ears flop contentedly in time with his gangling stride.

'*I'm too old for that shit*', Hilary mimicked as I looped the bottom of the ring past her cantering horse.

'*He's married and has two kids*', smirked Diane, trotting by in the opposite direction.

'Does it strike you that this arena is alive with estrogen today?' asked Colin innocently as we crossed paths across the center.

What else could I do? I laughed all the way up the long side.


People kept offering me new horses to ride, like all my rhetoric made me a swell horseman. Not even my own father was immune to the trend.

'I have a proposition for you,' he boomed through cyberspace as I tried for a quiet late afternoon cup of tea.

'What kind of proposition?' I asked suspiciously. 'A father-to-daughter proposition or a horseman-to-victim proposition?'

'Now, 'Chelley,' my dad chided, 'you've no need to be so bloody cynical. This is your own father speaking to you.'

'I know,' I said baldly. 'That's what worries me.'

He had the grace to laugh. 'Well, all right,' he admitted. 'It's a bit of both, actually. I was just over in Galway, you see, visiting the family. And I found this horse.'

'Uh-oh.'

'By that lovely runner that did so well for Da's people in England the last several years, you know the one.'

'Yeah', I breathed. 'I know the one.' And my heart started to do a few preliminary gymnastics.

One of the last sons of the same stallion that had given me Jake and his full sister all those years ago, this horse had been a Group winner in Ireland and England, which meant he had won the kind of Classic races that require stamina as well as speed. He'd run successfully through the age of six and retired sound, which meant he was tough. Beautifully bred and strikingly handsome on top of these juicy attributes, he'd been syndicated as a stallion for a sum that might have supported a minor Third-World country.

'This colt is from a first-year test breeding,' my dad was saying. 'Out of one of the best Registered Irish Draught mares in the country. Won at Royal Dublin Society. Grey, four, 16.1 and growing. Tasty animal, 'Chelle.'

'I thought you only did Thoroughbreds,' I said, trying to remain calm.

'I watched him jump out of a pasture bounded by a five foot bank and ditch. Nothing between he and it but clear blue sky.'

'I thought you only did Thoroughbreds.'

'He's an investment horse if there ever was one.'

'I thought it was you told me never to invest in anything that eats or rusts.'

'*And* I was correct. But when you see the creature…'

I started to laugh. 'Da,' I said, 'I'm beginning to get it. You mean you went over to The Auld Sod, let that romantic mist get into your brain, and allowed an even aulder sod to talk you into bringing home a grand souvenir for yourself.' Shit, I was even taking on the accent.

'Now 'Chelle, that's your grandda you'd be talking about,' he warned, scandalized.

'That's the whole *point*', I spluttered, weak from hilarity.

There was a dangerous silence, then my dad began to chuckle, and the chuckle grew to an honest laugh. 'Chelle, you've a mean tongue in your head,' he said. 'Maybe that mist did have more than a pair of black-and-tans to it. But I've got the colt, and by the way, he's still a colt.'

I stopped laughing abruptly. 'You want me to take on a *stallion*?'

'Well, that's the point, you see. Bred the way he is, I want to stand him when he makes a career for himself. Which I think he will.'

'Yeah, but there are other people up your way that are far better equipped...'

'I'm not expecting family favors, it's a business deal. I want you to start him slow-like, and go wherever he's capable of going. *And you can have a piece of him, too.*'

I was stunned into speechlessness by this generosity from my old man. While I searched helplessly for something appropriate to say, he added, 'You've your grandda to thank, actually. He wouldn't let me have the beast unless I agreed to give it you. Made me put it in writing. On my own I might have been inclined to go to that client of mine who has the fag husband, you know, the boy who won the Gold Medal.'

'Michael Draper?' I hazarded, wincing at my dad's unrepentant crassness.

'Yeh-yeh, that's him. For Christ's sake don't tell him I said that, though.' He hesitated. 'Should I even have said as much to you?'

'No, Da. It's okay,' I said, trying to pretend his zingers didn't have the power to hurt my adult self. 'For a minute I thought I was talking to a stranger. But thanks, and thanks to Grandda. When do you want to send the horse to me?'

'Well now, I'm hoping you can take delivery in two days. I had a friend shipping to Ocala with some mares and he had an extra stall, so I loaded him just before I called.'

I gagged on my tea and tried to choke out an expostulation, but before I could regain control of my scalded vocal chords my dad rang off.

Building on the day's capital, I met George's friend Gerry Dirk for supper, to discuss his intent to buy a couple of nice jumpers.

'They for yourself, or for somebody else to ride?' I asked through a big bite of juicy mushroom-smothered steak.

'Both', said Gerry. He was eating a Greek salad. Cultured kinda guy. Sensible diet. Probably obsessive-compulsive. But he didn't live with his mother, I'd already checked that out. And he was truly, legally, divorced. 'I have a couple of good packers that have been taking me through the Adult Amateur Jumpers – the best schoolmasters in the world, and I wouldn't trade them for anything - but I want to move up to A/O and these guys don't quite have the scope. So I'm looking for a horse with some mileage that's sound enough to go on with, if we all stay healthy. Then a younger horse with real class that might make the Grand Prix. That'd be for you to ride.'

'Why me? I've never ridden a Grand Prix.'

'Yeah, well, I'll bank on you for the first steps and then we'll see. George says you're the best with green horses. Harry Daly thinks you walk on water.'

'*Harry* does? You're kidding, right?'

'No, really, he does. And I've seen you on that nut case of Darcy Noriega's. Or Dancing Fool, she's a complete lunatic. Horses go for you.' He smiled at me winningly. 'I know you think I'm just a rich aging yuppie on some ego trip. But I grew up in Kentucky, you know. My daddy was a stallion man and I prepped yearlings for the sales and my mama cleaned houses for the rich folks in the big house and I swore I was going to have some of that one day. And now I do. I happen to love horses. I can afford nice ones. I want to maximize my time in the saddle and minimize hosing legs and treating tendon injuries. So I want somebody honest and careful. I want to ride as far as I can while I can, I want to watch a nice horse that belongs to me do some upper level winning, and I don't want to kill it if it doesn't pan out the way we thought. You with me?'

Well, I was flattered - who wouldn't be? Besides, this Gerry guy was sincerely good looking in a way that wasn't too sleek to be digestible. I mean like maybe the tan that deepened the sexy cinnamon hue of his skin wasn't just from lying around on a yacht in Aruba or wherever it is that disgustingly rich people go to get that all-over café-au-lait tint. He looked like he might have a couple of calluses on his hands and could maybe use his nice muscles for something useful, too. I munched my potato and contemplated the possibilities, which were not all of them horse related.

'So?' he asked. 'What do you think?'

'I think I know where to find your green horse,' I said. 'If you've got serious money.' It sounded casual coming out of my mouth, but my heart was beginning to race and I had to stop eating.

'Yeah?'

'Yeah. You remember Ivory Gardner's Ice Cream?'

'The grey jumper that colicked. I cried like a baby when they put her down.'

I nodded. 'I think I can get you her full sister.' I couldn't believe I was saying this. I put my hands in my lap and squeezed them together, my head ringing *oh please say yes, please please say yes*.

Gerry Dirk put his fork down and forgot to close his mouth. 'Ice Cream's sister! Are you serious?'

I nodded. 'Big, grey, scopey, four years, ready to start Pre-Green or do the Futurities.'

'How much?'

I named an enormous figure that I thought might cover the purchase and my commission and the guy didn't even blink. By this time we were both hyperventilating. We cut dinner short and set land speed records to get to his car phone and call the Morgans right-away-that-second before the Cosmos got wind of our desire and found a way to thwart it. I swear, we couldn't have moved faster or breathed more heavily if we'd been ripping each other's clothes off to have mad, unbridled sex.

The mare was still available, and the Morgans said they were delighted to have her come to me. I sent Gerry Dirk up to see her and put a leg on her, but I knew he'd fall in love. I knew it was only a matter of days before the mare they called Dreamcatcher would be in my barn.

I'd promised Jake and Jennie out for an evening hack. But the combination of gambler's rush and anxiety over being responsible for something costing more than my farm made me so dizzy I had to lie down for an hour before I could contemplate riding without falling right off.


Even Harry's eyes lit when I told him my latest stories and asked, as was my increasing habit, for his advice. 'I don't get it,' I complained. 'Here I've been struggling along for yonks in complete obscurity and now all of a sudden all these horses are falling into my lap. It's so weird.'

'That's the way it's supposed to work, darlin'. You've earned your rides, built up a good reputation the hard way. And you have a pretty high profile these days. Good media never hurts.'

I groaned. 'It makes me want to die of embarrassment, honest to God, Harry, it does. Soon as I get nervous it's just *blah blah blah* like I have no control over my mouth. I wish I could be like Colin - *'Aw shucks, ma'am, twu'nt nothin'* - you know, Jimmy Stewart with an English accent.'

Harry roared. 'That's good, babe. I like that,' he said. 'But you got passion, you know. That's pretty good, too.'

'Yeah, well, there's a difference between passion and ability. Sometimes passion is just passion. *Full of sound and fury, signifying nothing.*'

''Chelle...'

'I know, I know, you're going to tell me if I can't stand the heat to get out of the kitchen, right? I know.'

'*No*, I wasn't going to tell you that. That what you want to hear? That's what you want to hear, that's what I'll tell you. But it wasn't what I was going to say.'

'You weren't?'

'No. I wasn't. I was gonna tell you not to start with the Shakespeare, is all. How'd you grow up with such a low opinion of yourself anyway, doll? Smart, tough woman like you. I'd think you'd be on cloud nine, all these nice horses to ride.'

'Is it cloud nine or cloud-cuckoo-land?'

'Not a lot to choose between 'em sometimes, darlin'. But I'll tell you what I know for sure. I *know* you better ride this wave as far and as long as it goes, 'cause another one this size may be a long time coming.'

I grinned. 'You've caught your share.'

'Yeah, but we won't talk about the slides between 'em. For chrissake *enjoy* it. You got some great horses, some wonderful opportunities, and you're hot. Tell you this, though: you'll sure have a lot of other people drooling over those horses, the next few weeks. And there's more than one rider around here'd be tickled to pieces to tell your owners you're not feeling up to the job.'

'Like Hilary?'

'Like her, and worse than her.'

'*Why?*'

'Cuz there aren't enough nice horses to go around, doll. We got every amateur in town with the doe-ray-me wanting to ride their own instead of hiring us like they used to, and the shows filling up with divisions of *cross*-rails so they can do it without turning ass over teakettle. More and more big horses are locked up in the three-foot divisions and we'll never see 'em over the kind of fences they oughta be jumping. We'll never get the chance to ride 'em. So it doesn't matter how well everybody likes you if you got horses they want, babe. You'd best watch your ass. And *ride*.'


As it happened, Dreamcatcher arrived a lot faster and my dad's colt (which was inexplicably called Ottawa) much more slowly than expected, so they unloaded within moments of each other on Monday as I was entertaining my mother, The Rev, and his lady friend Beverly for a tent-side picnic lunch. Dreamcatcher was just as perfect as I remembered her, and Gerry was on hand to get in the way and caper around and generally fall over himself like a kid getting his first bike on Christmas morning. My family entered giddily into the spirit of the thing, too, with The Rev extolling the virtues of a well-made horse from *Venus and Adonis* as he strolled through the barns, oblivious to everything but the combined sensual beauty of horseflesh and words: '*Round hoof'd, short-jointed, fetlocks shag and long, Broad breast, full eye...* something something... oh, yes... *straight legs and passing strong/ Thin mane, thick tail, broad buttock...* I particularly like a broad buttock, myself... where was I... ah! *Tender hide/ Look what a horse should have he did not lack/ Save a proud rider on so proud a back...* now I've been meaning to ask you, 'Chelle, what precisely is a fetlock?'

The Rev has a great voice. I noticed both Beverly and Gerry eating his performance with a spoon while I threw in 'scuse me,' and 'can you hand me that shank' and 'watch out behind you, Gramp', and 'Ma, don't step there in your good shoes' and other such practical and largely unheeded interjections, and one way or another we got the new horses settled.

The colt was something a bit different. Irish Draught horses are not as heavy as Clydesdales, Percherons, and Belgians, but like many big, scopey horses they're slow to mature. Ottawa, despite his royal sire, was just plain ugly. His head was too big for his neck, his feet huge, his body small, he was about a hundred and fifty pounds underweight, and he was completely exhausted and unkempt, with a long, bushy mane and tail full of witches' knots and hack marks where somebody'd tried to cut burrs out. I imagined the poor sucker had been dragged straight off the side of a stony hill in Galway, shoved on a plane, shunted through quarantine, shipped to my dad's clinic, and sent down here more or less without a breath drawn. His eyes were large, liquid, and troubled. When I took hold of the lead to bring him into yet another strange place, he nuzzled my shoulder worriedly with a prehensile upper lip. My heart went out to him. I patted him soothingly, told him he was going to be okay, and put him in a corner stall with Jake on his other side, a safer location for a stallion than mid-aisle where he'd be surrounded by too many distracting horse-ladies. I left him with a flake of hay to sleep off his trip and come to whatever arcane conclusions horses arrive at when they realize their lives suddenly resemble nothing they've ever imagined.

The Rev was still quoting *Venus and Adonis* to the rapt Beverly and an awed assemblage of other riders and grooms as my mother shepherded them out of the barn to their car. Then, blue eyes gleaming wickedly, he told Beverly how he'd always thought the phrase *all for the eye/ of the fair breeder standing by* referred to a human horse breeder until his granddaughter had enlarged his knowledge by explaining that in fact it referred to a mare in standing heat, ready to be mounted by the stallion. My mother, Gerry, and I inhaled sharply and didn't dare look at each other. Beverly turned bright pink and squeaked, 'Thomas *Roche*, that's *obscene!*' and then she giggled and shoved him playfully and the rest of us laughed until we had to wipe our eyes.

'You have a very unique family,' observed Gerry when I finally waved them out of sight.

'That's the understatement of the year,' I agreed. For some reason, watching them disappear into the dusty distance brought a lump to my throat. I wished momentarily more than anything else to run after them calling *wait, wait, take me, too!* But there were horses to ride.


Dreamcatcher hadn't had quite so arduous a trip as the poor colt, and she was more used to travel. After I'd dispatched my other charges I took Gerry and one of his trusty old boys for company and rode her out to see her new surroundings. As expected, she was on the squirrely side, but the Morgans had given her a good start in life and she wasn't going to self-destruct. This was a relief. A horse with an advanced sense of self-preservation always makes me feel safer - it means I can concentrate on riding and unlocking its mind rather than wondering if it's going to kill us both by mistake first.

Even so, the first dance with a 1,000 pound blind date that doesn't know whether to trust your control or take steps to save its own skin is nerve stretching stuff. Trust from a horse takes time. You have to earn it. Until you do, their obedience to your commands has to suffice. So by the time Dreamcatcher and I reached consensus about my suitability as a leader, I had the blind staggers. I was glad to end the ride, say goodbye to Gerry, and take her home.

It wasn't just Dreamcatcher, of course. The cumulative effect of all these horses was beginning to tell on my middle-aged body. Wearily, I contemplated the evening's round of straightening blankets, pulling manes, trimming whiskers, tails, and fetlocks to keep them tidy, cleaning stalls, dishing out grain and hay, lugging water, and hand walking. I longed for a hot bath, a drink, a handful of ibuprofen, and the solace of my bed. Somebody to stroke my head and read me a story wouldn't be bad, either, I thought, though it seemed even less likely than the rest.

But instead of uncompleted work, what I found when I got to the stalls were horses contentedly munching, lights cheerfully turned on, and the harmonic sound of a human whistling tunelessly to the accompaniment of soft rock on the radio and water buckets being filled. Blank with astonishment, I slid off the grey mare and led her to the open door of her stall, from whence both the whistle and the water hose trailed.

'Santé!' I exclaimed.

The wiry ex-jockey looked up and grinned. 'All done here, 'Chelle,' he said. 'You want me to take the mare, I walk her and rub her while you take off your boots. You look like you need to sit down some.' He crimped the hose, coiled it up, and turned off the faucet with a flourish. 'Nice bunch you got.' He nodded with satisfaction. 'Yeah, nice bunch. Even that big colt down there the end, now where you got that thing?'

'Santé... What are you doing here?'

''Chelle now, don't you get funny, see? I got to work. I can't stand it no more, sit around the house nothin' to do, and Ivory you know, well she don't know what happen with Mr. Desmarchais and that. So I gotta *do* something, see. I gotta be busy so's I don't... you know...'

'Yeah, yeah, I know. You clean?'

'Yes ma'am, I am. I go to them meetings every day, I don't do nothin' bad. But it ain't easy, see? Now I come 'round here today 'cause I miss all the horses, I gotta be near 'em, and I seen how hard you working. I seen you need help like I need work. Okay? That right?'

'Yeah. I'm swamped. But Santé...'

''Chelle, you just think on it. Ain't no unemployment money gonna be okay for me. I need a job. You need help. I stay here, I don't drink, my wife don't throw me out, you get some sleep and ride better. Anyhow,' he reached reverently for Dreamcatcher's reins and took them from me, 'you got this beautiful mare.' He crooned to her and stroked her neck. 'Something special, this mare.'

I nodded. 'Ice Cream's sister,' I said, and sank gratefully into a folding chair.

'That right? Ice Cream's sister?' He looked at me hard and then back at the mare and silence stretched between us.

'You know anything about that, Santé?'

He shot me a quick look from under his eyebrows as he busied himself untacking the grey horse and putting on her halter. 'Well now, maybe I do,' he said finally.

'Santé...'

He ignored me and began rubbing Dreamcatcher's sleek body from the base of her ears, down her neck, to her lean shoulders and so on backward, working out the sweat marks and the stiffnesses of travel and work. The mare leaned into him sighing, her lips wiggling in pleasure. They all loved Santé. I'd never seen a horse that didn't respond to him the same way. 'I done some big thinking, 'Chelle,' he said finally. 'But maybe we don't talk about it here, see? Maybe we wait a little bit. Okay?'

'Sure. Okay,' I said, though I wanted to jump on him and shake out of him every deep thought he might have had about Ice Cream, the accident, Ivory's current legal troubles, and whatever other snippet of half-heard conversation he might have been privy to.

'But first, do I got a job?'

'Did Harry and Ivory put you up to this?' I asked suspiciously.

''Chelle now, honest, I never…' but he blushed.

'You fuckin' liar,' I laughed. 'Yeah, you've got a job. I'll figure it out somehow, and you've got yourself a job.'

He grinned all over his face and I watched him relax into the mare the same way she'd done to him. Until I saw that release of tension I'd had no idea how well he'd disguised his desperation.

I wondered if mine was as evident and suspected from the way he glanced at me from time to time that it was.


I'd barely been back in the rig for five minutes before my phone rang. 'Honey, I am calling you from a public phone in a motel in beautiful downtown Atlanta,' Ivory crowed, without preamble.

'Ivory! That's wonderful! So does that mean you're off?'

'Well, not exactly. The feds decided there wasn't enough evidence to hang the whole thing on me, but they weren't sure enough to let me off altogether. They figure I won't bolt, since I'm in a wheelchair and expecting and all, so they're letting me out on bail. Harry and you got that all taken care of, so thanks and… here I am! And the suits are going to have themselves an investigation.'

'Winston still under?'

'They say he's been upgraded from 'coma' to 'stupor', whatever that means. But he's still pretty much out of the picture. I went in to see him, you know. It… um… it was…' her voice cracked. I could hear her breathing, and she tried hard to clear her throat. 'It was not so good, 'Chelle.'

'I'm sorry, Ive. Really sorry.'

'Yeah. Me too.'

'Um… How's… um… Janna?'

'It's okay, doll, you can say her name. Maintaining best she can. We actually chatted a little bit, you know? She's not so bad.'

'I thought the same thing.'

'I took over Morning Glory and Heavensent, 'Chelley, if you don't mind. Now that I can do something.'

'Go for it. Is it okay?'

'Well, no. I don't suppose it'll ever be okay. Janna drove me out there this morning, to see them. Shit, 'Chelle… it was… I just don't…' her voice cracked again, and I listened to her cry for a bit. I wanted to say something, to comfort her. But there was nothing to say, and there was no comfort. 'Anyway,' she continued after a time, 'they're doing okay. They can be moved soon. So I was wondering if maybe they could go on up to your place? Would Jimmy mind?'

'No, we've been through all that. Go ahead and call him, he's expecting it. You need any help?'

'You've done plenty. It'll give me something constructive to work on. Janna's paying for it. She's okay, you know? She gave me those horses, 'Chelle. She'll get the insurance on 'em, and it's not like they're going to be any use to her, you know, even if… even when… anyway. They're mine now. They're safe. We're riding south together, and one of my old clients has offered me her condo on the water to stay in yet awhile.'

'A condo on the water! Honey, you move in the right circles.'

'Yeah, well, it helps to know people, for sure… I don't suppose you've heard anything more, have you?'

'No. Few more hints, but nobody'll come right out and say anything.'

''Course not. Too much shit on the line. Well, maybe we can shake a few trees when I get down there, see what kinda rotten fruit falls out. Anything else new?'

'Yeah, there is. Santé just started working for me, did you know that?'

'Santé? Well now that's great, 'Chelle, I'm glad to hear that,' said Ivory a shade too enthusiastically. 'He needed work and y'all needed help. How'd you find him?'

'Ivory Gardner, you cheating slut. I think you and Harry put him up to it.'

'Well now,' she said, 'I *did* have a little bitty notion that you were pretty rolled-up down there, sweetie.'

'How'd you figure that? Talking to Harry, no doubt.'

'Well naturally, 'Chelley, he *is* the guy in charge of my defense fund.'

I started to splutter some nonsense about being able to take care of my own affairs, which made Ivory laugh.

'Shit, 'Chelle, you are just the honest end, you know that? Harry said you were gonna be like this if we took steps. But you just stop being so righteous and let your friends help out once in a while, you might survive this season in one piece.'

'Ivory, I have every intention of surviving this and many other seasons! And if it's your silly *mare* you're worried about, let me tell you...'

'Uh-huh,' said Ivory, sounding unconvinced. 'Gotta go, honey, I got fish to fry. So I'll see you soon, huh? Love ya, bye.' And she hung up in the middle of my bluster. I chuckled in spite of myself. Sometimes friends meddle even better than families do.

# SEVEN

*...For through his mane and tail the high wind sings,*
*Fanning the hairs, who wave like feathered wings.*
-William Shakespeare, ***Venus and Adonis***

I had a juicy cantaloupe on hand that hadn't rotted yet, and Tommy Essex arrived with croissants. After we'd laughed over the week's accrued gossip and compared injuries and embarrassing moments, I bluntly asked him why he'd come.

'I don't think it was just for the pleasure of my company.'

He grinned. 'Now, how can I respond to that and still be a gentleman?'

'Okay, I'll get you out of it. I *think* you're here because of all these hint-hint remarks Craig keeps almost not making.'

'Yeah, he's pretty good at that.' Tommy took a breath and thought for a moment, then began. 'Do you remember that drug thing Craig was involved in a few years back?'

'That bust that happened in... when was it... five? Six years ago? When Craig got caught coming back from Europe with weed in his luggage?'

'Yeah. That's the one.'

*Click-click-click*, went the slot machine pictures. All lemons. 'Yeah, I do remember now. He was ruled off for a couple of years, right? And dropped out of sight. Ruined his international career. Did he do time for that?'

'No. I think he made some kind of deal. I don't know what it was.'

'Probably better not to.'

'Whatever. Anyway, I believe it bears somewhat on Ivory's predicament.'

'I don't follow you.'

'I have to go back a little here. See, Craig was carrying the stuff for Michael Draper. Michael was getting paranoid. Thought someone was out to get him, you know? Rat on him. He had a lot on the line. The World Cup standings and then the Olympics and all... So he asked Craig to carry the stuff...'

'Hold on, Tommy, Craig was a user...'

'C'mon, 'Chelle, are you going to tell me you're any different than him? Or Harry Daly's any better than him?'

''Course not. Harry's in the program. And shit, when I was your age...'

'So, yeah. It's a lot of pressure at that level, you *know* what it's like. You have owners breathing down your neck to win big, you have horses going lame before International competitions, you have trying to make the Team, then staying on it, then not letting it down when you're in Europe, and all that *explaining* when things just don't go the way your owners hoped... You have to be pretty tough to deal with all that. So yeah, Craig smoked some to unwind. Maybe did a line here and there, okay. I'm not saying he's a saint. But Michael... well, Michael's real sensitive. Stuff *matters* to him. He couldn't deal with that kind of pressure all the time. He never drank much, said he got too heavy, but he'd blow some dope to unwind. Then the further up the ladder he got, the higher the pressure, the more he had to lose, the more he smoked. Then he started sending more and more garbage up his nose to keep himself sharp.'

'I'm not feeling too sorry for him, Tommy.'

'No. But you should feel sorry for Craig, is what I'm saying. Michael, he panicked when Craig got busted. Said anything he could to get as much distance between them as he could. Denied everything. *Everything.*'

'Everything meaning, like, the relationship?'

'Yes'm. Went back to Margie and swore he never had anything to do with Craig-the-fag. Never knew Craig had a drug problem. And then he let Craig take the fall.'

'How do you know that? Is that what Craig told you? I mean, he would, you know. Addicts... he might even believe it, after awhile.'

'I'm saying it wasn't like that, 'Chelle. I was a working student in their barn when it all came down. Lived with them. Traveled with them. Went to Europe. I saw Craig keeping the horses going when Michael was too messed up to get it together, and then lying about Michael's 'health problems' to his clients so nobody'd know. I heard the fights. I couldn't believe how Craig just took it.'

'So when Michael went back to Margie...'

'Her deal was straighten up, come home, I'll never say a word. Stick with Craig, all bets are off.'

'She'd have blown the whistle?'

'She said she would.'

'And Craig never said anything. Just took the fall.'

'I don't know what he was thinking. What he's thinking now. But he was carrying the stuff, all right. Not Michael. And Michael Draper... well, you know, he's *Michael Draper*. He's got money, he's got connections, he's got a wife and kid, he's got Olympic Silver and Pan American Gold, he's got fourth in the World Cup standings and his face on magazine covers. Who's going to believe queeny old Craig Oppenheim, eternal side-kick?'

'So then Michael goes off and rides on the World Cup team for the U.S. and he's a hero and Craig is ruined.'

'Pretty much.'

'That's ugly, Tommy.'

'Tell me.'

'I don't get how it relates to Ivory.'

'Well, see. Michael's been in a slump, you know the buzz. He needs a couple of good horses to pull him out, he hasn't got the caliber or depth he had before. He's getting a little freaked. And there's his old buddy Winston Desmarchais, who could say just about anything he wants to blow Michael's life all to hell, and all these nice horses.'

'Yeah, but Ivory...'

'Yeah, but Ivory. Yeah, but riders get dumped all the time. And I'm guessing Michael owed Winston a lot of money. From before.'

'He must have been in pretty deep.'

'He was. Deeper than most people know. 'Chelle... I've got no hard proof, but I think Michael got into... ' he pressed his lips together, searching for the right way to say it. 'I think Michael got into the *insurance* business, you might say.'

'The *insurance* business,' I echoed. 'Holy *shit*.'

'Uh-huh. To pay Winston off and keep his family out of the mud. And I figure there had to be some other big payoff for Michael, because he's no born horse killer. So there had to be a carrot. Like...'

'...Ivory's Dream Team.'

'Uh-huh. And no word about their - um - *previous* connection.'

I winced. 'How many people know this?'

'Without the van wreck, it's totally on the q.t. But you know how it goes, like that whole other insurance thing a few years back. If they hadn't caught the one guy and squeezed him probably nobody would have come forward. Only everybody sorta *knows*. Like it's hanging in the air or something…'

'… And maybe that's part of Michael's problem. Why he's not getting the horses anymore.'

'Yeah.'

'Oh my god, Tommy… I mean we're talking about our *Michael*. I just…' I struggled for words, looked for the way out. 'He couldn't be that desperate. He's got *everything*.'

'Except Olympic Gold, World Cup Gold, and a horse to get him there. He's not getting any younger, even as riders go. And there's his family to think about, *and* the fact that he's playing for the other team. He never came out. Not like Craig. It's a lot.'

'People make stupid decisions,' I said, floundering. 'If anybody checked out *my* past…'

'I doubt you ever set your best friend up, or killed a horse, 'Chelle. I doubt that.'

'I'd like to think not, Tommy. Not for my career. But what if there was a threat to my family. To Camille. Who knows what I'd do. What any of us would do.'

'Yeah. But that's all theory. This is real. We're not just talking about people blowing dope to unwind, or people snorting their way out of careers, 'Chelle. Shoot, I'll inhale if it's offered, I'll drink more bourbon than I ought, who's perfect? But we're talking about horses' lives, here. *Good* horses' lives, that ought to have happier endings than Ice Cream, or Memphis, or Rougère. And nobody saying anything because we've all got something to lose. So it's like, *I don't talk, you don't talk, bad things happen, wink-wink nudge-nudge*. It makes me want to vomit sometimes. I'd like to see it end.'

'So Michael Draper kills a horse to pay Winston Desmarchais off so Winston doesn't take him down and ruin his career.'

'And his family.'

'And people just shut up.'

'And other people get stuffed. Like Craig and Ivory.'

'But Craig made a deal. And we still don't know what kind of deal.'

'Possibly.'

'So… what's this about, then. Are you asking me to fix it, Tommy? Are you saying I should be the one to rat out the people I work with? Without real evidence. Because you say so. C'mon, man. You could do it just as well. So could Craig. Maybe he already is.'

'You've got the visibility right now. You've got the reputation.'

'But no evidence. It sucks, but it's true. *No evidence.*'

'So you'll be just like the rest of them and let it go on because you don't want to stick your neck out.'

'No! But... Oh my God, Tommy, you're telling me that Michael Draper killed Ice Cream.' I started to cry, like a child with no Santa Claus, like somebody just told me the relationship was over.

'I know,' Tommy said. 'But I'm not lying to you.'


My morning of joy didn't end with Tommy's departure. My distraction and upset telegraphed itself all too clearly to Dancing Fool and she summarily dumped me by making a giant leap over a small schooling fence and popping off an equally wicked buck on landing. Unfortunately it was Hilary that caught her.

'Too bad Michael's not here', she said silkily. 'He could probably turn this mare into a great jumper.'

'I guess that's up to Ivory,' I said grouchily. Then remembered to add, 'Thanks for catching her.'

Hilary wasn't going to let me off that easily. 'I heard your old man sent you down a really nice Irish horse.'

'Yeah.' I collected Dancing Fool's reins and remounted.

'How come? It should be Michael's horse. Somebody who can take it to the top. That's what I hear, that your dad wants the horse at the top. And Michael's his *client*.'

'Michael's *wife* is his client,' I snapped. 'But he's *my* dad. And what's in it for you, Hilary?' Then I realized too late that I had said exactly the wrong thing. Hilary would now say that even my dad was giving me horses out of pity. Pity for what, I wasn't certain.

I turned Dancing Fool over to Santé and headed back to the rig in despair, thinking that half an hour to weep and rail in private might help. As it turned out, I shouldn't have bothered. Just as I'd pulled myself together and was dragging myself out the door to ride the rest of my horses, the phone rang and it was Joe-don't-call-me-Josie.

'Camille's about to be thrown out of school,' he said without preamble.

'Ohhhh, no. What this time? Smoking in the bathrooms? Or sneaking out at night after curfew?'

'She was caught smoking pot in the boathouse with a bunch of her low-life friends.'

All the breath went out of me like from a balloon. I sat down heavily on the floor and wept myself empty.

I spoke not a word while I went through the motions of riding all my charges for the rest of the day. Santé sized me up silently and simply handed me horses, took horses away from me, did more work than I would have believed possible, and otherwise ignored me. But when I'd finished with Clyde and returned him to a groom, Harry sauntered over instead of disappearing with another horse and rider and offered me a cup of coffee.

I was so stunned I nearly fell over backwards. I accepted, followed him into his tack paradise, and sank into a chair with a cup of hot, steaming java hinting of just enough hazelnut to make my nostrils quiver. It tasted as good as it smelled, too.

'You want to talk?' Harry asked, when I'd drunk off the top third in blessed ecstasy.

'Is it that obvious?'

'Yeah.'

I took a deep breath. 'Well... I had a visit from Tommy Essex this morning.'

'Uh-huh.'

'Saying some things about some things that reflect really poorly on people I love and admire. If you read me.'

'Uh-huh.'

'Makes me think there are some questions I need to ask Ivory, once she's here and I don't have to worry about phones being tapped or whatever. Shit, I can't even believe I said that, it sounds like a fuckin' made-for-TV movie.'

'Uh-huh.'

'So then I ride Ivory's stupid mare like a fucking novice and get dumped. And of course Hilary catches her and you can imagine how she turned that into an opportunity.'

'Uh-huh.'

'So I go back home to get my shit together and my ex calls to say my daughter - you remember Camille?'

'Uh-huh.'

'Just got busted at school for pot. Shit. I mean, she's a *kid*. Just six*teen*. 'Course, Josie thinks it's all my fault even though this friggin' school was his big socially acceptable idea and he's paying for it.'

'Uh-*huh*.'

I finished the coffee, put down my cup, and buried my face in my hands. 'Ohhh, fuck, Harry. Life is just too complicated sometimes.'

'*Uh*-huh.'

'Is that all you're saying today? '*Uh-huh*'?'

'Well, I'm in listening mode, darlin'. That's what I say in

listening mode.' He got up, took my cup and refilled it, then casually rubbed my neck with strong fingers and a vibe that tingled right through to the soles of my feet.

'You're wound up tighter than an eight day clock, babe,' he said. 'When was the last time somebody got you loosened up?'

'Too goddamn long, Harry,' I sighed, floating on the sensation. 'Harry… you're not putting the make on me, are you?'

He stopped rubbing, went back to his chair, sat in it. Looked at me poker faced for a long moment. 'What gives you that idea, darlin'?'

'I dunno. You never offered me coffee before. You're listening to my problems. You're rubbing my neck and sending me vibes. I mean, I'm just asking. Because my life is really, really upsetting right now and I am afraid that every time I turn around something else is going to break apart.' I could feel tears ready to flood the dam again.

'Nah', said Harry, after a long stillness. 'I'm not putting the make on you, doll. You're too much like my first wife.'

'What's that mean?'

'Smart-assed and skinny.'

'Thanks a bunch.'

'Old guy like me wants flesh and the milk of human kindness.'

'Good,' I said, not sure whether I was relieved or disappointed.

'But - just out of interest - what *are* you going to do about Camille?'

'Shit, Harry, I don't know. You've had kids. What would you do if your kid got busted?'

'Well now, happens one of my sons did get busted, fifteen, twenty years ago. We don't speak anymore.'

'Why?'

'He was real arty. Wanted to be a writer. I thought he was a lazy sombitch. Gave him my take on longhaired, pinko slackers like him. *What kinda stupid job is that. When're you gonna get real.* You know the drill. When he got busted I threw him out the house and told him I'd no part of him, he had to face the music himself. Which he did. Real well. He became a successful writer just like he wanted, and I admire him. I've read every word he ever published. But we don't speak. He's not too proud of his old man.

'Thing is, see, I was drinking all the time myself then. Took my boy's mama leaving me to get me into rehab. And that was my second wife. First one left me for the same reason. That, and I was already screwing around with number two.'

'*Jesus*, Harry.'

'Oh, yeah. I was just some kind of prince, huh?'

'Do you regret it? Not knowing your son?'

'Every single day of my life, doll. Every single day.'

It was much later that I realized Harry hadn't said a thing about my conversation with Tommy Essex. Not one single thing.


I spent two hours on the phone, first with Josie, then with Camille, then with the dean of students, and back through them all again. In round one, Josie was loud and abusive and Camille was loud and defensive. The dean of students was at least quiet. She referred to Camille as undisciplined, angry, and brilliant, as if this were news to me. She said Camille needed help, which I agreed was a good idea. She said Camille suffered from an inconsistent family life, which I agreed was exactly the case. She said, after I'd worn her down by agreeing with her for an hour, that Camille *might* stay until vacation week, *if* she'd see a shrink. No promises.

In round two, Josie blamed me for our daughter's problems, shouted through the fiber optics that he'd disown her (*what, again?* I asked helpfully), and added that no daughter of his would set foot across a psychiatrist's threshold as if she were a mental case. Camille, just as predictably, shouted that the school rules *sucked*, that the laws of our land were *fucked up*, and managed to intimate that somehow I was responsible for all of it. She flatly refused to see a shrink. *Fine, go to jail*, I said. *You wouldn't dare*, she said. *Try me*, I said. She called me a fucking hypocrite. I agreed that this described me perfectly, which made me an authority. She agreed to see the shrink. Josie agreed to pay for it. I agreed to let her ride Jennie over break. The dean agreed to keep her until then.

In round three I opened a bottle of very expensive pinot noir I'd been saving for a special occasion and got completely and sublimely smashed in the forgiving dark of the aisle by my stalls. On balance it would probably have been better just to talk to my mother, but I suspected she'd say something unhelpful about reaping what I'd sown. So I unburdened my soul to a row of sympathetic horses and my dog. They blew through their nostrils, pricked their ears, and (in the case of Spring) whined in all the right moments. '*I would there were no age between ten and three-and-twenty, or that youth would sleep out the rest*', I griped feelingly from *The Winter's Tale*; '*for there is nothing in the between but getting wenches with child, wronging the ancientry* – not that I'm all that ancient, mind you –

*stealing, fighting* – well, shit. At least she's not a wench with child. Or I don't know. Maybe she is. Maybe it'd be easier.'

*Exit, pursued by a Bear...*


I woke up next morning with a hangover the like of which I had not experienced for more than a decade.

Wouldn't you know, the first people I bumped into - literally - were Colin Rutherford and Diane Gambarini. I was groping my way around one corner of the barn with my sunglasses on to block the blinding light of the shadowed aisle as they strode around the same corner from the opposing direction, deep in animated conversation. We collided smartly mid-aisle and Colin had to wrap his arms around me tightly to stand me up straight. If we hung on a fraction longer than necessary, who was going to notice? When we'd all exclaimed, *oopsed*, laughed awkwardly, and apologized, I noticed that Diane was looking awfully pleased with herself and Colin was looking slightly embarrassed. And they were both looking at me oddly.

''Chelle,' started Colin, 'you look dreadful. Are you alright?'

'Yeah, fine,' I lied, and straightened the shades so they'd shield my bloodshot eyes. 'Just keep your voice down.'

'Looks like you had a little too much fun last night, Chelley,' Diane giggled. 'That it? A little too much *par-tay*?' She squeezed Colin's hand and gazed at him meaningfully. Colin frowned a little and pulled his hand away. I mumbled something completely inarticulate and scuttled away with my eyes squinted against what seemed to me to be klieg lights aimed straight at my eyeballs.

I loaded up with 400 mgs of 'vitamin I' and began the riding part of my day with The Ploughboy, which was what everybody was calling poor, clunky Ottawa. I really liked the horse. He was like a giant adolescent whose feet and hands are too big for his body. He clearly felt he was too big for every space he went into, from his stall to the largest schooling ring. Corners defeated him entirely. When I tried to turn him he tripped over himself and ran into things. Sitting on him was sort of like riding a camel. I stayed up in half-seat to try to save my throbbing skull from too much contact with my spine, my arse, or the saddle. I was motion sick, too. But Ottawa was affable and earnest. He really tried to get the program.

''Chelle, are you *sure* you're all right?' asked Colin again, riding up beside us on something graceful and brown. 'You look green.'

'I've got a terrible hangover, thank-you very much.'

'Why?' He looked at me searchingly. 'What's gone wrong? Ivory? Something at home? Something here?'

'All of the above,' I said, and the fucking lump in my throat was growing again.

'Anything I can do?' I shook my head, but he didn't look convinced. 'Come on, 'Chelle. We're supposed to be friends.'

'We were. We are.'

'Then why be so bloody prickly? Why not talk? I *might* be able to help out, you know. My shoulders are broad.' He smiled invitingly. I wanted to fling myself into his arms and cry on his lovely chest.

'Thanks, Colin, I appreciate it. Really. But I don't think there's anything.' Even to me it sounded like a stiff brush-off.

His smile hardened at the edges. 'Right. Be a frigging hero. But you've only to ask.' And he trotted off.

It was going to be that kind of day.


Sweat and hard work cleared the alcohol poisoning by around noon, which helped. Santé studied me assessingly when I came back with Dancing Fool and nodded briefly.

'I know,' I said, reading his mind. 'I am a stupid slut and ought to know better than to drink myself into a stupor like I thought it was going to help.'

'*Yeah*,' agreed Santé feelingly. 'You need help, you got friends, you talk to 'em. Be doing that stupid shit. You one impossible woman, do everything yourself. Hold it all in like that. You gonna come all to pieces, *ffft*, like a bomb, you go on like that.'

'Thanks, grandma.' I sat with my head in my hands while he tacked up Jake, then I accepted a leg up and rode back out into the heat. When I returned, drenched with sweat from a tightener that proved my little bay horse serviceably sound, Santé was gone. But Michael Draper was standing in front of The Ploughboy's stall.

'*Michael*!' I yelped involuntarily, and flinched as if I'd seen a ghost. 'I thought you were in Europe!' I slid off of Jake and busied myself untacking him to cover the adrenaline shot of seeing Michael unexpectedly so soon after Tommy's visit.

'Yeah,' he smiled. And it was a sad smile. It was my friend Michael Draper, the consummate horseman I'd admired and learned from for years. Not a thing with horns that smoked sulphur. 'I had some bad luck. The big horse colicked and had to go into surgery. The brown mare - you remember her? - injured a stifle. Nothing to do but get them home.'

'Oh Michael, what a disappointment. I am so sorry.'

He shrugged resignation. 'Happens.'

'But you're over on the Coast, doing the big circuit, aren't you?'

'Oh, yeah. Plenty to ride. But - you know how it is. Europe…' His voice faded and he looked into Dreamcatcher's stall. 'You look good. All these nice grey horses, you've got yourself a dandy hunt team.'

'Yeah, we could line 'em up in order of size and they'd look like a perspective drawing.'

'What's this thing of beauty?'

'Dreamcatcher. Ice Cream's sister,' I said without thinking, then froze. Michael looking at me very oddly.

'*Ice Cream*'s sister?' He turned back to her, stared at her silently for a very long time. Rested his head against the bars of the stall. I could see tension jumping in the muscles of his jaw, but his face was a mask. Finally he moved to the next. 'And Dancing Fool, too. Lucky you. I'd have thought…' He shook his head. 'I mean. How's Ivory? I was hoping I might find her back here.'

'Okay. She went to ship…' my throat filled up again, and suddenly Michael was cloudy. I cleared my throat and tried again. '…to ship Heavensent and Morning Glory. Up to my place.'

Michael was resting his head against the bars of Dancing Fool's stall, now. Looking tired. Looking… *well of course he looks tired, you dweeb*, the sane part of my brain saying, *he just got back from fuckin' Europe*. The other part wondering why he was here, by my stalls.

'How are they?' he asked. 'Will they be okay?'

'Dunno yet. Time. You know.'

He nodded. Wiped his face. 'God. What a mess. What a *waste*. Those nice horses… and Winston still in a coma.'

'Yeah.'

'Any word? He going to come out of it? I was already in Europe when… and there was nothing I could…'

I shook my head. 'Ivory says he's been upgraded. Something called a stupor. But it's still up in the air. It's not like he's conscious or anything.'

'So he still can't talk?'

'No.'

'What's happening around here, then? I mean, besides all the bullshit that always gets into the papers. Good thing none of it's true, huh.' He looked at me sideways, like he wanted to see if I was the one spreading the stories. *No*, I wanted to blurt. *No, it's not me, never me...*

'Um... yeah. Really good thing.' I said.

'Are the feds crawling around? Investigating? Do they have any ideas? Is Ivory officially clear?'

'No. Nothing's set that I know of. I guess there's an investigation happening, but there's nothing spooky going on. You know, stalls bugged, guys with no necks lurking around, whatever. Just, y'know. Some guys in suits. We avoid them, unless they ask a direct question.'

'Guys in suits?' He was a master at the bland expression, my old friend Michael. But I could see alarm crease his eyes, and the muscle in his jaw turn rigid. He stared at Dancing Fool.

'Yeah. Feds, maybe. Winston's friends, maybe. I don't want to know.'

Michael gave me another laser scan with his eyes, then moved on to the Ploughboy's stall. 'Well, it's an ill wind, as they say,' he said neutrally. 'You're doing okay out of all this. Big media star, big horses coming your way...'

I blushed. 'Well... I *hope* I'm *earning* it, Michael.' I decided I wouldn't want to play poker with this guy. And I didn't want him studying me or my horses the way he was. 'I don't like the media stuff much,' I admitted.

'Why? I hear you're a natural. Sara Wychoff thinks you have a brilliant career ahead of you as a commentator. Thought for awhile it might have been a job for me, but it didn't work out.'

'How come?'

'I dunno. Scheduling. Voice. Some dumb shit.'

'Michael, I'm...'

'*And* you've got these horses', he added. 'A little different than your old pony show, isn't it.'

'Michael...'

'Look at this guy, now.'

I stopped trying to cut in and decided to go with whatever flow we were on. 'Yeah. Ugly sucker, isn't he? He'll come, I think.'

'Oh, yeah,' he breathed, studying the big horse's angular frame. 'Hang your hopes on this guy, 'Chelle. Forget the rest of them and hang your hopes right here.' His eyes devoured the horse.

'You think he'll go Grand Prix?'

'I think so, yeah. He could fool me. But I think so. He'll be your first, huh?'

'Yeah. If I do it.'

'Oh, you'll do it. Dancing Fool and this horse in your barn, you'll do it. But if you don't, I hope you'll give them to me.'

'You'd be my first choice, Michael. Always.'

He gave me another odd look. 'Thanks,' he said. 'But I was kidding.'

'I wasn't', I said.


The first class of Dreamcatcher's show ring career took place under a drizzly sky that had scared away every spectator that didn't absolutely have to be there. But Dreamcatcher's fan club were not to be denied, and so, as she cantered her very first competitive courtesy circle, she was greeted by a fluttering of applause and some quite audible if not necessarily educated comments on her beauty, grace, and deserving nature. I laughed out loud as I went by the assembled throng - The Rev, his squeeze Beverly, and my mother, all beaming at the lovely grey appreciatively. They were completely unaware that their bright raingear and a sudden inspiration to wave their programs at Gerry Dirk and his parents across the ring blew the poor mare's concentration so that she spooked and was a little wobbly to the first two fences as a result.

She jumped the remaining six as if they were four feet high instead of a straightforward three. She jumped so round, and with her legs pulled up so tight and square, that she just about launched me out of the tack. When she finished, her little cheerleading squad made so much noise that she spooked again. You'd have thought she'd just won the last jump-off of the World Cup final instead of simply completing her first Pre-Green class. To my delight and Gerry's, she managed to get a call, though there was no ribbon. The peanut gallery thought she'd been robbed because, as Beverly put it, 'She looked so much *prouder* than the others'. Gerry's parents, much better educated in equine ways, graciously agreed that Dreamcatcher was lovely and talented and left it at that.

As we began to stroll *en masse* back to the barn, there before us, big as life and twice as bright, appeared Ivory Gardner resplendent in a souped-up chrome-deluxe wheelchair with a big, multi-striped umbrella over the top. Harry pushed her with his best Cheshire Cat grin, and Ivory held court in a procession of friends, admirers, well-wishers, and the odd rain-hardy fan. With shouts of delight we joined the throng and I twirled my friend around in a little wheelchair jig while she yelled names at me and laughed her raucous, husky laugh, tried not to get tangled in Dreamcatcher's reins, then came to rest directly in front of the startled mare and stared at her in open-mouthed silence.

'Ice Cream's sister,' I said.

'Wow,' Ivory said. She reached up and gently touched the mare's soft muzzle. 'Wow.' The mare brought her head down and smelled Ivory's face, and Ivory held the lovely head to her and wept. Then the rain started to come down in earnest, I clucked to Dreamcatcher, Harry whirled Ivory's wheelchair around, and we all sprinted for cover.

It was still pouring when it came time for the speed class. This is usually Jake's bread-and-butter, but though he did his level, gutsiest best in the slop the old oomph wasn't quite there. He came out feeling just enough 'off' behind that I could feel it in his gait.

'Could be a soft tissue thing,' offered Ivory, as we studied him trotting on a longe line later. 'They can be like that - hard to put a finger on.'

'Yeah,' I agreed despondently.

'You know,' she added carefully. 'I know you love him, and nobody could have kept him sound and happy longer, but... he's not getting any younger.'

'What are you saying?' I bristled.

'I'm saying he's put up with a lot of pounding for a little guy. C'mon, 'Chelley, don't bite my head off. You know it's true.'

I nodded, brought my faithful horse down to a walk, and invited him in. *'To me, fair friend, You never can be old,'* I told him. *'For as you were when first your eye I eyed, such seems your beauty still'.* I pulled his brown ears and rubbed the white stripe between his eyes and scratched his chin and loved every molecule of him.

We all understand that horses only have so many jumps in them before they start to break down. Using their hindquarters to push off over a big fence puts a huge strain on their hocks and especially their stifles, which are built like a human's knees, with a patella that slides and helps tendons and ligaments slip across the joint. Then landing from a big fence, with all that momentum and the weight of a rider piling onto two front legs held together with ropy tendons and brittle bones adds over two tons of compression on the front end. It's asking a lot of any mortal being.

But I couldn't imagine my competitive life without Jake. He'd brought me to the upper levels and helped pay for me to stay there. He'd helped make me the rider I was now. 'He's not old enough to retire,' I said.

'I'm not saying retire him. He's not ready for that while he still loves his job. And he does still love his job, 'Chelley. It sticks out all over him when he goes. But maybe he should drop back a notch or two. Be a great junior horse.'

'For who?'

'For Camille.'

'Camille's in school.'

'She could use some time off. She hates it. She's in trouble. Chip off the old block. You remember what we were.'

'How do you know all this? You been in touch with her behind my back?'

'She calls me. We talk.'

'She's only sixteen.'

'Kids grow up faster now.'

'I don't want her to be like us, Ive.'

'You'd rather she was like Josie?'

'I want her to get a decent education. Have a decent shot at some kind of life.'

'You sound just like your mother did twenty-five years ago.'

'*Fuck* you, Ivory Gardner.' I stalked off to put Jake away, then went to the office and withdrew him from the rest of his week's classes.

Sara Wychoff took this as a sign and asked me to be the commentator for the big Saturday night televised program, instead. She knew I had no other horses entered in the big classes, the bitch.

'Please say yes, 'Chelle, you've no *idea* how important it would be, how *desperate* people are for somebody with your - well, your *charisma*, your *way with words…*'

'Sara, *stop*! You're laying it on way too thick, man. I thought you were using Jory Devenant.'

'Chelle, you *heard* her, she was *hopeless*. She could no more explain what goes on than fly to the *moon*. She's too used to *doing* it. And *don't* suggest Michael Draper, because we tried him last week at Wellington, and he has that *twang*. *Dreadful. And* he's got three horses between the Open Stake and the Grand Prix.'

'How about Colin Rutherford? He's everybody's hero right now.'

'He would be divine,' she admitted. 'But he doesn't know enough of the people and horses over here yet. And it's *commentating*, 'Chelle. You have to have people that *talk*.'

Then she pulled out her trump card and told me what she'd pay me, if the evening went well and a contract for the rest of the season was forthcoming. It wasn't enough to put me in a new tax bracket, exactly. But…

'I'll think about it,' I said… *It meant I could turn down another*

*stout offer for Jennie and accept one on her three-year-old sister at*
*home, instead.*

'Oh, just *say yes,* Chelle. It's so much *easier.'*

*It meant I could pay Santé without missing any meals.*

'Chelle...'

'Yes,' I said.

And you know, I really enjoyed it. I sat with Sara Wychoff in the press box. I told funny stories about the horses and the riders – at least, I thought they were funny, and the people in the press box laughed - and described how the fences went and got all hot and excited when, in the big Grand Prix that featured enormous jumps bordered by giant whales, beer bottles, and every other visual distraction you can think of, Michael Draper, Hilary Knowlton, Harry Daly, Jory Devenant, Alvaro Baeza, and three other superheroes from the Grand Prix stratosphere all had double clear rounds. They jumped off over a shorter but equally huge, twisting course under the lights with only split fractions of seconds to give Hilary the class over Baeza, currently one of the best riders in the world and favored for the World Cup. It was a thrill, all right. Then I got to do little interviews with some of the riders with cameras and sound equipment trailing after me.

By the time I'd finished, gotten my clean duds all disgusting by mucking out stalls in them, tucked my horses in, and gone to bed, I was flushed with joy. I almost felt like I'd ridden the class myself. And in fact I had done something that was just as challenging, and fun, and new. I didn't exactly want to admit that last bit to myself. After all, talking to a camera is not death defying in the way that jumping large fences is. But it was true. I really liked talking about my favorite subject while cameras rolled.

The glow lasted me through the next day's riding and showing. It was as if talking about horses and riders and competition to other people helped me remember how much I loved my chosen life. Each time I rode a horse into the ring, each time I asked for an adjustment of stride, a jump, a turn, I felt as if I were a part of a continuum of noble horses and extraordinary riders that stretched backward through human history. A couple of times I almost burst into song in the middle of a line of fences, I was having that much fun.

I was still in afterglow that evening, sitting in the aisle with Santé, cleaning tack and watching the world go by as the watery sun faded westward. Santé had told me not to bother, he'd get it; but I love the smell of leather and saddle soap, and the mundane daily chores of grooming, cleaning stalls, and caring for saddlery - especially when

I'm not trying to cram it in sometime between the hours of midnight and 2:00 a.m. There's a particular rhythm to cleaning stalls and tack that is exactly suited to the sound of horses stomping and munching hay and swishing their tails. Exactly suited to letting your mind drift while muscle-memory goes through ancient and ingrained motions. It's as soothing as white noise to a librarian. And companionable, to sit around with your friends and co-workers, attending to the details of horse husbandry and gossiping lightly as daylight slants rich and warm from the west and the air begins to cool. It's a tribal rhythm, even now. It still lives deep inside our souls and begs for an outlet.

Life on the winter show circuit sometimes seems like a modern extension of the movements our earliest ancestors made thousands of years ago, to me. Celts, Scythians, Nubians, Mongolians. People of the horse. Nomads. Maybe we're all re-incarnated and still living the old rhythms of the herders. We go north in the spring, south in the winter, taking our chattel with us as we travel. Setting up gypsy camps away from home, then returning to our native lands to recuperate, foal the mares, break the youngsters, plan the next migration. To those of us connected with the noble horse, the materials and topics of conversation are probably not even that much different, except that we aren't riding around in war chariots or sacrificing victims to our gods. Well... not with goats or slaves, anyway. Mechanization aside, Santé and I could just as easily have been sitting on a central Asian plain in 3,000 B.C., discussing this horse's pulled tendon or that one's prospects as a broodmare; this one's extraordinary speed and agility, or that one's dependable nature; all while rubbing dirt and slime out of leather and iron to keep one supple and the other untarnished and sleek.

'Look at Ivory there, acting like a Queen,' Santé broke into my reverie. I looked. Ivory was being wheeled across the horizon in her pasha-mobile by Craig Oppenheim, with whom she was deep in conversation.

I shook my head. 'You know, I've seen her run that thing herself. She goes a million miles an hour. What a manipulator.'

'She like the attention okay,' grinned Santé. 'She always good at that.'

As we watched, Michael Draper appeared and joined the pair. Santé's smile evaporated. I watched with interest to see how this little meeting would express itself. I could hear Ivory laughing, making some joke. I guess it didn't work. Craig stiffened, his body language finding reasons to leave. Ivory began wheeling herself along, Michael keeping step beside her.

'No guts asshole,' muttered Santé.

'Who? Craig?' I asked in surprise.

Santé shook his head.

'You can't mean Michael,' I said lightly, 'so that leaves Ivory. And I *know* she's got guts. Now if you wanted to criticize her taste in boyfriends...' I shrugged.

Santé looked at me sideways and hunched over his bucket of soapy water to fish out a shiny steel snaffle bit that had been soaking. Methodically, he rubbed every imagined grass and slobber stain off it, dried it, and polished it to a mirror shine. 'Mr. Desmarchais, he pretty mean for sure. Don't like to be told what to do. Don't like when somebody owe him money too long. But Michael Draper... jump a big fence, shit, that just learning. Guts, now... that come from inside. And Michael Draper, he ain't got 'em.'

I leaned over my bucket seat so I could see Santé's face and stared into it. 'Santé,' I said seriously. 'Don't feed me bullshit. Tell me what you're telling me so I can understand it.'

He stared back at me, silent.

I sighed. 'Okay, then. I'll fill in the blanks. You're telling me that Michael owed Winston a lot of money, and Winston came to collect. And said a lot of things about what might happen to Michael and his family if he didn't pay up. And then Ice Cream died.'

Santé nodded. 'You got it.'

'But is it true, Santé?'

He nodded again.

I closed my eyes. I wanted so badly for Santé to tell me that my information was cruel and untrue. I wanted to throw up into my bucket. I wanted to go to sleep forever, and never wake up. I wanted to go back to a month ago and change careers so that I would not ever end up here, listening to the evidence mount against a horseman I had looked up to all my professional life.

'Was Winston going to pull the plug on Ivory and give her horses to Michael? That's what Tommy Essex said.'

Santé nodded. 'Soon as they got down here. Last thing Michael had to do, pay off the rest of his debt, that shit, was help bag up some product, you know what I'm saying. Load it on the van. Come on down here.'

'You know that for sure?'

'I seen it. I come back the barn, see, last check on Rougère, he didn't clean up his grain so good and I wanted to make sure he's okay. And I seen Winston and Michael with that Elliot, loading bags of shavings. Now why they do that? I ask myself, cuz they got other guys do that for 'em, but Mr. Desmarchais, he do what he want. So I just kinda lay low 'til they done. I don't want no trouble.'

'So why don't you tell the Feds?'

He shook his head. 'I got me a wife and kids, a job I like, I'm clean... I known Mr. Desmarchais a long time. Look what he get Michael Draper to do. He got a family, too, he's a famous guy, lots to lose. I seen it all before, at the track. Guy with money want something. Exercise rider or jockey, into him for some money maybe, some product. Got to do a favor so something bad don't happen. Throw a race, dope a horse, you know how it work.'

'Michael Draper, he never rides again, this gets out. Then what? What's he gonna do?' Santé stared at the tack sponge in his hands, the shining steel bit. 'I been that road, see? Maybe once or twice I don't ride as hard as I should cuz I owe some money. Then I feel bad, see, cuz I know that horse, he want to win that day. And I don't let him. Then I have a little drink, a little snort, make me feel better. And I got to make the weight, see. I got these pills, I don't feel so hungry, I feel like I can do anything. Only then there's some trainers look at me funny, my horse don't win. They won't ride me no more. I only stopped a couple, honest, but nobody gonna believe that. So I drink some more and snort some more and I drink myself, snort myself, right off the big horses, got suspended, right off the track. Tried to get straight. Couldn't do it. Finally wouldn't nobody give me my license back, in no state. Never ride those beautiful suckers again. Never feel that muscle, that big horse shift into another gear, never have that hard wind in my face down the stretch, never hear that crowd...

'I get this dream sometimes, 'Chelle, honest to God, I dream sometime I'm in the winner's circle and they layin' that carpet of red roses across my horse's neck, it's like the best moment of my whole life, it's better than the best junk, it's so high. Then I wake up again. I got tears all down my face. I got my wife askin' me what's wrong. And I'm working here for you, rubbin' horses like I was a kid. Hackin' 'em out. Which is good, don't make no mistake. Only it ain't riding no Derby winner.

'I say Michael Draper got no guts. I got none, neither, I guess. Not while Mr. Desmarchais alive.'

'What if he dies?'

'I dunno. Ruin people's lives like that. I already did that to myself, you know? I dunno could I do it to somebody else.'

'But he killed a horse. At least one. He deserves...'

'Yeah, I know what you gonna say. And you know what? You're

right. But 'Chelle, he don't need no law. He never gonna forget what he done to that good mare. There ain't nothin' he can snort, ain't nowhere he can go and forget what he done. He gonna burn for that, his whole life.'

# EIGHT

*Well could he ride, and often men would say,*
*'That horse his mettle from his rider takes:*
*Proud of subjection, noble by the sway,*
*What sounds, what bounds, what course, what stop he makes!'*
*And controversy hence a question takes,*
*Whether the horse by him became his deed,*
*Or he his manage by the well-doing steed.*
-    William Shakespeare, *A Lover's Complaint*

Jennie collected a group of neighborhood children that followed her like a comet's tail wherever we went. They patted her and crooned to her and fed her peppermint candies and she never so much as stepped on a little foot or nibbled a tiny finger. Every now and then I'd let some lucky kid sit on her for a minute and watch them turn pink and speechless with joy.

It made up for the fact that my timing was off this week. My horses were taking rails we shouldn't have had. Clyde stopped at a fence for the first time in his life, and wouldn't you know, there was a potential buyer watching. Darcy Noriega's whacko jumper had two knockdowns in the same class. Dancing Fool was just plain wild. And I fell off Ottawa in a schooling session when he put his feet in the middle of a little oxer instead of jumping it.

I wondered if I was losing it, if I couldn't handle the pressure, if all this recent exposure was more than I could process. It was different with my own horses, or horses I'd bought for resale. The heat there was internal, me for myself. But outside owners don't just hire you because they like the way you ride; they hire you because they like the way you win. So the stakes were ratcheted up a few notches. More questions to answer, more skill to prove every minute of every day, more split-second decisions out on the narrow limb of competition over large, scary fences on horses whose attitudes vary as widely as the weather. The world watching every step because I was Somebody now; because the announcer said, 'and as we all recall, it was this rider, Michelle Martin, who rescued two horses in a recent...' every time I came on course. Ivory watching me critically from the sidelines. Michael Draper foremost on my mind when the fences should have been. Camille imploring me almost nightly to get her out of school. I lost my concentration; I fumbled.

After a straightforward First Year Green class where I'd had an unheard-of bad fence with Jennie, Ivory reamed me out and declared that I was riding like a frigging amateur. I snarled something back about being burnt to the socket that just put more wind in her sails.

'You're not *cooked*,' she said scathingly. 'You're just not *focused*.'

'I've got a lot on my mind!' I shouted. 'Not the least of which...' I stopped mid-sentence and bit down on my lower lip before I made some stupid crack about Ivory's legal and health problems. Then, just as I'd thought of some other lame thing to say instead my eyes were drawn irresistibly to the figure of Colin Rutherford strolling across the horizon with a gaggle of adoring ladies and teenaged girls in train.

'So that's where your brains are', Ivory said drily, totally ignoring any of the other factors that lent weight to my recent screw-ups.

I looked skyward and fervently wished to be teleported to a distant solar system. 'Don't be a mean bitch, Ivory Gardner.'

She laughed heartily, the cow. 'Always have been. Why stop now?' Then her eye took on a dangerous gleam. 'Honest to Christ, 'Chelle. You want to ride horses? Ride fuckin' horses. You got Dancing Fool yet tonight. By-Christ I'll fire your ass, you screw my mare up. *And* I'll give her to lover-boy over there, you just see if I don't!'

Nobody can push my buttons like Ivory. Take me off Dancing Fool! Who the *fuck* did she think she was, anyway? Fury coursed through my veins, heating my ears. I stalked away fuming to get the bay mare ready for her class and gave her the ride of my life over an Intermediate course that had as many twists and convolutions as my overloaded brain. And I won it, coming fourth with Darcy's nut case, who nobody'd ever seen go so fast, and which paid for the two rails of our last outing. Then I galvanized myself for the Knockdown and by-god got three rides in the top ten there, too. And I was *still* pissed off by the next day when I couldn't find Ivory anywhere to tell her exactly what I thought of her fucking high-handed, prima-donna, grandstanding, southern-fucking-belle ways.

So I kept on taking my anger out on the fences, and it was amazingly, headily, transformingly cathartic. *Fuck 'em all*, I was thinking as I drove down to each bright colored oxer hanging suspended in the rarified air. *Fuck the Winstons, the Ivories, the Drapers, the Josies, the fucking private-ass schools, the fucking Rutherfords of the fucking world and take fuckin' **that***. And I'd punch it and the horses would leap in the air like stags and it got to be like a battle song out there, full of bright rage and powerful joy and galloping and jumping and turning and jumping and galloping and jumping some more, and *WOW!* I'd say to whatever horse it was, *Let's do that again Now!* And they would. I felt a little like Cuchullain, that Bronze Age Irish Hero-guy who got so warped-out during battles that it took seven cauldrons of cold water and a bunch of naked women to chill him out of his battle fury and make him safe for the world again.

Well, maybe that's an exaggeration. But I was smokin', for sure.

'Nice going, darlin'', said Harry when I handed him a yellow ribbon to add to his collection. 'You got your attack back. Keep it up and you might not lose my horses yet awhile.' I snarled and handed Clyde to Cam, whose toe he immediately stepped on, then strode off to ride again before the effect left me high and dry.

'Does this mean I'm going to have to spend the rest of the winter antagonizing you just so you'll ride right?' asked Ivory later, reappearing as if by magic well after all my horses were done for the day. We sat in the shade under the eaves of the tent, with an impressive-looking collection of multi-colored ribbons riffling above us on their baling-twine rack. Ivory had arranged them in order of color and importance - first Jennie's Reserve, then blues, reds, yellows, whites, pinks, and greens. Me, I always let them sit in the order they're won, a colorful hodgepodge that makes a book of days. But Ivory's always been anal like that.

'I hope the Christ not', I said, admittedly pretty satisfied with the effect she'd created, a little rainbow of color with the sun shining through it. 'It'll ruin our friendship.'

'You know what *fat chance* means?'

'Um... Plump opportunity. Corpulent fortune. Portly...'

'Yeah, fuck-you very much.' She was silent for a moment. ''Chelle,' she started, gently enough for her. 'D'you think you've got the fire in your belly to ride like that all the time? That's what it takes, you want to reach the stars.'

'I never aspired to the stars, Ive. I've been perfectly happy in the lesser planets. I like playing with the babies.'

'You don't lack the skill.'

'Maybe I lack the ambition,' I admitted reluctantly. 'That's the key, isn't it? But I've wanted this - done this - so long I don't know what I'd do instead.'

'Maybe '*instead*'s' the wrong word. Maybe *in addition*'d be better.'

'You got any bright ideas?'

'Be a commentator.'

I groaned. 'Oh, Ive, that's just a stopgap.'

'Not the way I hear it, sweetie. I hear Sara's dangling a big-ass contract at you. I hear people saying you were a big success out there the other night. And you were, too. You were great. Born to it. Might be it's a meal ticket. So don't try to tell me you didn't like it.'

'Okay. I liked it.'

'I been doin' a lot of thinking, you know, since the accident. Since this,' she stroked her belly. 'There's a limit to how long we can do this shit. It's not just the horses breaking down. It's us. I don't know about you, but every time I take a spill I have a harder time getting up.'

'Yeah. But look at Harry. He doesn't seem...'

'He's got a whole support system here, a bizillion clients, a business back home that you and I could dream on, and a bunch of assistants that ride almost as well as you and me, with lots less age and lots more resources. What have we got? I mean, between us and ending up like Santé? One bad fall. We're not so young anymore, 'Chelle. It's not like it was when we were in Galway.'

'Galway.' I sighed. 'We were so young. It was so cool.'

'Yeah. Well, I'm not saying we're circling the drain or anything. Just... looking at the future.'

'You never used to think like that.'

'I never had to. I'm gonna be a mama, now. Feeling more mortal, I guess.'

I looked at her in alarm, my best friend Ivory Gardner, the queen of *sang-froid*, the rider who made every horse she sat on look like a gazelle, whose career was among the sparkling stars. 'But Ivory... you're going back to riding, aren't you? After all this is over. Aren't you? You *can't* give it up. I have all these horses you gotta ride if I can't make...'

'I dunno, 'Chelle. I plain old don't know yet. I guess it all depends on how this trial nonsense plays itself out.'

'What would you do instead?'

'Dunno. Teach, maybe. Train. Maybe try to make a business like Harry's. Think on it, 'Chelle. You've got the farm already. We've got the reputation and some nice horses, between us. I bet we could pull it off, if we wanted. We could call ourselves 'Grey Horse Enterprises'. After the hunt team here. Huh?'

I went to bed deeply thoughtful, lay there looking at the ceiling with the sad, harsh words of Prospero cycling through my head:

*But this rough magic*
*I here abjure; And when I have required*
*Some heavenly music - which even now I do -*
*To work mine end upon their senses*
*That this airy charm is for, I'll break my staff,*
*Bury it certain fathoms in the earth,*
*And deeper than did ever plummet sound*
*I'll drown my book.*

The next day, I told Sara Wychoff I'd sign on the dotted line. She was far more delighted that I would have thought the decision merited. I reminded her that the stipulation was that I was still a rider, first. She agreed. Then she packed me off to Palm Beach to make good on the next installment before I could change my mind and rip the whole thing into teeny tiny pieces in a fit of abject cowardice.

I exercised all my horses before I left, of course, which meant getting up earlier in the morning than seemed strictly necessary, even by equestrian standards. Jake especially thought the change in routine a bit beyond the Pale – *what! Work before breakfast?* – and tried to launch me at the first opportunity. When that didn't work he set about spooking violently at every post, bush, shadow, and dog he could find to spook at. One thing was eminently clear through these shenanigans – Jake was ready to rock 'n' roll again. So I left just after dawn with a smile on my face and contentment in my heart, knowing that the next week would see me back in action on my best buddy in the classes with the big fences.


The Grand Prix at Palm Beach was part of the World Cup tour, a purse worth six figures and full of both legitimate international stars and stars-in-the-making whose horses were as famous as The Rolling Stones to a nation of horse-crazy kids. Some of the horses had already been immortalized in plastic statuettes that rarely bore any resemblance to the real animal. Strolling the alleyways between colorful trade booths that helped give the show a medieval festival air, these appealing effigies sat in boxed lines on shop shelves, a plastic hall of fame, all horses I have loved and admired over the years. There were the racehorses: Seabiscuit, War Admiral,

Secretariat, Seattle Slew, Affirmed, Cigar, Smarty Jones. Barbaro. Then the Jumpers and Hunters: Rox Dene, Milton, Charisma, Big Ben, Gem Twist.

In the barns and schooling rings their breathing counterparts trotted and cantered and jumped little grids in interlacing patterns while trainers shouted and riders exhorted and grooms and by-standers laughed and traded stories and speculated on the eventual winner of the evening's big money class. So much of it depending on readiness and technical skill. So much – with little to choose between the qualities of horses and riders - hanging on the luck of the night. Each horse seemed to have its fierce fan club, and the grounds were crowded with teens and avid adults clutching programs and pointing out their heroes, eyes large with excitement.

Despite the stresses on their bodies and limbs, jumpers generally have longer careers than racehorses, and thus more time to build a following. The average racehorse is like a teenage athlete who burns out after winning Olympic gymnastic or swimming or skating titles by age 16, never to be heard from on the world stage again. At least the human athlete gets a chance at having a useful career as an adult. The racehorse – which will not even be a mature adult until it reaches the age of 6 - has fewer options. Decently bred fillies and colts might go to the breeding shed and spend their lives fuelling the racing industry's future. Other fortunate ones may find new careers as hunters, jumpers, or eventers, if they are sound and sane enough.

Sometimes, though – and far too often – the Thoroughbreds that started out as somebody's dream just go down and down the ranks until they hit bottom and end up in the auction ring to be bid on by the pound. All because they didn't run fast enough for long enough, and didn't earn enough money at the track.

The unpleasant shock wave of public outcry that resulted after some illustrious stakes winners - famously including Kentucky Derby winner Ferdinand - went to the killers having 'outlived their usefulness' has resulted in breeders and trainers taking more responsibility for the long term well being of the animals they sell. Suffolk Downs in Massachusetts even instituted a rule preventing resident trainers from sending horses that have raced at that track to the killers. Meanwhile numerous organizations do yeoman's work in haunting auction yards to rescue useful horses for retraining, new lives, or just a quiet equine old age home.

It's only fair that, once they have finished providing us with a means of making a living, we should give our horses the same honorable retirement we accord our human public servants. But that's a lot of horses. If you think that only about 3% of the 30,000 or so Thoroughbreds that are foaled every year in the U.S. will ever win a classic stakes race, what happens to the, say, 60% that never win anything? Or the thousands of Quarter Horses, good, bad, and indifferent, that are registered with their society every year whether there is a market for them or not? Or the hundreds of Mustangs incarcerated in holding pens because their range has shrunk and knowledgeable new owners are too rare? How do we fund retirement, reclamation, and retraining? Where do the new owners, or the quiet pastures, come from? And - murky thought, but legitimate – what do we do with the ones that really are crippled beyond usefulness? Rescuing horses is a noble enterprise, but it takes a lot of money. Horses eat a lot, working or not.

Sara caught up with me as I hung over the schooling ring rail, admiring horses like some star struck kid and thinking these uncomfortable thoughts.

"Chelle! What on earth are you doing?'

'Wondering how many of these beautiful creatures came off the track.'

'Oh, quite a few, I think. See that chestnut on the other side? A grandson of Secretariat. They say he couldn't outrun a woodchuck, but as a jumper he's been superb.'

'That'd make a great story.'

'I could talk to Jory.'

'Not just that one. All the others, too. I mean, how you can take a Thoroughbred racehorse that's basically sound off the track when its career is done. School it, care for it, compete it, give it a life. No reason to think it won't last competitively well into its teens.'

'Hmmh.' Sara looked speculatively at the horses circling the ring.

'Who were your jumping heroes when you were younger?'

'Oh, well. Gem Twist, Milton, Big Ben, Jet Run – my superheroes! Better than movie stars!'

'Doesn't it make you happy to see it all happening here? A new generation of horses and riders, a new generation of eager fans...'

'Michael Matz training a Derby winner after a sizzling show jumping career...'

'Yeah! Maybe we could, you know, bring attention to the way horses get treated. How they deserve better than the killers or the camps.'

'You're sounding a little rabid, 'Chelle.'

'C'mon, Sara. Think of the publicity. It's the kind of thing people get media awards for. The big exposé, the solutions...'

'You're right. I will. But today we're doing jumpers. C'mon, quick.' She dragged me to the big arena where the Grand Prix would be held under lights. With the afternoon classes over and the ring cleared and raked, truckloads of enormous jumps with their attendant gigantic beer bottles, whales, trees, pots of flowers, panels with investment company names blazoned across them, and the other assorted paraphernalia of professional commercial sports were unloaded and erected with the aid of an army of volunteers with tape measures and head sets. I am not the tallest person in the world, and I could barely see across some of the widest oxers on the course. Sara had me walk the course as if I were going to ride it, telling the camera about the fences, the course, the crowd, the lines of jumps, how the whole thing might ride, what it might look like to a horse, what kinds of questions it would ask of both horse and rider.

I did my best to describe how the course would challenge not only speed and jumping ability, but also a horse's obedience to the rider, its ability to listen well enough to make rapid changes of direction and pace and striding, and its ability to focus on the fences rather than the broad crowd that seethed and muttered just beyond the lights. Then how the riders must stay completely 'in the zone' with nothing but horse and fence on their minds while they answered the challenging technical questions: go forward on a longer stride, or collect, go from a shorter one, and add steps? Cut this corner and risk a rail in the interest of saving time, or take a longer corner and don't risk the rail? Take this fence at a slight angle so the horse doesn't feel like it's jumping into the stands, or trust his bravery and go straight for it? The thousand things confronting riders facing a course of this size.

I walked it again when the riders came out, but I flatly refused to let Sara talk me into asking them about their strategies. When riders walk a big course they have to be almost Zen about it. Because no matter how many times you walk between the fences and gage the options and plan your ride, once you get on your partner and get out there under the lights, your plan will require minute high speed adjustments every step of the way that mean the difference between fences that stay up or rails that fall; time that is unmatchable by any other horse and rider, or time that is shaved by somebody that hair faster who goes home with the glory. I wasn't going to feel responsible for screwing that up. But I loved being a fly on the wall. It gave me a lot of material to use when I described the rounds as they went, from up in a booth with an incredible view of the arena and monitors that showed us close-ups of every horse so that I almost felt I was riding each one myself.

And the oddest thing happened, while I was playing god up there. As I analyzed the rounds and the course and the horses' and riders' performances... I began to think that the fences looked jumpable. That maybe Michael Draper had been right, all those weeks ago in Virginia, in what now seemed like a different life. Maybe Jake and I could handle a smaller Grand Prix together.

Handsome young Alvaro Baeza won the class on an enormous bay horse from somewhere in Holland that jumped as if it had wings. Baeza's extensive female fan club was so deliriously hysterical over the win that I nearly got trampled trying to interview him while guards tried somewhat fruitlessly to keep him from being mobbed. I don't remember much about the interview except his wide sparkling smile and wonderful eyes and the beauty and poise of his enormous horse, who was about the size of Ottawa only every inch muscular and gorgeous. But I felt so buffeted that I asked Sara later if we might do these interviews mounted, in the collecting ring, head and shoulders above the mob like the lady that does the Triple Crown races. Sara looked thoughtful, and asked if one of my ponies was quiet enough to do the job. Of course I said yes.

And I drove into the steam of a developing rainy night, wipers flapping time to Mary Chapin Carpenter singing about windshields and bugs, thinking that maybe I wasn't too old for this life, after all.


Two days later, as if he was channeling my thoughts, Jake won a big open class under the lights and at the end felt bouncy and full of himself, almost like he could do it all again. His victory lap was like a tango, like we were dancing on the roof of the world, and I laughed and cried at his pride, his ability, his courage. Victory is so, so sweet when it comes.

And yeah, well, there's the number on the check, too, which paid for an awful lot of entry fees.

'Maybe I was wrong, honey,' admitted Ivory, grinning hugely after cheering herself hoarse on our lightning fast second round. 'He sure rocked tonight.'

All I could do was laugh in utter joy. I let Ivory think it was just because of our success, and not because I was harboring the thought of a nice smaller Grand Prix that was coming up toward the send of the series. There was a huge one over in Tampa the same weekend that would draw off all the biggest and the best, leaving this one open to a somewhat less lofty echelon of riders and the greener horses. Not that Jake was green, but I thought the course might suit us, as a one-off.

And it would be a one-off. I knew Jake needed to drop back a level if he were to retire sound, as I intended him to. Not even his ironclad Connemara legs could put up with this sort of pounding forever.

But somehow it seemed important to ride my first Grand Prix on the partner that had gotten me to the level I now inhabited. Somehow it felt like a fitting graduation ceremony, win or lose. Or, as Marc Antony put it, *Who seeks, and will not take when once 'tis offered, Shall never find it more.*

The point was just to try it together.

I knew Ivory would tell me I was crazy, so I didn't tell her. I hoarded my dream and kept it to myself.

Well. Almost to myself. I discussed it with Jake in the dark beyond the tents as I grazed him after he'd cooled out.

'What do you think, buddy?' I asked him. 'One Grand Prix? See if we have what it takes? Jump the big jumps? Spook at a whale?'

Jake sneezed happily and rubbed his face all over me in contentment, which I took as a 'yes'. The air was soft, the moon nearly full, the gods in their respective parts of heaven. A moment to relish and be happy for.

Because on the other hand, Ottawa's show ring debut was not as auspicious as I would have hoped. He was perfectly affable, and looked much better for some weight and a few weeks of steady grooming and work. But he was more interested in rubbernecking at the sights and sounds than looking where he was going, and took down a bunch of rails. One he even got between his front legs somehow, and fell on his knees on the landing side. This time, I stayed on. Barely.

'What am I going to do with this animal?' I wailed to Harry. 'He can't even stand up!'

'Well, he's still growin', babe. Gonna take him awhile, big guy like that.'

'I could die of old age, waiting,' I grumbled.

Harry pursed his lips. 'Bring him out here awhile,' he suggested. 'He might be one of those animals just needs a bigger fence to wake him up.'

'A *bigger* fence? Are you *kidding*? Harry, I'm not suicidal.'

Harry just laughed and had Cam set up a little grid - a vertical to a vertical to an oxer to a vertical, all one short stride apart. I told Harry The Ploughboy looked longer than the space between the jumps.

Harry said it was to make him rounder and I should shut up and ride. I was sure I was going to die, but I kicked Ottawa into his galumphing canter and tried it. The first time through, he ended up wearing most of the grid, and scattering the rest like pick-up sticks. But the second time, he picked up his feet. Harry raised the fences. Ottawa looked at them briefly and hopped through with a little more care. Harry raised the grid again. Ottawa pricked his long ears and boinged through as if it had been cross rails. Harry raised it once more, to 4'6". Ottawa began to look positively interested, moved forward as if his breakfast was on the other side, and landed crow hopping, like he was The Man.

I laughed so hard I almost fell off. Harry looked thoughtful. 'What now?' I asked. 'This is amazing!'

'Take him for a hack, put him away while it's fun,' said Harry. 'Then we start him in Schooling Jumpers so's we don't over face him. But no more pre-green for him. He's beyond that stuff already. Then,' he sighed. 'Then we gotta be careful not to screw him up before he grows up enough to win every Grand Prix you ever heard of.'

'Are you serious, Harry? You think he's that good?'

'Yeah, I do. 'Course,' he added with an old horseman's fatalism, 'he could colic and die tomorrow, too, so don't count your prize money yet, doll.'

Still, he had that gleam in his eye, and when I took Ottawa back to Santé's tender care I reflected that the enormous colt seemed to be as constitutionally sound as he was physical rugged. I said a little prayer to Epona, the Celtic goddess of the foals, and asked her to protect her young giant of a son from all the lamenesses and accidents that cause horses to break, and to break our hearts.

Jennie continued her winning ways and looked as if she would end the week with her second tri-color ribbon of the series, another nice reserve championship with pretty red, yellow, and white streamers to add to our collection. Dancing Fool had decided to stop embarrassing me, and her efforts, while erratic, got steadily better and gave larger and larger hints of the incredibly fine jumper she might become. I bought another young horse I'd liked the look of, to school and resell sometime in the summer – a better quality horse than I had been able to buy in the past. Darcy Noriega was back on her old boy, and with my help was learning how to unlock a decent performance from her jumper. When she asked me to help her sell him and find a more stable replacement that she could actually enjoy riding to the big jumps, I about sang. I'm not the kind of person that trades on buying and selling horses for my clients like they were peanuts just to line my own pockets, but I sure wanted to see her mounted on something safer. And George Andros had just the horse for a price that wouldn't sink her.

When I talked to him about it, he agreed to sell, and told me about a couple of Dutch horses he had his eye on.

'Sure,' I agreed when asked. 'I'll come take a look.'

'If you think they're what I'm looking for, I'd like to send them up to your place at the end of the series.'

'What about Diane?'

'Well... I'm finding that situation a little uncomfortable right now, to be honest. Too much other stuff in the way. You know.'

'Um,' I said, more than a little depressed about the other side of that situation myself. 'I know. So... if you send them to me does that mean I get a break on my insurance?'

'No,' he laughed. 'But I'll pay my training bills on time. Then you can afford to *pay* for your insurance.'

All things considered, this sounded like a pretty good deal. Though I wasn't sure I wanted to be around when Diane found out she was going to lose a client and some nice horses. Especially not to me.

'Okay,' I said. 'I'll think about it.'

'So will I.'

Dreamcatcher was as good as her name, a dream to ride and looked as if she might catch some stars, in the future of her promising career, if she stayed sound. When she won her first class, Gerry Dirk was so ecstatic that he pulled me off her back, wrapped me tightly in his muscular arms, and kissed the bejesus out of me. He was a really good kisser. His arms felt really good around my body. Giddy, I accepted his invitation to a bang-up dinner to celebrate. The mare's victory, that is. Not the kiss and the arms. Or that's what I told myself. But I couldn't deny the possibilities that might exist. Life with horses is pretty tactile, and intensely sensual. Success in competition adds an electric charge that can easily cause a super-heated situation to ignite.

And besides, I hadn't had any sex since...

Well. Never mind.

So we sparkled at each other through dinner, wine, and candlelight, reliving the day and hatching plans for the future. We went back to Gerry's digs and practiced some more deeply luscious kissing on the sofa while keeping half an eye on a funny little video featuring Alan Rickman whose rich-as-molasses voice made Captain

Hook sound as devastatingly evil as Richard III. I surfaced briefly from the warm sinuousness of Gerry's body to comment on this. 'Richard who?' asked Gerry, exploring the best entry into my shirt.

'Richard III', I said.

'Who's that?' he asked, from somewhere in the vicinity of my bra straps. 'How the hell does this thing work, anyway?'

I guessed I didn't really want to have an affair with Gerry Dirk. I disentangled myself from him as tactfully as I could. I said I wasn't quite ready for this. I told him I needed to check on my horses. He was disappointed but philosophical. He told me he'd call me during the week from New York, be back on Friday to ride, and we'd go out again. I said that'd be fun. And I went home to my horses, my dog, my house on wheels. And after I'd done the last barn check and curled up in my little over-the-cab bed with Spring on one side, a lamp on the other, and a few pages of *The Hamlet Trap* to read, I realized that I was really pretty content. Which I suppose should have made me suspicious.

I woke up thirsty for Shakespeare and on the afternoon I had off thanks to Santé, I took myself to the town library and checked out a copy of *Richard III* on audio. They didn't have it on cd, only an old dusty copy on tape, so I bought a bunch of blank tapes at the drugstore to copy it and dug through the junk in my rig's storage box until I found Camille's old tape-to-tape deck. Ancient technology, but advanced enough for me. I was going to have myself an orgy of Shakespearean passion, and a glass of red wine. Maybe two. *And there's an end to't.*

It was balmy dusk by the time I finished the evening chores. After Santé left I set my tape deck on a couple of bales of hay and tried to read its instructions by the dusty light of the fly-specked bulbs strung from the ceilings of the aisles until I thought I could recognize at least a majority of the machine's parts. I held my breath and poked a series of buttons that looked like they ought to play and record something. When all the wheels obediently moved in the same direction at approximately the same rate of speed, I cheered. Jennie and Jake poked their heads curiously over their doors at the noise, blew through their nostrils, decided that nothing required their direct involvement, and returned to munching hay. I tilted my folding chair back against the stall wall with a contented sigh, and closed my eyes while the words of Shakespeare washed over me, inspiring me to mouth and taste the fullness and bitter cynicism of the crippled, evil Duke of Gloucester: '*Now is the winter of our discontent/ made glorious summer by this son of York; and all the clouds that lowr'd upon our house/ in the deep bosom of the ocean buried...'* Lowr'd. What a great, deep, growling word. I tried to make my voice as low and resonant and dripping with bile as Ian McKellan, but I had a lot going against me, not the least of which were gender and talent.

After a few minutes of this pleasant occupation I thought a cup of decaf might be nice. I left the tapes running and wandered back to the rig.

I was gone - what? - maybe fifteen minutes, and left Spring asleep on the bed. But as I strolled back toward the stalls I saw by the pale moon that Jennie's door was cracked open, and from inside there shone the briefest gleam from what must have been a penlight.

'*Hey*!' I yelled and started to run. '*Hey you*! *What the fuck are you doing in there*!' I spilled scalding coffee on my hand, swore, flung the cup away and sprinted. '*Hey*!'

Someone in the stall cursed and shouted a warning and another someone muttered something. We all three collided at the aisle but they didn't give me a chance to recognize them. One caught me hard with the door and slammed me back against the wall. The other grabbed me by the neck and punched me so hard that I couldn't even cry out, just gasped and clawed at his hands, his arms, tried to twist free.

'Careful!' hissed a female voice, high with fear. 'Don't hurt her!'

'She shouldn't be here!'

'I never signed up for this!'

'*Shut up!*'

'You stupid son of...'

I lashed out with a foot and caught somebody in the shin.

'*Ow! You fucking...*'

'*Get the fucking car!*'

I tried to hit, tried to bite, tried to kick again but whoever it was that held me was strong and tough. I heard footsteps running down the alleyway, Jennie and the others nickering in nervousness, Jennie running against the back of the stall looking for an escape, the sounds of my own grunts and whimpers while my captor flung me in with her so hard that my head cracked against the wall and I heard him hiss urgently, '*It didn't have to be like this! You brought it on yourself, you stupid bitch!*' As I slithered to the ground he kicked me and as I gasped and cried out some kind of explosion went off inside my skull and I died.

Don't let anybody ever tell you that pain is bad. Pain is very, very good. It means you're alive.

That was my first thought on swimming slowly back to consciousness with Jennie's sweet, anxious breath and prickly lips on my face.

The second was that death was the better alternative. I hurt everywhere, exquisitely. I hurt with a fierce, white-hot intensity that drained color from the landscape and turned it into a red-edged haze. Somewhere far, far away I heard a small puppy whimper imploringly. I vaguely wondered who'd left a poor little puppy in the barn all by itself overnight. Then I realized the sound was coming out of me. I attempted to breathe gently enough not to move a ribcage apparently full of carving knives. I moved my head and the only thing that kept me from fainting was dizzy nausea. I fixed my eyes to the most stationary object I could focus on, which was the door. I gazed at it longingly. It seemed farther away than a mere two feet; it could have been as far as the moon. I panted shallowly, sweating from the pain that pulsed through my body in waves.

*Okay*, I thought dimly. *Isolate*. Find the pain, find where it's coming from. Shimmers emanating from my shoulder. Broken? No. No bones poking out, no crunchy noises. Dislocated, I guessed. Ribs? Cracked, maybe, if I'm lucky. My head... probably concussed, the haze I could barely see through seemed about right for that. And shock – yeah. Definitely shock.

Whoever attacked me had been really pissed off. Or really scared. But why?

I heard footsteps coming down the aisle, a light tuneless whistle. I tried my voice. A whisper; not good enough. Tried again. Lips dry and feeling swollen, *help help help help help* I managed to croak, over and over. The footsteps drew level, went by…

*Help help help help help please help…*

…stopped, turned, came back. Listened. 'hurthurt', I mustered from my aching vocal chords. 'Hurt.' The bolts shot back, the door opened. Santé, peering into the darkness.

"Chelle?' he asked incredulously. 'Jesus man, what happen to you? The mare, she do this?' He stooped down to look at me, glancing doubtfully at Jennie, who hovered over me protectively, like I was her foal.

'Unh-unh… Long story… Not Jennie… Don't touch me…' I whimpered again.

'Don't you worry none, man, I go find somebody we can move you. Still a couple people hangin' roun'. You be okay a minute? You look pretty bad.'

'Mm-hmm.' I tried to nod. Nearly threw up.

While Santé was gone, I floated in and out, in and out of reality. Heard the scuffle again, relived the blows, whimpered a little more, Jennie's breath on my face, nostrils fluttering, the voice *You brought it on yourself, you stupid bitch* and knew I knew that voice from somewhere, if I could just remember where.

I could not think what it was that I had brought on myself.

Santé came back with Colin Rutherford, whose reaction was predictably horrified. 'We've got to move you out of here,' he added to his first exclamations. I begged them hoarsely to let me die where I was, but Colin was firm. 'If the mare gets upset she could step on you.'

'She won't', I mumbled uselessly.

They moved me as gently as possible onto some horse's folded dress sheet and slid me into the aisle. I tried not to cry too much, panting the way you're supposed to when you're giving birth. They shushed me and stroked my sweaty brow and said the rescue squad was coming and carefully went over my body to find their way around the broken pieces. The hands of good horsemen are healing hands. I rocked in near-oblivion and said 'yes' and 'no' and 'ow-ow-ow' to questions like whether I thought my ribs were broken and if I thought there might be internal damage and did this hurt here, and felt comforted by their presence.

At the hospital I got a massive dose of Demerol, then people in scrubs x-rayed and probed and generally made my life miserable until I was taped up like a mummy, stoned to the gills, and completely exhausted. A nurse with tired eyes asked me how I was. '*Hell is murky*', I mumbled.

'Shakespeare', said Colin helpfully.

The nurse rolled her eyes and told me severely that I was to do absolutely nothing but rest and then added to my friends that she could tell I was the kind of person who wouldn't do what I was supposed to even though I'd solemnly promised I would. She said she hoped they'd see to it I took proper care of myself and they said poker-faced that they certainly would do that and the nurse looked at us in disgust.

'You riders are all crazy,' she said. 'All y'all walk around with busted up bodies and pain that'd cripple most folks, and y'all think it's funny. Then you stand there lying through your teeth and smiling like old devils, like I don't know you're going to ignore everything I tell you. Well this stuff is *not funny*, you hear? You just better stay off those old horses awhile, my lady, if you know what's good for you. Don't you go 'round being a hero.' At that Santé and Colin started to laugh uproariously while I wheezed and tried *not* to laugh. And the nurse turned on her heel and said, 'Oh, *honestly*,' and left. But I saw the smile. I know I did.

In the back seat of Santé's ancient low-riding station wagon I lay dozing under the horse blanket, my tender head cradled on a yellow plastic inflatable duck belonging to one of his numerous kids. I could hear the men talking up front without making out much of what they were saying. It sounded worried; and Santé said something about hanging around my stalls a little bit extra tonight and Colin agreed to do something later. I tried to frame some kind of question about what was going on but either they didn't hear me over the radio and the car's ailing muffler or they were ignoring me.

I spent the night in Colin's apartment. We stopped first at my bus to pick up a man's idea of a woman's overnight needs, which fortunately included a roomy button-down shirt left over from some forgotten lover. My knights in shining armor then carried me to bed and stood there for a moment, looking at me.

'Um...' said Colin, embarrassed. 'I guess she probably can't dress herself tonight. Should we...'

Santé looked at him derisively. 'You 'fraid of seeing a woman, man? I tell you this one hardly count, she too small.' This from an ex-jockey.

'Thanks, Santé,' I mumbled hazily. 'I always knew you had the hots for me.'

'Hunh,' he grunted. 'See, she so drugged she don't know what she's saying. Tell you what, I could sure use some' that stuff time to time. Get me some sleep.'

Somewhere in the dim recesses of my fogged brain I recalled that Santé and his impossibly young wife were working on about their seventh kid. I tried to think of something snappy to say about abstinence and birth control but couldn't string two words together and kept drifting in and out of dreamland.

They unromantically got me out of the few clothes that hadn't been cut off in the ER, and into the shirt. And Santé left.

'I always wanted to spend another night with you,' I muttered to Colin in a brief drift nearer consciousness. 'Didn't imagine it like this.'

'No', he said shortly. 'Nor I.' Then he took a pillow and left. I guess he slept on the sofa; I was back in never land by the time he got to the door.

I woke up to a chorus of pain from my beleaguered body parts, and a mockingbird's lyrical song emanating from a bush outside the window. Sun streamed across my eyes. I opened them carefully, tried to locate a clock without moving my head too far, and found an old fashioned wind-up on the bedside table with blessedly large numerals that told me I'd slept through midmorning. Next to the clock several prescription bottles were neatly arranged. I groped carefully at them with my good arm until I managed to grab one, squinted at the directions, got the lid off with the aid of my teeth, and choked down two tablets in the hope that they were the right ones and the right dose. Then I dozed fitfully and waited for them to work.

For years after I cleaned my system of the byproducts of a hallucinogenic lifestyle, I was such a hard-ass about drugs that I wouldn't even take aspirin. Middle age, the beginnings of arthritis, and the wear-and-tear of life with horses cured me. I now revere NSAIDs as gods, and welcome them in combination with red wine when my body says it won't take any more real life. I know it's not p.c., but there it is. Drugs are useful. They give your broken body a chance to rest and heal without getting the parts that are still okay all seized up in sympathy.

But they also make you braver than you should be. They make you think you don't feel as rotten as you do. Which is why there are strict rules about giving drugs to the horses that are our companions, competitors, and tickets home. And why there are a few people out there every day trying to circumvent those rules to get one more mile out of sore and pathetically willing animals before they become an insurance claim.

Drugs and horses. Drugs and horse people. These go together. They always have. We use drugs to enhance performance. Drugs to alleviate pain. Drugs to cure disease. Drugs to make us feel younger. Drugs to raise self esteem. Drugs to keep us awake, to send us to sleep, to lift us and our horses that tiny notch above the competition to give us the win. Or kill us. Or see us cast off the highest peak we ever aspired to. Where is the line, really? At what point do we cross into dangerous territory and forget how to get back? In any of our barns, at any time, there are horses and people on some form of drug. A horse with old leg injuries might live and work for a long time on Bute. And if that's what you're used to, it doesn't take long to get to the point that we feel a leg and start to think a degree of warmth - signaling inflammation - is normal. We forget the benchmark, that 'normal' is a cold leg, tight, with no inflammation at all. We just don't see that benchmark very often anymore.

And then we say to ourselves, well of course. My joints are pretty inflamed, too, it's a side effect of a working life. So what's the problem with taking care of it? And if anti-depressants and alcohol and tobacco are okay, then why not marijuana? Cocaine?

Which is a good argument.

Only horses can't make it. And they can't stop us from making bad decisions on their behalf.

The thoughts that drifted through my wool-filled head as I awakened again weren't half this coherent. Mostly they ran along lines like, *I used to do drugs. Don't do 'em anymore. Terrible for your brain cells. Doing drugs now to get well. Heehee. Oww. Not so good for horses, though. Drugs. People on drugs. Your brain on drugs. Scrambled eggs. Say no. No drugs. No killing horses. No drugging horses. Only getting better.* Well, you get the picture.

I decided to try some affirmative action, anyway, and struggled to squirm gently to the edge of the bed.

It's amazing the things we take for granted before we get hurt. Simple acts like getting up and putting on clothes are no-brainers until we don't have the use of some critical appendage like an arm, a hand, a shoulder, a waist. Achieving a sitting position took a painful eternity. Taking my shirt off once I got there proved a sweaty, agonizing impossibility. I gave up and wept limp tears of frustration, pain, and helplessness. Then spent another whimpering hour getting into jeans and a pair of socks. By then I was panting from dizziness and exhaustion and had to admit that I felt really and truly awful. I maneuvered myself carefully into Colin Rutherford's sofa and stared dejectedly at the ceiling until I fell asleep again.

This is where he found me sometime later. After he'd run out of epithets to hurl at my aching head about the lunacy of trying to get out of bed he assured me that Jennie was just fine, gruffly plonked my tape deck on the coffee table 'in case you want some music or something', and heated me up a can of soup with about a gallon of hot tea to accompany it. While I sipped life-affirming hot liquids, he told me that George wanted to know if he could have all my horses, that Sara wanted to know if I would still be able to commentate that weekend, and that the police would put off speaking to me until I'd had a chance to rest. Then he ceremoniously unfolded a get-well picture colored for me by Santé's five-year-old daughter, which featured a long-bodied, short-legged, scaly thing with a smiley mouth full of pointy teeth and a red palm tree next to it.

'Cool!' I said. 'A purple speckled alligator!'

'Actually,' he said, 'it's meant to be Jennie. 'She is... um... eating coconuts for lunch.'

'What's that little brown thing in the corner? A coconut getting away?'

'No, that's Spring.'

'Omigod! Where *is* Spring?'

'With Ivory. She'll be up to visit as soon as Santé can give her a lift, but I didn't want her jumping all over you.'

'Yeah, Ivory's like that...' I examined 'Jennie's' teeth with interest. They were all different colors and shapes. Maybe eating coconuts for lunch does that.

Colin shot me a look that redefined 'foul'. 'You can be a real pain in the arse,' he said.

'I'm sorry.' I put the picture down. 'I really appreciate everything you've done, you're...'

'That's *not* what I meant.' He sighed, and stared at the ceiling in exasperation. Then changed the subject. 'Now, about your horses.'

'They're all right, aren't they?' I demanded in alarm. 'I mean, if they didn't get to Jennie...'

'No. No, they're all fine. Santé and I kept watch last night to make sure. But. We did find an empty syringe in the aisle. Still had a needle attached. Pretty unlikely anybody using one in the course of a day would have left it like that, so I assume it may have been emptied and thrown aside by whoever was there last night. We gave it to the police, at any rate, to check for fingerprints and see what was in it.'

'There won't be fingerprints. If it had death juice in there they'd have worn latex gloves.' I started to shake, to feel waves of hysteria start to work my nerves.

''Chelle, listen. It was only 12 cc's, right? Not nearly enough to do the job. And they'd have had to get the stuff from a vet who'd *never* let a controlled substance out like that. You know what they go through to get the stuff. That's grounds for losing a license.'

'There are ways... they could steal... there are people...' I shivered again, and fought down a lump that threatened to close my throat. Struggled with a long breath, and another one after it. 'No. You're right. Thanks. I'm just... feeling pretty helpless.'

'Right. 'Course you are. But let's keep thinking, shall we? I wonder if they meant to incapacitate her. Make her test positive, tip off the steward, get you ruled off.'

'But that's what I don't get. Why my silly little hunter? What could possibly be gained by hurting her?'

'To get at you.'

'You mean like revenge? For what?'

'Think of all you've been saying, the last few weeks. Standing up for professionals against ignorant animal rights people, standing up for animal rights against dirty professionals. You haven't exactly been coy about it. Even on the air. You've managed to alienate practically everybody. It's quite remarkable, really. If you were a politician, I expect you'd have been assassinated by now. So perhaps somebody wanted to make you an example. Show your clay feet.'

'They wouldn't have to drug my horse to do that. All they'd have to do is look at my life.'

'It's still worth considering. So do it, right?'

He left me and promised to look after my horses with extra care. Santé would exercise them, the police were doing their thing, and I was to stay put for another day. And try not to worry.

Hah.

My brain seethed with horrible scenarios and probably more than one hallucination, not the least of which was a grotesque semi-dream in which I watched helplessly as Michael Draper herded all my horses into a big knot, then drove them into a long, black tunnel. Then another that harked back to the van wreck, only it was Jake twisted and broken in the crazily tilted stall, mouth wrinkled in a hideous grimace, eyes glazed in death yet somehow staring at me, *how could you I trusted you how could this happen*. I jerked awake, sobbing, reminding myself that it was a dream, that my horses were in good hands. And then I slept and dreamt again.

The cops woke me up moments after I had finally stopped dreaming and twitching. Or so it seemed. In reality I'd slept for several hours. They were kind and concerned and asked the usual questions to which I gave the usual answers. They said they really didn't have much to go on right now, unless I could identify my attackers. I couldn't. They left assuring me that despite the trampled area by the stall that left no distinct footprints, despite the lack of finger prints, despite the unlikelihood of finding anything on the barrel of the syringe that was now being tested at a lab somewhere, despite the long trail of people who might like to wring my scrawny neck right now, they would keep making enquiries. And I should rest up and keep trying to remember something helpful. I thanked them and said I would.

The unending pain in every inch of my body made further sleep useless after they left. I exhausted myself by struggling to make more tea, then took more painkillers and snapped on my tape deck to try to doze with Shakespeare's rich language easing my tender ears.

But instead of the rolling thunder of *Richard III*, what I heard over the top of the recording was my own thin voice in an unbelievably bad imitation of Ian McKellan. In my ignorance I'd apparently done something completely bizarre that resulted in my voice being overdubbed onto the tape. In the background I could hear the crunching and rustling of horses in their stalls, the clank of a water bucket, Spring scratching at a flea. *Honest to God,* I thought in disgust. *You can't get one fuckin' thing right, can you...* I reached to turn the embarrassing thing off.

Then with a flash that hurt my head I realized what else would be on that tape. And sat, glued to it, hearing myself leaving with Spring, hearing nothing but rustling and sighs and the thrilling, tension-filled rise and fall of Richard's iniquity, then there it was, voices whispering as they approached, words I couldn't catch, then closer,

*'...friggin' tape deck. What's this shit?'*

*'Don't touch it! Good (mumble mumble) hear us. (Mumble mumble mumble) stuff?'*

*'Yeah. Here. (mumble) sure about (mumble mumble mumble)...? (Mumble) gonna do it?'*

*'Stop worrying. Here's a (mumble mumble) get the (mumble) to (mumble mumble) grey mare...'*

I sat, chilled to stone. Heard more words that I couldn't catch, interspersed with the things people say when they're trying to soothe a strange horse. Heard, in the distance, the beginnings of my frantic entrance. Heard above the voices of actors in a play the curses of my attackers, the shouts, the stall door slamming against me, then the tape ran out.

And still I sat, shaking from head to toe, shaking as if I would never be warm again. Because I knew those voices.

Michael Draper. Hilary Knowlton.

I barely made it to the bathroom before I lost my lunch.

# NINE

*A horse! a horse! My kingdom for a horse!*
- William Shakespeare, *King Richard III; V.iv.13*

*...My horse is my mistress.*
-    William Shakespeare, *Henry V., III. 7*


'Christ,' breathed Ivory, when I played the tape to her later. 'Oh my fuckin' Christ. Michael Draper and Hilary Knowlton. *Why?*''

'To warn me off, I think. I talked to Tommy Essex, Ive. And Santé. I think I know how the song goes.'

'But it's not enough to hang a man.'

'Are you kidding? Santé saw them load the shit. It's enough nail Winston and Michael. It's enough to get you off.'

Finally she shook her head. 'You gotta make a copy of this tape, 'Chelle. Then deep-six it somewhere real safe while you decide what to do.'

'I already know what to do, Ive. Turn it over to the cops.'

'The cops! But Michael and Hilary... I mean, they're... Michael is... fuck, 'Chelle, he's fuckin' *Michael Draper*. This is no ordinary slime bag we're talking, here. He's us. He's our people.'

'*Look what he did to me, Ivory!*' I shouted. 'Our fuckin' world hero tried to get at my horse!  And he killed Ice Cream!'

'*No!* He couldn't... he wouldn't... Don't, 'Chelley...'

'Don't *what*, Ivory! Don't *say* anything? Pretend it isn't so? What am I, gonna close my eyes and say he didn't? Hope he'll be a good little boy? It only gets easier, Ive!'

'You don't even know what's behind it!'

'*Winston's* behind it! Am I born yesterday all of a sudden? Are you gonna wait 'til he dies so we can all go back to *normal*? Are you *crazy?*'

'Come on, 'Chelle.' Ivory stared hard at me and reached for the tape deck. With a motion so fast that I yowled in pain I beat her to it and, crying from the hurt, clutched it to my chest.

'You'll have to fight me for it, Ivory Gardner.'

''Chelley,' she implored, 'Chelley, don't! You don't have any idea what it's like, what Winston had over him, how he could turn the screws. 'Chelley, it's *Michael*. He's tried so hard to get straight, to work his way out...'

'And you'll go down to let him get off? Like Craig did? What *is* it with you guys?'

'It's loyalty, 'Chelle. Loyalty to our own.' She started to cry.

'*Loyalty*! My ass! It's fuckin' royal *stupidity*. This guy has never been loyal to you, to Craig, to his wife, to anyone but his own little famous self! He deserves to fall. He deserves to find out he can't stomp on other people and walk away like his shit don't stink. What is he, *God* all of a sudden? *He killed Ice Cream.* He was gonna take away your best rides. He tried to dope Jennie. What does it take to piss you off, Ivory?'

'You're holding a man's life there in your hands, 'Chelle Martin,' Ivory insisted. 'He's gonna to have to live with himself the whole rest of it. Live with what he did. Even if the Feds don't find out about him and Winston, his soul is dead. What are you gonna do about that? Take away everything else because you're so right? So pure?'

'I never pretended that!'

'You just copy those tapes and keep 'em safe, 'Chelley. But do some thinking, okay? It's gotta stop somewhere. All this shit has got to stop. I am just so sick of watching people fall.'

I had this horrible sense of *déjà's vù*, a flashback to the bad old days of our youth. But things had seemed etched more clearly, then. And we hadn't been dealing with a group of animals whose lives hung daily on our dreams. Our whims.


'This is dynamite, 'Chelle', said Colin, some hours later. He snapped the machine off. 'You're *sure* that's who it is?'

'You recognized them well enough, and Ivory picked it up right away. Lots of other people would, too.'

'Yeh. And would you like to hear something interesting? Hilary Knowlton packed up her horses and her kit and left for Georgia early this morning.'

'She *did*? Are you sure she wasn't just moving over to Wellington?'

'Sure. I asked her. I thought she seemed a little... I dunno.

Distracted. Tense. Said it was a family issue.'

'Fucking bitch.'

'Mmm. So. What will you do?'

'I should take the thing to the police.'

'Yeh, but what do you *intend* to do?'

I sighed, and thought. 'First I guess I'd like about four copies. There's a bunch of blank tapes in my rig. Can you do that without erasing it? I don't trust myself.'

'I'm sure I'll manage. We're not all of us electronically challenged.'

'Yeah, well be glad I am. I'd never have gotten this.'

'Touché.'

We copied the tapes, sealed them into their cases, and mailed them. The original and one copy went to my brother Jimmy, with a letter explaining what exactly they were and instructions on getting them into a safe-deposit box. Another to Ivory's lawyer, Guy Carmouche, 'to be opened in the event of…' The others, I kept.

That evening, Harry came over for a check-in and to help with the vital topic of how to keep my horses going. They were all entered for the week coming up. I didn't want to lose the entry fees, and even more I didn't want my mounts losing their competitive edge. They would if they were left inactive for days on end, just like human athletes who reach a certain peak of fitness in time for a specific event. Darcy Noriega was easy – she was back to riding her horses again, and I could coach her from the ground. Gerry, ditto. He would leap at the chance to ride Dreamcatcher, and she was uncomplicated enough that the change wouldn't unsettle her too much. Clyde looked like he was about to change hands anyway, and the other couple of horses I'd been riding for Harry's owners could go to Cam. 'But I'll tell you what, babe,' Harry assured me, 'I'll put you back up again soon's you're able, okay? So don't you worry about losing anything.'

I was so absurdly grateful for this vote of confidence that I cried, which made Harry turn red and awkward.

'What about the ponies?' he asked, once I was back under control.

'I dunno. I'm kind of stuck there.'

'How 'bout giving 'em to Camille? She's good, she could use the miles, and it won't be too heavy on 'em.'

'She's in school 'til next week. Santé can keep them going and I guess she could have them then. Ottawa won't suffer with Santé showing him where to put his feet, either.'

'Ever think of giving him a shot?'

'Santé? In a class, you mean?'

'Yeah.'

'Think he can find his way around?'

'We'll stand at the corners and point. He doesn't weigh much. Your ponies'll hardly know he's there.'

'If he says yes, I think it's a great idea.'

'That leaves Dancing Fool.'

'You?'

'Too busy. Don't want to die, yet, neither.'

'Right. Next.'

We rejected Craig, Tommy, Diane, Cam, and several others in turn. Harry never mentioned Hilary, and I sure wasn't going to. The name 'Michael Draper' hung between us unexpressed, too. In the past, the logical - really the ideal - choice for a mare like Dancing Fool, and one which Harry would not have hesitated to mention. In the past. I waited, tense, for the suggestion to be made, and wondered how I would react. Harry waited, too, and stared at the ceiling in silence.

'I'm not sure how she'll take another rider,' I ventured, deciding not to broach the issue. 'That's the problem. Not that I'm so great. She's just used to me.'

Harry shot me a radar glance that felt like it peeled my soul bare, then went back to studying the ceiling. 'Hmm. Someone tactful.'

'...Colin?'

Harry frowned. 'He's quiet enough, he might. I'll check it out with Ivory.'

'It won't be long,' I said. 'I'll be okay in a couple of days.'

'Weeks,' he said.

'Days,' I repeated stubbornly.

He laughed sepulchrally, and shook his head.

As Harry was leaving, Colin arrived with Chinese take-out, agreed to try the crazy mare, and told Harry that yes, he would indeed make sure I laid still even if it meant chaining me to the sofa. Before we'd had a chance to get through half the food, Gerry Dirk appeared at the door with a huge bunch of roses and territorial exhortations that I should be moved instantly to his condo, to be waited on hand and foot. I could see Colin's hackles rise. He did *not* think I should be moved, just yet. I watched them spar with interest, thinking of Mistress Page with Falstaff's letter, *What, have I 'scaped love letters in the holiday time of my beauty, to be a subject for them now?* Nobody'd ever argued over me before. I wished I'd been blonde, younger, and beautifully made up instead of disheveled, stoned, and all taped up like a turkey, so I could really appreciate it.

After several frigidly polite moments during which Gerry and Colin reminded me of nothing so much as two terriers with their hair on end, no progress had been made and the doorbell rang again. This time it was Diane Gambarini, and I nearly fell over in a fit of giggles. When she heard that Gerry wanted to take me away, her troubled expression lifted like clouds after a storm, and she lent her voice to Gerry's in support of my being moved out of Colin's apartment immediately, if not sooner. A few minutes of this was all I could stand; I lay down, and closed my eyes against the ridiculous din. Gerry hovered. Diane spirited Colin into the kitchen. I swallowed more pills and told Gerry please not to get too close to my pain-aura, that I appreciated his concern, and that I really, *really* didn't want to move anywhere or do anything more that night but sleep. And that, by the way, Dreamcatcher was his to ride. This lifted his spirits to cosmic levels. He was bubbling by the time Colin and Diane reappeared. And miraculously, she and Gerry left together.

Colin closed the door on their backs and leaned against it. 'How does life get so complicated?' he asked the air.

The laughter I'd been trying to suppress exploded out of me with a snort that made every inch of my body hurt and the next thing we knew we were both collapsed, Colin doubled over on the floor next to me, me wheezily trying not to move my ribs. When we'd finally regained control of ourselves, he looked at me out of the delicious hazel eyes that made my stomach weak and said, 'You know, if it hadn't been...' and then the doorbell rang again. Colin cursed fluently and creatively, and went to answer.

And there, lined up outside, were my family. I mean the whole unit: my mother, The Rev, my father, and Camille. 'Oh, my God!' I breathed weakly, and tried to struggle to a sitting position as they all descended on me with expostulations, greetings, questions, speculation, and orders, all at the same time. The Rev hung back politely, shook Colin's hand, and introduced the rest, who belatedly remembered their manners and turned on my startled friend with the same intensity they had showered on me. They thanked him and questioned him and triumphantly brought out the food they'd picked up - more Chinese. My mother and dad escorted Colin to the kitchen to heat it up while The Rev looked around the room.

'Not a single bookcase,' he said, peering reprovingly over the rims of his glasses.

'It's a rental,' I said.

'That explains it,' he said, and sat down with a copy of *Horse And Hound*.

'Camille,' I said helplessly to my daughter, '...*look* at you!'

She touched her hair self-consciously. It was buzz-cut, and dyed maroon, with large yellow polka dots. Some of the dye had gotten on her ears, making them a sort of pale burgundy. She had two studs in one ear, three in the other, and a small ring in her left nostril. A minute tank dress just covered her crotch and displayed an extraordinary length of leg clothed in red and white striped tights. The Doc Martins she'd saved for months to buy finished off her wardrobe.

'Everybody keeps giving me these strange *looks*, Ma,' she said. 'Like I'm a *freak* or something.'

'Well,' I said cautiously. 'You have to expect that, down here.'

'They're all like, so *straight*.'

'Camille... why are you here?' I asked bluntly.

'Grandpa brought me. Because you were *hurt*. Ma, these weird *things* keep happening to you, it's like... really scary. You know, so I... well, and anyway, vacation week was gonna start in three days, so I just came. It's okay. GranEllen called the school and all that. And anyway, you *need* me.'

'Does your father know you're here?'

Camille giggled. 'Grandpa fixed it. Dad's afraid of him, you know? You look like shit.'

'Thanks. I feel like it, too. How did you guys know?'

'Well, *duh*, Ma. *Ivory* called. She's like the original jungle drum or something.' My daughter started to say something else, changed her mind, and jumped up to help serve the latest batch of take-out.

'You want me to feed you?' she asked.

'I can eat left handed.' I illustrated, and dropped a cup or so of chow mein on my chest.

'*Gross.*'

'I didn't say it was pretty.'

The next half hour passed before my eyes like a movie, everybody talking over and around me like I was a corpse and this was my wake. I half expected my dad and The Rev to break out the whiskey and drink toasts to the dear departed, but instead Colin got up and said he had to get back to the barn and my dad jumped up and said he wanted to check on his colt, and Colin said *oh is that your colt, the grey?* and da said it was and what did Colin think of it, and they were out the door together, with Camille shouting at them to wait for her and galloping off in their wake.

'What a lovely man,' remarked my mother, to no one in particular.

'*Why, he's a man of wax,*' quoted The Rev from *Romeo and Juliet*. What, exactly, is a JA Jumper, 'Chelle?' and he disappeared into *Horse and Hound* again.

'He's married,' I said neutrally. My mother looked at me assessingly.

'Michelle, there is a horse here advertised as being green, with no vices,' said The Rev. 'What on earth does that mean? It sounds to me like a piece of lumber.'


'You don't have to go, yet,' said Colin, two days later.

'You shouldn't be sleeping on the sofa. You need your bed back.'

'I have no objection to your being in it,' he grinned. His eyes crinkled so nicely at the edges, it made me ill with desire.

'I think it's best,' I said.

'Probably,' he agreed, more matter-of-factly than I could have wished.

Camille, my dad, and Ivory – now a demon on crutches that she used with deadly accuracy as weapons if she felt the need for attention - made a procession of my return to the rig. I was glad to be home, surrounded with my own clutter and my ecstatic little dog. I was barely settled when the police stopped by for another talk. The syringe had come back from the lab. It had traces of flunixin meglumine, they told me, a common pain reliever that wouldn't harm Jennie but would have made her test positive and made me liable for a stiff fine and possible ruling off from competition for several months. No prints on it, no surprise.

When they asked me again if I had any idea who might have done it I looked them straight in the eye and said I didn't know.

'It was too dark to see. It happened too fast. And they were whispering.'

I described the whole sequence of events as I remembered them, again, in detail. 'It was a man and a woman, I think,' I added. 'I've been kind of high profile lately. I guess it could be anyone. Even the animal rights guys, they get pretty nasty, and they sure don't like my attitude.'

'Do you think it might have been anyone connected with the recent findings surrounding Winston Desmarchais?' one asked.

'That would seem logical,' I said. 'Only I don't know why.'

'High profile. You said it yourself. You're close to it. And from what we understand, you've been pretty vocal.'

'Yeah.' I grimaced.

When they left Ivory appeared as if by magic, large with anxiety. 'Well?' she demanded.

'They're looking for a connection with the Winston Desmarchais affair.'

'And? Did you…'

'No.'

She expelled a gusty sigh and deflated a size or two. 'Generally speaking I'm really glad you're straight as you are, doll,' she said. 'You're still the best liar I ever met.'

'I didn't lie,' I said uncomfortably. 'It was more a don't ask, don't tell arrangement.'

'You're good, sweetie.'

'Yeah? Been years since I was proud of it.'

'Hey,' she changed the subject casually, 'I put Camille up on Jake today. Give her a tightener, you know, since she's been at school.'

'Yeah? How'd she do?'

'She could do a Children's/Adult Jumper this weekend. She's awful good, 'Chelle. The real thing. Just needs competitive mileage.'

'What about Santé?'

'He's real flattered, but he says God didn't intend him to be flying in the air like a bird. Also, his wife had a lot to say on the subject, but it was in Tagalog or something, so I didn't understand it.'

I sighed. 'I hate to think what Josie's going to say about this.'

'Don't you worry about him. Your mama's got him right where she wants him.'

I giggled. 'Does she! I wish I'd heard that one.'

'It was choice, I'll tell you that,' said Ivory. 'That is one lady I would not want to get on the wrong side of.'

'Believe me. I know.'

When I struggled out the next morning to watch my horses go, I had to agree with Ivory. Camille was preternaturally good. And in her chaps and helmet she looked like any other pretty teenage girl who could really ride. Except when the accrued tribal hardware that adorned her face caught the sun and glittered, that is.

Now… having been a good hippie in my colorful youth I grew up believing that I would never so much as raise an eyebrow if my kid's appearance strayed from what I consider to be the norm. On the whole I'd done pretty well. But we weren't just talking about personal choices, anymore, I told myself, looking at Camille's piercings. We were talking about creating the right impression among a bunch of Republican, arch-conservative, often influential and wealthy, horse people, in a state I have always thought of as leaning politically somewhere to the right of Ghenghis Khan. Not maybe the best place to flaunt one's determined individuality, as my own past experience had shown me. But how to get this across to my daughter? Not gracefully, I supposed.

'You're gonna have to lose the jewelry, if you're gonna go in the ring,' I heard myself telling her.

Predictably, she bristled. 'No!' she said. 'That's totally not okay!'

'You're not going in the show ring on my horses looking like that. It's totally unprofessional, discredits a beautifully turned out animal, and nobody in their right mind will pin you.'

'What is *with* these people, anyway? That is such *bullshit...*'

'Camille, watch your mouth, you're in public...'

'What the fuck do I care about...'

'Get off my horse, Camille!' I demanded. 'If you can't hold by a few simple rules long enough to get the job done, I'd rather find another rider!'

'You would not!' she flared.

'*Get-off-now.*'

She suddenly realized I was serious. 'That's not fair, Ma!' she complained. 'You know it's not!' She looked desperately to Ivory for help. Ivory studied the ground with deep absorption. Rescue came in the unlikely package of Colin.

'Maybe not,' he said reasonably, coming to ringside with Dancing Fool in tow. 'Sorry to interrupt', he said to me. 'You were getting rather... um... loud. But it's not safe, you know, Camille. The studs - okay. But the rings'll get caught if you get in trouble. You could rip off your earlobe, or your nostril.'

'But we're not, like, in the woods or something,' she said mulishly. 'It's not, like, a *rule.*'

Colin shrugged. 'Read the rulebook, if you want. There's a whole list of what's appropriate in the hunter ring and what's frowned on, yeah? No point wasting money on a class if you won't get looked at. And like it or not, it *is* your mother's horse. I'm sure you want to do your best by it.'

Camille looked from Colin to Ivory to me in uncertain defiance. 'Yeah,' she said finally. 'I guess you're right.'

'Whyn't you go put him away and get Jennie, honey,' suggested Ivory. Then, when Camille had gone, turned her anger loose on me. 'You coulda maybe told her how good she looked, first. Before you nailed her,' she said. 'Sometimes you have the tact of a rhinoceros, doll. Okay, Colin,' she said, turning pointedly away again. 'Let's go see what the bay bitch has to say about you.' She crutched off to the middle of the arena. I put my head in my good hand and felt useless.

'What are you gonna do about that daughter of yours?' asked Harry, coming up beside me. 'I dunno how they dress up your way, but down here she's trouble on legs. I wouldn't let her out the house, she was mine.'

'Yeah, well it's a good thing she's *not* yours, Harry,' I snapped. 'Then you'd have *two* runaways that wouldn't speak to you.'

Harry looked at me as if I'd just landed from Mars. 'Thanks for reminding me. Talk like that, babe, I don't know whether to hit you, or...'

I grabbed his arm so he couldn't turn his back on me as the others had. 'No. No, Harry, I'm sorry. That was out of line. *Please* forgive me. I'm just... I don't know. Not doing too well.'

'You hurt?'

'Body and soul, Harry. '

'Wanna talk?'

'I wouldn't know where to start. I just feel all beat up and confused. And I don't know what to do next.'

'Well, *that* was clear as a puddle.'

'Harry... what exactly do you know? About the other night, I mean.'

'I know Hilary's put a lot of geography between herself and her good friend Michael Draper and Michael's timing's way off and he blew a couple big classes yesterday and his owners are pissed off. Other than that I don't know anything. That good enough? 'Til you feel like telling me more, I mean.'

Which is how I knew he knew. 'Sorry I came off sideways.'

'Rest up, will ya? Learn how to get along.'

'I'm trying. But honest, Harry, I don't think I know how to relate to people at all.'

'Well, you got no tact, babe, and that's a fact. Beats me how you ride so good. But Camille's not so bad. Even with the...' he wiggled his fingers around his face and head, '...y'know. Okay?'

'Yeah. Thanks.'

'So cheer up. By the way,' he fished in a pocket, 'Clyde's sold. Here's your share.'

'My share!'

'Well. You got the sucker going. *I* sure didn't think he'd do that good.'

'*Thanks*, Harry. I guess I should come say goodbye to the big oaf.

I'll sort of miss him.'

'Oh, you won't miss him that much. Not once you cash that check. Besides, might be the new owners'll need a little advice from time to time, and you know the horse.'

My day suddenly looked a little brighter.

It improved another notch when I saw Dancing Fool pull the kind of airs-above-the-ground on Colin that I thought she only saved for me. Mind you, he looked a lot smoother pulling her back together since he could just wrap his long legs around her, stick like glue, and ride it out. But I still chuckled all the way back to the tent.

I met Camille and Jennie on the way. My daughter scowled and would have ridden by without a word, but I caught Jennie's bridle in my good hand and stopped her.

'Yeah?' she asked scathingly. 'You got something *else* you want me to change?'

'Yeah,' I said, steam rising again. 'Your attitude.' Then I took a deep breath. 'No. Stop. Let's just... stop for a minute. Look, Camille, I'm sorry. I shouldn't have come off sideways like that. I really like the way you ride Jake. I'd like you to ride him in the Junior Jumpers, if you want.'

'Yeah?' She looked at me suspiciously. 'What's the catch?'

'No catch.'

'I can really do it? The Juniors? On Jake?' Sunshine broke through.

'Yeah. And you can do the Junior Hunters with Jennie, if you want.'

'*Cool*!' exulted Camille. 'Oh, Ma, that's *so cool*! I think he's okay. I mean, he feels pretty good. And Grandpa's in the barn now, looking at him. If there's anything to find, he'll find it!' She walked off to the schooling arena, humming to Jennie.

There's a benefit to having a vet for a father.

'What do you think?' I asked him as he stooped over my bay horse's legs.

'I think he's just showing the effects of age and miles,' he said. 'Little creaking in the joints. What is he now? Seventeen? Eighteen? Amazing legs on him. Done you proud. He's a tough little bugger.'

'Yeah. He is.'

'You don't want to be riding him into the ground, now. Now you've these others. The big horse cleaned up nice, eh?'

'Well... for the *ugliest* sombitch I ever saw, yeah,' I laughed.

'He is that,' grinned my dad. 'He'll be a swan, give him time. I'm glad I sent him to you. You're doing good things, 'Chelley. Don't think I don't know.' He stood in front of me awkwardly. Always more relaxed with horses than people, my da. Runs in the family, I guess. 'Be careful, yeah?'

'Always.'

'Never. See all this grey hair? You give it me. Every one.'

'C'mon, Da. Jimmy gave you a few.'

'Not he. Never a moment's trouble, that one. But my darling daughter, now...'

'Get outta here.'

'Well, I will, at that. Now that I've checked up on your charges here and seen you alive.'

'Oh no! I was kidding. You're not really leaving so soon?'

'Got to. I left young Will in charge of the practice. God knows what the boy's prescribing.' He studied me and my medical bindings. 'I'd give you a hug, love, but I can't think how.' He cradled my face with his big, callused hands and kissed me gently on the nose. 'Call if you need anything, will you now.'

'Sure,' I said, amazed. He'd never offered that before.

'Come up to Saratoga in August. Bring that Colin fella with you. Not bad, for a Brit.'

'He's married.'

'Oh, well.' He laughed. 'Bring him anyway. Fit right in with the rest of us.'


I read somewhere that mothers and teenaged daughters spend an hour or so fighting every couple of days, on average. I guess that made Camille and me above average, because we took fighting to a new level. We fought over her clothes strewn all over the rig and my wardrobe. We fought over my habitual facial expressions and her pout. We fought over the dirty dishes. We fought over lights out. We fought over the amount of schoolwork it seemed reasonable to do, about the hours she was expected to be 'home', and about the nature of her riding.

Ivory had moved in while I was at Colin's, to keep Camille and Spring company. They didn't fight. My mother arrived every morning, far too cheerful, to tutor Camille. They didn't fight. My rig – set up perfectly to suit me alone – was suddenly very, very small. I snarled a lot, like a caged animal. Every time I moved, something hurt. Every time I turned around, I bumped into another person or that person's stuff. Every time I watched other people ride my horses, I worried that they weren't doing a good enough job. Then I worried that they were doing a better job than I could. Everybody seemed to be having a swell time without me. After three days, I was exhausted from insomnia, teenaged daughter-itis, and yeah, a healthy dose of self-pity.

'Honey,' Said Ivory in exasperation, 'why don't you just go and get *laid* or something, huh? Help us all out.'

'That will *not* solve my problems!'

'Oh, yeah? Well I bet it'd sure as hell *help*. You got to do something, before we all go nuts.'

'I'd like to just get some peace and quiet around here. That's all.'

'Well, you can't. Not right now. So get over it.' Then she added, grinning, 'You know, I really like living all piled up with your family. Takes me back to when I was a kid having slumber parties with my 25 best friends.'

I growled something incomprehensible, even to me.

Gerry provided some rescue. He took me out to dinner after one of our daily training sessions, to exclaim happily over Dreamcatcher and what a wonderful time he was having on the mare. Afterwards we went back to his place to have a drink, see the video he'd just gotten on a horse he might want to buy, and indulge in some more of that world class kissing he specialized in. Maybe Ivory was right. Maybe I did just need to get laid.

But everywhere Gerry touched me was bruised and sore, and my shoulder throbbed like a beacon. I was tired from the effort of acting like everything was okay. And I wanted to go home, crawl into bed, pull the covers over my head and dream the kind of dreamless sleep that is common only to children and those who are lucky in love.

Gerry dropped me off near the rig. I heard laughter and music wafting from the open windows and screened door almost before I saw the lights. I stopped and listened. Lights and cheerful voices – isn't that how most people spell 'home'? I was merely disgruntled, and hated myself for it. *This lack-love, this kill-courtesy… Churl!* Without conscious thought (or so I insisted later) I turned around and walked in the opposite direction, out the main gate and down the road.

I don't know what kind of welcome I expected when I found my way to Colin's digs. Light conversation and a nightcap, maybe, or even some hint of awkwardness. But he barely said hello before he pulled me in the door, wrapped his arms carefully around me, and started kissing me and pulling my shirttail out while all good intentions melted entirely out of my body and into the receiving earth and I was unbuckling his belt one-handed while shedding my shoes. I couldn't believe the warm smell of him, the warm touch of him, the pressure of his hands...

'*Ow*! Careful of my shoulder...'

'Sorry... how does this hook... *aghh, mind* the knee...'

'You feel so... *echh* shift off that leg a little...'

'...watch the elbow...'

'Sorry... *upphh*... ribs...'

Well, it was that kind of middle-aged-riders-making-love-around-injuries-old-and-new sort of affair until desire and oblivion took over and an eternity or so later we resurfaced, having somehow ended up on the rug in front of the sofa, laughing ourselves silly.

'I d-don't remember all those aches and pains, the first t-time,' I stammered through my hilarity.

'Adrenaline's a great anti-inflammatory', he said, wiping his eyes. He sat back and studied me. 'You know, I've never tried sex with a woman trussed up like the Christmas goose before. There's something vaguely S/M about it.'

'I never took you for a pervert.'

'Well... let's just experiment...'

We began again, more slowly, more deliciously, more cognizant and caring of the knots and knobs and bruises and hurts, his and mine, brand new and ancient history. 'How did you know?' he breathed into my neck with his beautiful rumbly voice much later, and I was thinking of saying that I didn't, it was all a huge surprise, but the words never came out.

'I thought you were seeing that guy what's-his-name Gerry Burke...'

'...Dirk...'

'...Prick... Whatever... I thought you were seeing him.'

'I thought you were married.'

'I was. Am. Sort of. I think.'

'What's *that* supposed to mean?'

Colin turned onto his back and sighed. 'It means that I am married, legally speaking, though officially separated.'

'Your choice or hers? I've never known.'

'Hers.'

'Why?'

'She doesn't want to be married to a professional horseman anymore. I don't fit the growth profile.'

'Ah. Too many demands, not enough pay-off, misses the concept of upward mobility, wants the dinners out?'

'Yeh, summing like that. And there's that bit about horrible accidents at unexpected moments that keep you out of work for unspecified periods.'

'Do you still want to be married? Don't bullshit me,' I warned. 'I'll know.'

He was silent a long time, staring at the ceiling. 'Yeh', he said finally. 'I do still want to be married. I care for my wife. I love my children. I miss our life together... I've been having a lot of fun over here, but it's not the same, is it?'

'Yeah. Well, so I've been seeing Gerry Dirk.'

'He's a prick.'

'Why, because I go out with him sometimes? How about Diane Gambarini, oh by the way?'

'That's different.'

'It is *not*. Honest to God, you're worse than my brother.'

'Diane threw herself at me. I didn't want to be rude.'

'*Jay-sus*, Mary, and Joseph, me beads.'

'I don't understand the attraction, that's all. Is it his money?'

'He does happen to have a lot of money. He likes to spend some of it on me.'

'Ah. Flattering, that, eh?'

'Let's say it makes a nice change. We can all use the occasional dinner out, you know.'

'Yeh, so what else? I don't see you dripping diamonds.'

'No. I got the ride on Dreamcatcher.'

'Must be he's good in bed, too.'

'Colin, don't be an asshole. That is just none of your business.'

'So he's not good in bed.'

'I really wouldn't know, if you want the honest truth. I have not boinked the guy.'

'You haven't done! Really?'

'A few meals. A few dates. Very pleasant, but no chemistry. And you can just goddamn well stop looking so pleased about it.'

'Am I? Sorry,' he said, without looking less pleased.

My turn to sigh. 'So. I guess I should go. This was probably a mistake.'

'No!' He rolled over and put his arms as tightly around me as my bandaged situation allowed. 'It was most definitely *not* a mistake. I've been wishing for this ever since... well, ever since the first time. I thought you weren't interested. I've met hedgehogs that were more comfy.'

'You haven't exactly starved for female company. You've had

every woman on the circuit trailing after you, looking hopeful. Speaking of flattering, I mean.'

He snorted with laughter. 'Yeh, quite a scene, innit? But I like you better.'

I leaned up on my good elbow and studied him. 'Are you really that ordinary? It doesn't seem natural.'

'Well... yeh. I am. I mean... maybe there's been the occasional lapse. I am human.'

'Like Diane.'

'Mmmm, yeh. Like that.'

'But you're still married and want to stay that way.'

'Oh, hell, 'Chelle. What can I say to make you stay? *Make me a willow cabin at your gate/ And call upon my soul within the house...?*'

'You're so full of shit your eyes should be brown,' I said.

I guess my life hasn't really changed much in the last thirty years. It's still drugs, sex, and rock-n-roll. Horses have replaced the drugs for the most part, but I rock to the same old weird beat I always did. As for sex... well. Who'd want to replace that?

I wouldn't have expected any big wins from Camille at this juncture, but considering the amount of time she'd been away from riding she brought in enough decent ribbons to keep her elated. And she was a pleasure to watch, graceful and possessing that indefinable quality called 'feel' that allowed her to communicate sensitively and effectively with her horses. Her sense of pace was impressive, her eye for a distance to a fence instinctively good, and she had nerves of steel. In a conceited moment, I might grant that she had developed a lot of her ability from hanging around her old lady. But I envied her the absence of nerves. And I knew it would only be a matter of time before she became a much better horsewoman than I ever was. If her interest held.

In between schooling and classes, she spent long hours with the horses grooming, grazing, and strolling around the grounds. 'Put me out of a job,' grumbled Santé, though he was pleased to teach her everything he knew about turning out a sound and beautiful competition horse. And for several hours a day, as good as her word and without my constant presence to rebel against, she did schoolwork with her erudite grandma.

Nobody said a word about my having moved back to Colin's apartment. I think they were all glad to be rid of me.

I was so pleased with Camille's demeanor and commitment that I let her help out with my latest sale horse, a nice dark bay gelding my dad bought off the track with the idea that it might like being a children's hunter better. I even let her sit on Ottawa and galumph around on him a little.

But I drew the line at Dancing Fool. And of course it was Dancing Fool she wanted to ride more than anything.

'I know I can manage her, Ma. I *know* it,' she pleaded for the nth time.

'No,' I said firmly, also for the nth time. 'I'm sorry, but she isn't safe.'

'Well, *you* can ride her,' she said, with a scathing arrogance and badly hidden contempt that left me speechless, my mouth hanging open like a striped bass. 'You just think I'm no good!' she continued, building herself into a right fury. 'You just don't want me to succeed!'

'Don't be an asshole, Camille. You're my daughter and I love you. And I won't let you ride a crazy mare like Dancing Fool because I don't want you to be killed.' Then, the tumblers all clicking on oranges at the same time, I blurted, 'That's it, isn't it? All this great behavior, all the studying, all the butter-wouldn't-melt-in-your-mouth... it's all about that damn mare, isn't it? Jee-sus, Camille. Did you think I could be *bribed* into letting you ride her?'

'You are ruining my life!' she shouted.

'Hey, *I* wasn't the one kicked out of school for smoking weed in the bathroom! *I* didn't put that on your record!'

'Why am I even *talking* to you?' she yelled without answering my accusation. 'You don't even *own* her!' She flounced out with a martial glint in her eye, straight to Ivory.

When Ivory turned her down flat, she stormed out of the barn, white with fury, and disappeared from view for two hours.

'Should we worry?' asked Ivory.

'No,' I said. 'She'll come back eventually.'

'You think she might... you know... hurt herself?'

'Camille? Ha. She wouldn't want to miss our reaction.'

But I was more worried than I wanted to admit. When Ivory sauntered off 'to have a look around', I was relieved.

Some mom I am. I didn't want to look for my own daughter and be accused of spying on her.

But she finally returned, pale and quiet. Without a glance or a word, she sat on a bucket and started cleaning a saddle as if her life depended on its glow.

'What the hell is that about?' I asked Ivory as we hobbled our way to the schooling ring and left Camille to sort herself out.

Ivory smiled knowingly. 'She just got back from talking to Harry.'

'To *Harry*!'

'Yeah. 'Bout what a dweeb her mother is and what a big shot her daddy is and how she can ride anything, anytime, anywhere. I just *happened* to be walkin' by, you know. At the time.'

'Ivory, you *eavesdropped*. If I'd done that she'd never... What did Harry say?'

Ivory chuckled. 'Well, let's just say he had a lot stored *up*. You know what he's like.'

'Oh my God.' I rolled my eyes. 'He must have really laced her.'

'There were some home truths spoken. She needed to hear 'em.'

I sighed. 'I feel like I do everything I can. It still doesn't seem like it's enough. And I sure don't do it very well.'

'That's because you're her mama. Everybody *knows* their mama is as dumb as a box of rocks. *And* the worst bitch that ever walked. Especially when Daddy's telling her bad stories and using his money to keep her out of trouble so she thinks she's special.'

'Yeah. That's no help.'

'Anyway, she's basically a great kid. She'll figure out how cool her old lady is one of these days.'

'I was amazed how smart and kind my mom got when I was about 25. I hope I live that long.'

'Uh-huh.'

'I just wish she didn't have to learn as hard as we did. I wish I could just tell her stuff.'

'Sometimes it's gotta come from somebody else. Somebody you think sits on the right hand of God, you know. Remember how you were with your Grandda?'

'*Please*. Don't even remind me!'

'What I really want to know... is Camille what I have to look forward to in another sixteen years? Cuz if it is, I'm sending this baby away to your Grandda when she turns ten!'

'Nah. You'll have a boy. Then you'll just have to worry about him killing himself in a car wreck or getting some girl knocked up.'

'That's supposed to be *easier*? Cam, honey,' she called, 'Long as you're out here, could you square up this little oxer for me? And maybe shorten that bounce a foot-and-a-half? You're a dollbaby.' She smiled deliciously and Cam, all attention, couldn't help her out fast enough.

We made quite a pair, Ivory and me, standing in the middle of the schooling ring - her on crutches, me with my collarbone and ribs trussed - and lording it over everybody like we were the queens of the May. It was great to have strong young men and women scurrying to do all the heavy lifting of poles and standards and buckets and so on for us, I have to admit. Ivory loved the attention and dispensed charm in all directions. I wished I was half as gracious. But I was chafing to get back on my horses.

Not that they were suffering much. Gerry Dirk was still in heaven on his lovely Dreamcatcher, and if she wasn't quite as consistent as she might have been with me, the pair excelled in enthusiasm. The jumper we'd found him suited him nicely, and he and Darcy both did well in their Adult divisions, which raised my reputation as a trainer another notch. Ottawa bumbled around happily with Santé under Harry's eagle eye, though he wasn't competing at the moment. And after a rough beginning in which she took down the better part of an Intermediate course, Dancing Fool agreed to let Colin be her cruise director.

Diane found good reasons to school at the exact moments that he might be found in the ring working any of his horses. Then she hung on him like a terrier, even when she was mounted. I found myself remarkably unmoved by her actions, for once. But then, I was happily ensconced in his room like Titania in her bower, *where the wild thyme blows... with sweet musk roses and with eglantine... Lull'd in these flowers with dances and delight.* Ivory found the scenario so funny that she nearly wept. She wasn't alone. Diane's actions were beginning to cause an undercurrent of humor more generally, too, but George Andros was not among the amused. So far from it, in fact, that he told me he'd decided for sure to send his two new warmbloods up to my farm later in the spring with an eye to sending them out for the Vermont Summer Series.

'That's what I need,' I said to Ivory. 'Another enemy. Diane'll be ripped.'

'She's young yet. She'll live and learn.'

'Is that the bitter voice of experience talking?'

'Believe it, honey. See over yonder? She's learning as we speak.'

And in fact, Diane and Colin had moved off to a secluded spot under the live oaks outside the ring to have a tête-à-tête, with horses attached. Their voices were quiet, but the body language was clear. Diane's was possessive, angry, importunate. Colin's was comforting but firm. In the end, Diane stormed off holding back tears of rage, with one of George's horses jogging along obediently beside her. Colin stared at the ground reflectively and absently patted Dancing

Fool's neck.

'How can we be so stupid?' I wondered aloud. 'I mean – thinking we're better than animals?'

Ivory giggled. 'Where sex is concerned? We are nothin' but base flesh, honey. Like the noble horses we ride. Oh, Cam?' she crutched across to the other side of the oxer and Cam all but fell over himself to get as close to her as he could while she whispered in his ear and touched his arm. And here she was, almost old enough to be his mama, pregnant, and it was still all about sex.

There aren't that many mammals that mate for life, after all. Mares are a perfect example of the old 'love the one you're with' adage, and if they're in heat they don't much care where they get their sex as long as they get it *now*. And while a stallion in the wild may prefer certain mares to others, he's not going to say no to a randy female who wants his attention. It's not unlike the average Saturday night singles-bar routine, when you think about it.

Of course, in this day and age our horses don't get much say in the matter of mating choices. We arrange matches on the basis of pedigree and performance like feudal empire-makers. If the mare doesn't like our choice we go all Petruchio on her - *Will thee or nil thee I will wed thee, Kate* - and there's an end to it.

These days stallions generally live separate from their mares and interact with them only while breeding. This is chiefly because you don't want your zillion dollar stallion and irreplaceable broodmare getting into a fight, or having rough sex and beating the stuffing out of each other, which does happen. But since horses are herd animals that like hanging out and touching each other, it's a lonely old life for the poor stallion. Ponies are often luckier than Thoroughbreds and their ilk, and may get to live with their ladies. It's a happier situation all around, if you have a kind stallion and generous mares.

Lots of people still believe that a big macho stallion is at the head of every wild herd of horses. In reality, a mare generally runs the establishment. She maintains her position in the pecking order by means of stealth, aggression, and subtle threats, and she does not suffer competition gladly. She sometimes hen pecks the poor stallion mercilessly, too, like those 'honey-do' women who are constantly getting their husbands to lug the sofa to a better spot or throw out his favorite recliner. And by the way: mares, like women, vary in their attitudes and eptitude regarding motherhood. Some are really rotten parents. So maybe I'm not an anomaly there, either.

Two boss mares in the same pasture is really bad news. This happened to me once, and those girls spent an entire night whaling on each other until their hind legs were in ribbons and they were both dead lame. It took a lot of cold hosing, ointment, and bandaging to heal those legs. Fortunately, the mares came sound and arrived at an agreement after that. Even more fortunately, they were mine. I would have hated to have to explain legs like blood sausages to an irate owner who had trusted me to care for a six-figure show mare.

Not that Diane and I were going to act like that. Or... not openly. The hurts we inflict, the scars we carry, are all internal. The holes are all in that psychic thing we call our heart.

I even felt a little sorry for Diane.

Well. Not that sorry. I liked being boss mare, for a change. As long as she didn't come and shoot me or something.

I spent a certain amount of time in the rig to try to circumvent the inevitable nosiness and perennial raised eyebrows of the whole horse show scene, and to attempt to be a decent mother to my daughter. During the day Colin's and my paths crossed no more than they had before, in the ebb and flow of schooling, teaching, and showing our horses.

But the end of the evening was ours, barring any classes under the lights. When all the work was done, we'd take our beer and wine and find a grassy spot and lie on it and look at the stars. There in the warm, silky dark of Florida's spring we argued the relative merits of *The Tempest* versus *A Midsummer Night's Dream*, the relative durability of the Thoroughbred versus the Hanoverian or the Irish Draught, and the problems we faced as parents and by-products of failed relationships. All around us, lightning bugs flickered on and off and other unidentified insects made noises like chainsaws and sewing machines.

Ominously summer-like sounds. They couldn't but evoke the leaving season just ahead, when the winter series would end and we would all separate and take individual roads to other homes. I pretended it wasn't so, lived just for the moment, followed my lover into the blissful air conditioning of his rooms, ate supper, and went to bed, just like folks. We spent a beautiful week in perfect love, harmony, and denial. Oh, yeah. It was 'way too good to last.

The insistent, frightening jangle of the phone woke us at about 3 a.m. after a very long day. Cursing, Colin fumbled, found it, knocked it on the floor, cursed again, found the receiver, mumbled *hello* into it. Shot me a look of mingled shock, worry, and furtive guilt that told me better than words who was on the other end. I wrapped myself in the sheet and walked unsteadily into the living room, where I lowered myself onto the sofa in a sort of daze.

'She wants to bring Bryan and Sam over and meet me in Camden', he said, finally appearing in the doorway. 'She wants to try again. They miss me...'

Is sex sweetest when it's new and illicit, or when it's steady and known? Or is it sweetest when you're saying goodbye? People argue about this all the time, but I've nothing new to add. All I know about love is that Goodbye is written into the first Hello.

I left at dawn and wept myself dry in Jake's stall, wrapped in his cooler. Then I pulled myself together, went to the rig to collect Camille, and took the shuttle to the airport with her. She was headed back to Connecticut and her school, where she would pack her belongings and make her peace. She was armed with promises extracted from Ivory and me that she could come back to help drive the rig home as soon as she was sorted out. Thanks to my mother, Josie had agreed to the idea. I wept some more, watching my daughter – almost a woman now, even with the maroon-and-polka-dot hair – walk gracefully away from me and disappear through the security check with a cheery wave.

We are always saying goodbye, always letting go. Of love, of dreams, of horses, of children. *'Why that's my dainty Ariel! I shall miss thee; but yet thou shalt have freedom.'* I said it to the air, to them all, or maybe to my own captive soul, and got back on the shuttle. Back to my horses and their needs.

Sometimes this old life is its very own Trail of Tears.

# TEN

*O! For a horse with wings!*
-William Shakespeare, ***Cymbeline***

Michael Draper had three horses in the big featured Grand Prix at the end of the week, Hilary Knowlton had shipped back from Georgia with two, and I was the commentator. I prayed fervently that they wouldn't win, and Hilary didn't. But Michael did.

With my thoughts in a seething turmoil of fear, rage, and hurt, I did the post-win interview; mounted, as Sara and I had discussed. I sat on Jennie, pointed the mic, shook like a leaf, my thoughts twisted worse than a pretzel, thinking about his betrayal, about what I carried in my pocket. He wouldn't look at me, my old friend Michael Draper. I would ask about the big vertical with the whales and my mind would be saying *horse killer, horse killer, I should turn you the fuck in* and he would give this jerky smile and talk about the short stride between the oxer and the sharp turn to the combination and I would nod while my brain chanted *I trusted you looked up to you you were my hero you asshole my hero* and finally thank heaven it was over.

'Are you okay?' Sara asked. 'Your eyes are all red and wobbly. I thought you might *faint* or something.'

'I just hurt, Sara.'

'Of *course*. Go home and get some *rest*, will you? We *need* you.'

I gave Jennie to Santé and tried to lie down in the rig, but couldn't rest. I went to the barn and sat by my stalls but even the sight and smell of my horses couldn't calm me down. I paced and turned with my heart racing and my throat all closed and tight. *'I never hurt you'*, I said to the air. Romeo to Tybalt, in pain. The pain of enmity, the pain of no reconciliation. *'You drew your sword upon me without cause, but I bespake you fair and hurt you not'*. Then finally I got up and went to the stalls where I knew I would find Michael Draper, getting the big horses wrapped and ready to ship back to Palm Beach. He saw me coming and tried to go the other way, but I caught up to him.

''Chelle!' he said, trying to look surprised and happy. 'Hey, that was a nice interview there, you know you really do great as a commentator.' His eyes were shifty, looking for an escape.

And I just stared at him. Dry. I could not think of a single thing to say, except 'Why, Michael?'

'I don't know what you mean,' he said stiffly.

'I was never a threat to you. I never did or said anything that wasn't fair about you. Michael, I'm giving you a chance to tell me something, to explain it to me.'

The false smile slipped. I could see the nerve jumping in his temple. See the color coming into his face. 'I think you need to get some rest, 'Chelle,' he said, his face stony. 'You're talking crazy stuff.'

'You stupid *shithead*,' I said. I fished around in my jacket pocket and took out the cassette I'd been carrying with me. 'I got you on tape, Michael. I know it was you and Hilary. *Hilary*. For what? What did I ever do to you?' I let this sink in. Watched the color drain from my former hero's face, leave it chalky. 'I can take you down anytime I want,' I said quietly. 'There's more where these came from.' I slapped the tape on a bale of hay. And without another word, I walked away and left him staring after me, still as a marble statue.

After the big feature, the grounds began to empty. The weather was getting hotter; the rains would come soon; and a whole season up north beckoned. Deals were struck as horses changed hands, stalls emptied, ramps thumped and clattered, belongings, grooms, and horses disappeared into vans, people waved and hugged and swore eternal devotion, vans growled to life and ground their way off the grounds, out to the highway, on to the next adventure.

We figured we might as well stick around for the last show to give our greenies a little more experience, and give Ivory a little more time in case something in the legal realm could be settled. I got back on Jake and Jennie one day, then tried Dancing Fool the following, after cravenly letting Ivory tell Colin I was taking her back. I took a lot of painkillers first. Riding still wasn't pleasant, but I figured I could live through it.

After my first day back in the show ring, I wasn't so sure. I was in tears of pain by the end of my second class, which should have been an easy one, since it was Jennie. I could barely dismount. Harry met me at the out gate, got Cam to take Jennie from me, and dragged me over to a corner.

'What are you, stupid?' he demanded. 'You think a ball of tape and a bunch of drugs is gonna keep your body together?'

'Harry, c'mon,' I pleaded. 'It's the last week, I don't want to miss it.'

'You'd be better off to load up and get yourself home, babe. Take a little time and heal so's you can come back later and do more winning. Better winning. You're nothin' but a damn *passenger* up there.'

I smiled at him through my tears. 'Don't I remember you were the guy who rode that Grand Prix with a broken collarbone? I think I remember you had that horse Serpico and you were all…'

'That was different!'

'Why?'

'Cuz I'm a man. A woman shouldn't…'

'Oh, hell, Harry, you are the *worst* chauvinist I ever met!'

'And you're the worst little brat! Now *behave*, willya!'

But I couldn't. I had to have a place to work out my grief, my loss, my dreams, my soul. I had to ride.

By the time I got back to the barn after class number three I was throbbing everywhere, even in places that hadn't hurt before. I got a bottle of bute open and started to get some out for myself. Stupid, I know, but people do it. Santé came around the corner just then and grabbed it out of my hand.

'Don't you being doin' that shit! You'll rot your stomach out, you do that shit,' he said, furious.

'I am surrounded by mothers,' I complained. 'Between you and Harry…'

'Yeah, well you act like you need one, that's for sure,' Santé grumbled. 'And you don't know *nothin*' about mamas 'til you met mine.' With which unfathomable remark he stalked off to hide the bute from me, like I was a junkie or something.

I lay down on a stack of hay bales and grumbled mutinously to Spring about people who meddle in other people's lives. She cocked her head at me and panted cheerfully. And two hours later, I woke up, having slept through all the chores being done around me, and with Ivory and Santé staring down at me like I was an exhibit in the museum of natural history.

'You keep an eye on her,' said Santé, and turned to go home.

'Don't worry,' said Ivory. She put down her bag, pulled up two chairs, unloaded an opened bottle of Cab and two plastic wine glasses, served up, and offered me one.

'Better for you than Bute,' she said.

'Santé blabbed?' I staggered to my feet and resettled myself in a far more comfortable chair.

'Well, *yeah*. He knows I know that from bitter experience.'

'Your child is going to look like a bowling ball.'

'Prob'ly. But it'll be *my* bowling ball. Besides, Camille turned out all right, and you weren't even clean yet.'

'True.'

We sipped in silence for awhile and took in the nourishing sounds of horses munching hay, rustling bedding, and sighing in contentment.

'You know,' said Ivory after I'd safely consumed a glass, 'I've been thinking.'

'Ivory Gardener, this I've-been-thinking stuff could get scary.'

'Don't be a pain in the ass. *I've-been-thinking* that we do real well together. Better together than singly. We're like a really good team, you know?'

I looked at her suspiciously. 'Ive... are you about to propose to me? Because if you are, I gotta tell you, you've got the wrong equipment.'

'No, I am not proposing to you, fuckwit. I'm telling you that I am going to be your business partner.'

'Just like that? I thought I was going to think about it first.'

'Changed my mind. I talked to Jimmy about it, he says you got lots of room up there in the north. And your ma. She thinks it's a great idea. So does Harry. And I bet you haven't thought about it at all, you dumb mick.'

'Well, I... I mean it's been... um.'

'See?'

'You can't be my partner just like that. It's complicated. There's legal stuff. What if I say no?'

'You can't say no,' said Ivory bluntly. 'I need you. And you need me. What do you think?'

'I think I'm being railroaded.'

'Yeah,' Ivory smirked. 'We knew you would. Honest to God, 'Chelle, you're like fuckin' Rambo or someone. Anyway, listen up. A bigger lesson program. More horses to train. More help doing it. Working students. Maybe even some time off, with somebody covering. Santé'll come, too.'

'Where will we put his family?'

'We'll find them a little house somewhere. I mean it's not like y'all live in *igloos* or anything.'

'We'd need an indoor arena.'

'There are people who know how to build those. The technology exists.'

'But they're so expensive.'

'Well, you just signed that contract with Sara.'

'It won't build us an indoor.'

'You know, 'Chelley, after all this trial bullshit is done I'm still likely to have a lot of insurance money. The guy driving the car that hit us was drunk. There's a big case there. I figure I can use that money to set myself up somewhere and go back to work.'

'Oh my God. I see my whole life passing before my eyes.'

'It's called growth, honey.'

'You're serious about this.'

'Dead serious.

'You'd put your own money into it? You're sure?'

'Yeah, I'm sure. I don't want to do this alone anymore. I want to go in with somebody I like. And trust. We've got a good history, 'Chelle. You can keep me out of trouble and I can keep you in it. So don't hurt your brain thinking on it anymore, huh? Let's just plain old *commit*.'

She refilled the glasses and held hers out. I clinked it. We finished the bottle, made sure the horses were all snug, and wobbled back to the rig with our empties, Spring trotting along in front so we wouldn't get lost.

'You know,' I said, drawing a deep breath of hot air into my lungs, 'I'm ready to go home.'

'Me, too.'

'It's getting too damn hot down here.'

'That's for sure.'

'I could use a break. Bet you could, too.'

'Jimmy still as cute as he was?'

'Cuter. But he's way too nice for you.'

'Him and me'll be the judge of that... *partner*,' she said, and laughed her throaty laugh. 'How long a drive?'

'Three days, if we don't stop much.'

'Let's don't stop much.'


Pain or no, at the end of the last week of the series I rode Dancing Fool and Jake over the big fences under the lights. Dancing Fool went in the biggest Intermediate class she'd tried to date, like a graduation ceremony for all she'd been pointed for all spring. And I rode Jake in our first and his last Grand Prix.

Of course, all the big competitors had already taken their horses north or east. Of course my assorted self-appointed mothers thought I was insane. Of course nobody thought I was fit enough or Jake big enough or Dancing Fool sane enough to be ridden by a partial cripple.

Surprisingly, it was Harry who came through for me in the end. He fended everybody else off, consigned the combined voices of Ivory, Santé, Gerry, Diane, George and anybody else who had an opinion to silence with a few choice and authoritative words, spirited me off to his tack room, and demanded I take my shirt off.

'Harry!' I exclaimed. 'I never thought you'd ask!'

'Shut up and sit down,' he commanded. 'Here, take these.' He handed me two anonymous-looking tablets.

'What are these?'

'Don't ask. Just swallow. Jesus, you are one wiry little bitch. Don't you ever eat?'

He wrapped everything that was injured in tight purple stretch bandages until I felt completely unable to breathe.

'You cut off my circulation,' I complained, when he'd helped me back into my shirt. 'I can hardly move.'

'Good. Maybe you'll live through it,' he said. 'Now. *Think*, for chrissake. And don't take advice from anyone, hear? You know how to do this. Just listen to your gut and your horses.' Then he added gruffly, 'Good luck,' and gave me a walloping great kiss.

In her class, Dancing Fool responded to me like an angel, like a goddess of flight, and flew over the fences and spun through the turns and leapt in the air with one ear pointed at the fences and the other listening to me and she won the class with the conviction of a confirmed professional jumper. Ivory shouted and pounded the rail with her crutch, totally ecstatic. I punched holes in the sky with my good arm and laughed and cried. The crowd gave a big shout that sent the mare airborne and almost got me launched. It was worth every moment of pain, every hour of self-doubt, every embarrassing mistake, every mile of the long, slow schooling that got us here. When I got off her beautiful back, I was so high I could have done the course again, without a horse.

But there was still the matter of this Grand Prix, coming right up.

Did I say it was a smaller one? Even a small Grand Prix is huge. The fences are over 5 feet high and can be even wider than that. The distances between fences are longer, the turns to get to them are tighter. There have been other little horses that have succeeded in them. Way back in the 60's there were two half-bred Connemaras – Dundrum in Ireland and Stroller in Britain – who were sensations on the International circuit. They were so small you could barely see them approaching the fences – just their pointy little ears on the other side. But wow, could they jump.

The courses have changed since then. They're even bigger, more demanding, more technical. Smaller horses can get the job done sometimes, but the courses favor the large and powerful.

When I went out to walk the course, I was so ill with nerves that I could hardly walk straight. I told myself it wasn't that much bigger than the courses I rode every day, but it didn't work. The whole thing looked monumental. I walked the jumps, the turns, the distances with all the other riders in a daze: where we'd need to gun the engines, where we could cut a corner, where we'd need to adjust. Mostly for Jake it was going to be forward, forward, forward, and total balance on the turns. He'd never meet the distances otherwise, and there wasn't much latitude for adding strides without dropping rails. I hoped I knew what I was doing. I wondered if maybe I should scratch. If maybe I was asking too much. If maybe this was all a big ego-bound mistake. If my daughter would be an orphan. I walked the course a second time. Then a third.

Then I walked out of the arena and found my beautiful little horse stalking around the warm-up ring with Santé, every inch an athlete, at the absolute fittest and healthiest he would ever be. I took the reins from Santé and let him toss me into the saddle. I warmed my bay pal up carefully, getting into the zone, the partnership, the alignment of the million subtle sensations and signals that make up the conversation a horse and rider have together.

The loudspeaker crackled our number. We trotted into the arena and picked up a springy gallop, I settled into my horse's rhythm, and rode Jake to the first fence. He pulled me to it eagerly, sprang into the air like a small jet, landed, turned, galloped on. I rode him passionately, tearfully, thankfully. I loved every striped rail that came up between his little ears, I kicked and called to him '*Git, JAKE!*' for the long ones, I felt him turn under me like a Ferrari, like a Lamborghini, his bay neck arched in front of my hands, his muscular body surging between my legs while we made poetry, made a dance, out of running and jumping and turning and leaping and galloping to the drumming thunder of his hooves, of our hearts, of our breath. Everything that I am, that I have become, all due to

Jake, to Jennie, to The Auld Sow. The fences were as tall as my little bay horse, so broad that sometimes I felt we were airborne for days. He didn't care, he leapt, he soared, he surged, he spun, and did it again. He had a double clear, and because he was small and could turn so fast, in so little space, he shaved the time to a nub. And he won.

But he didn't try to buck me off in our victory round, this time. He didn't feel like he could do it all again. I had found Jake's limit, and asked for every ounce he had to give. And he gave it, without question, enthusiastically, just as he had always given me everything I asked. And I laughed and cried and told him all those people were cheering just for him, and he arched his neck and snorted. He knew he was The Man without me telling him.

When he trotted out of the arena we were mobbed by the other riders, all our friends, and a few strangers, too. Harry crowing like he'd laid an egg. Diane swearing she'd given the class to us on purpose. Tommy and Craig crooning over Jake and feeding him bits of carrots while he walked. Darcy positively squeaking. Gerry announcing his intention to break out the champagne. George spinning Darcy around in a dance. The Rev quoting appropriate Shakespearean passages while Beverly clapped. My mom timidly patting Jake, then throwing her arms around his sweaty neck. Ivory thumping me and Jake with equal enthusiasm and loudly pointing out to everybody that scaredy old 'Chelley wasn't even throwing up yet, what had God wrought. Finally Santé managed to lead Jake away from his fan club for a quiet cooling walk and a good medicinal soak for his tired body and legs. I watched him, concern, pride, and love washing over me in equal measure.

'No,' said Ivory to my worry. 'You haven't damaged him any, he'll be fine. But you've found his limit for sure, 'Chelle honey. What he just did he did on sheer will and guts. For you.'

'Maybe I shouldn't have asked him for it.'

'Sure, you should! Look at the little sucker, smug as a cat with a canary. Just don't ever ask it again, is all.'

And that is the epitome of the horseman's art, really: to know that your horse is so trusting and courageous and obedient that it would jump off a cliff if you asked it to; then never ask. Because if you do, you betray him.

We had a hell of a wild and wonderful party at Gerry's place to celebrate the successes of the two bays. We were royalty, Dancing Fool and Jake and I, dancing in the stars, dancing magic. In that one shining moment I could have been struck by lightning and died happy.

At the height of the party I dialed Camille, put her on speaker phone, officially announced Jake's retirement from the big fences, and said I intended to turn him over to my daughter as a schoolmaster after a few months of solid rest and grazing in our hilly New Hampshire pastures. I figured this would render her stunned and breathless when she heard it, and turn her face about the color of her hair. The latter may have been true; not the former. Her squeal of delight nearly deafened all present and everybody laughed uproariously and cheered and clapped and stomped and shouted their congratulations and I finally added my voice to the pandemonium and told Camille I'd call in the morning and hung up with my ears ringing just like they did after I sat in front of the speakers at a Grateful Dead concert in another life in Cleveland.

Much later, when the hubbub had died down and I'd gone back to the rig leaving Ivory to queen it over the last of the die-hard party animals, somebody's fist banged a tattoo on my door. I opened it to Colin Rutherford.

'Hey-*hey*!' I exclaimed with all the bonhomie I could muster, given the sick twisting of my gut. 'Did you come to celebrate with me? Wasn't Jake just so cool you could hardly stand it? I think it was your good work that turned that hussy Dancing Fool around. I never knew she could go so well...' I ran out of breath. I stopped.

'I've come to say goodbye, 'Chelle, actually.'

'Goodbye!' All my energy deflated. My shock and consternation must have showed, because he winced.

'Yeh. We've done what we intended here. Time to move the horses to Southern Pines to get ready for the summer season. My... um... Saundra and the boys will... um... meet me there. You know.'

'Oh. So. It's like... Goodbye.'

'For now. Yeh. But I mean, if you... you know.'

'Yeah. Come by Southern Pines, or whatever. I do have friends there. Actually. So, you know...' I shrugged.

While I watched and tried to think of what to say he scribbled something on the back of a card and handed it to me. 'This is my new address. Now for God's sake don't throw it away, will you?'

In spite of myself, I smiled. 'Promise.'

'Well...' he put his lovely arms around me.

'Careful...'

'Still hurt?'

'Yeah.'

'You shouldn't be riding.'

'I know.'

'You're impossible. But you kicked arse tonight. And by the way, Dancing Fool goes much better for you than she ever did for me.'

He held my sore places gently and kissed me lingeringly, and he tasted so good, and smelled so warm. And then he left and I just sat in my rig and cried for awhile, *a conduit... evermore show'ring*, like Juliet. Only I was supposed to be a mature adult, and this was not the end of a tragedy. Just the shredding of my stupid broken heart.

An hour later Ivory came in and sat wearily on her bed. 'I just got a call from Janna Desmarchais,' she said. 'Winston died this morning without ever regaining consciousness.'

'Oh, Ive,' I said helplessly. 'I'm so sorry.'

'Don't be, doll. He was a scumbag.' And she burst into tears. I never really knew whether they were grief, or relief, or both. I don't think Ivory knew, either.

Winston's death had the effect of a plug being removed from a drain. More men and more suits arrived almost immediately, and closeted themselves with Craig. Ivory talked to them for a long time, with Guy Carmouche at her side. I talked to them for a shorter time, all by myself. And then Santé went and talked to them longer than anybody else. I never mentioned Michael Draper, or Hilary Knowlton. I never asked Ivory or Santé if they did. I don't know who else the feds talked to. I didn't want to. But it seemed like a whole parade of people all over the industry suddenly had something to offer that they'd never had the nerve to voice before. And I didn't ask about that, either.

By the end of several days, rumors were flying fast among those of us who were still on the grounds. One was that Michael Draper had been taken in for questioning. Another was that he'd been arrested. And still others maintained it was all a mistake, it wasn't Michael at all, but some other rider who'd been arrested.

But it was Michael, our hero Michael who had killed a horse and betrayed a friend and God knows what-all. He was read his rights and taken away in hand-cuffs while TV cameras rolled and his family stood by with grief and shock etched on their faces and even if there were deals to be made – as surely there would be - we would not be seeing him on some beautiful horse, dancing on the roof of the world again for a long, long time. *But why?* people wondered. *Why?* The general emotion was one of disbelief and horror. And among others, there was satisfaction to see that justice was being done, that the guilty would be punished, that certain scores would be settled.

I was not among the latter. In the end, I was among those who wept.

The good news was that Ivory was cleared, and could go home – her new northern home - as planned. We promised to testify as required. They assured us that they already knew where to find us.

While I was pleased for Ivory, I still felt ill and sad. I wished that none of this had ever happened, and that my burgeoning career had not been boosted so high on somebody else's misfortune.

But maybe that's the way it always is. An actor friend once told me that you only ever get roles because somebody else wasn't available. The thought didn't make me feel better, exactly, but it wasn't so unlike Harry Daly's assessment of fortune, all those weeks ago.

The showgrounds were empty now but for us, nothing left but mud and echoes and tent roofs flapping in the breeze, sounding lonesome. We'd said all our goodbyes – *goodbye, goodbye* - and talked about the future, as we must, because there is always a tomorrow, always another show further up the road, new jumps to be jumped, new crowds to cheer, new ribbons and glory to be earned, new promising horses to discover. Virginia in the spring for some, maybe Devon for the big guns, a crowded circuit in Southern New England, the Vermont Summmer Series, all stretching in front of us. And maybe Florida again, next winter. Paths connecting and separating, weaving in and out to make the rich tapestry that is life and horses.

As I fed my buddies on our last morning in Florida I heard footsteps in the aisle and turned to see Hilary Knowlton standing there in acute discomfort.

'I came to say I'm sorry,' she said. 'I thought… it was supposed to be a prank, you know. You were so perfect. Too perfect. Shooting your mouth off. Getting all that attention. All those rides. It wasn't fair. I worked for Harry for two years. It should have been… I thought Michael was… that he just wanted to…' she stared at the ground and traced a pattern with the toe of her boot, then looked up again. 'I didn't know. I am just… so sorry.'

She stood and looked at me and I looked back and thought of all the million things I had wanted to say – no, to shout – at her, these last weeks, about the humiliations and the hurts she had doled out so freely. But… enough. Enough is enough. 'Okay,' I said. 'I accept.' We shook hands. We wished each other well. And she left.

I continued to pack the contents of our tack stall, the paraphernalia of life with horses on the road – tack, blankets, buckets, equipment, hay, medications, liniments, ribbons, and a million layered experiences that took up no physical space at all, anymore. Even if our departure was somewhat delayed by Winston's death and the accompanying legalities, I figured we might be well on the road and unreachable a vital few hours before the media figured out where we were and started to hound us about the latest chapter in the whole sorry can of worms that opened in a fatal van wreck. I hoped the public feeding frenzy might die down a bit by the time we got home. I thought maybe we'd dawdle a little, after all, and give ourselves half a chance at anonymity.

We sent one batch of horses home on a commercial van, Ivory supervising the loading from her crutches and driving everybody insane with her attentions and demands for perfection in the settling of the beasts. I'm sure she was thinking of the wreck, although she wouldn't admit it. We all were. We didn't bring it up since she didn't; just assured her that everything would be all right and got our heads snapped off in return. Santé rode with them, buoyed by the idea of being re-united with Heavensent and Morning Glory; and by the promise of a permanent home for himself and his family, even if it was to be 'at the north pole', as his wife put it.

Late that night, I picked Camille up at the bus station. She climbed into the dark cab without a word, pushed Spring over, and parked a heavy thermos on the dash. We rumbled silently back to the grounds with the rhythm of changing gears and the engine's growl punctuating the narrow dance of headlight beams on the curves and hollows of the road.

'I've been thinking of a perfect name for my colt', my daughter said into the darkness after a couple of miles.

'You've got a colt?'

'I will have. When The Auld Sow foals.'

'What if I want to sell it?'

'You can't. It's mine, and you can't ever sell it. Papers and all. Mine. You always said I could have one of The Auld Sow's foals, and you never kept your promise. And she's, like, *ancient*. So this one's mine.'

'Okay.'

'Promise?'

'Yeah.'

'I have the perfect name.'

'What's that?'

'Phoenix. You know, after that bird that rises out of the ashes?'

'Yeah, I know the one.'

'It's like a metaphor.'

'Got it. You going to have your own farm prefix?'

'I thought maybe I could use yours. Like we could share it. Like we could be, you know, partners.'

'*Partners?*'

'Yeah. You know. Like you and Ivory. And me.'

'I guess I'd have to think about that. I guess it sort of depends.'

On what?' She shot me a look full of anxiety and suspicion. The anxiety surprised me. I'd taken the pinched quality of her expression as a combination of weariness and the hour.

'On how hot that coffee is,' I said.

Her lips twitched. When we got to the highway, she opened the thermos and portioned out its contents, steaming and bittersweet. But...

'Sorry, Camille. It's not hot enough. Deal's off.'

'*Ma-a-a-a, c'mon!*'

'But it's really good hazelnut. That shows you're trying.'

'So c'mon!' she said. 'Are we partners?'

'You'll graduate on time?'

'I swear.'

'Even if it's the local public school?'

'Totally.'

'You won't get pitched out on your ass?'

'I'll try.'

'You and Jake gonna take the year-end Junior Jumpers?'

'*Ma-a-a.* Come *on.*'

'Yeah. Partners.' I raised my hand and we exchanged a high five and a grin.

We loaded Jake, Jennie, Dancing Fool, and Ottawa in a grey predawn, by the reflected rain-puddled lights of the tent aisle. Mud squelched under our feet and water droplets twinkled on the roofs and the grass. Breath blew little clouds. Hooves thumped hollowly up the rig's ramp. We settled the horses into their stalls, clipped chains to their halters, bolted the protective breast bars, and tied hay nets within easy reach. I patted their soft necks and kissed their silky noses and told them all the old things we always tell our horses, about how good they are, how much I loved them, how soon we'd be where we were going. By these small ceremonies we give shape to our lives. By these small prayers we keep chaos at bay.

Camille helped Ivory clamber heavily into the cab, crutches, growing belly, and all. With Spring squashed happily between us we drove slowly out of the silent grounds. *Goodbye, goodbye.* All that living. All those jumps jumped. All that love. Shadows, now. All gone away, like geese winging north with new songs to sing. *Goodbye*.

'I got the coffee,' Ivory said, and poured us cups that steamed the windshield to opacity. Camille choked on hers.

'*Jeez*, Ive, this is too fuckin' *hot*,' she complained.

'Just right,' corrected Ivory. 'You got to know this about coffee, you want to travel with us, girlfriend. It's not hot enough unless it cauterizes your vocal chords.'

'Or strong enough unless it corrodes a spoon,' I added.

'Right. So what've we got for music? And none of your Shakespeare, 'Chelle, hear?'

'Aw, c'mon, Ive. I got *The Tempest. You look, my son in a bemus'd sort, as if you were afraid...*'

'No, 'Chelle! *No-o-o-o*, 'Chelley...'

'*...Be cheerful, sir! Our revels now are ended...*'

'I'm not listening, 'Chelley! Hear, I'm singing a song, c'mon and sing, Camille, *la la la la...*'

'*These actors, as I foretold you...*'

'Shut up! Shut up! I don't want to hear it! Well... maybe not 'til Georgia, anyway, huh?'

'You got a better idea?'

'Yeah. Check it out. The Beatles *Anthology Three*!' She held it up triumphantly.

Camille laughed derisively. 'That's not *music*,' she started, but Ivory stared her into silence.

'You planning on hitch-hiking north, honey?' she crooned. 'Now here's the rule. *I* pick the music. That's cuz we *know* you have taste up your butt and your mama is obsessed with dead white poets. But,' she added magnanimously, 'y'all can each have *one pick* between here and Maryland. Fair enough?'

I agreed. Camille sulked. Ivory plugged in the disc. She and I sang to it raucously, doing all the harmonies. We laughed over *Obladi* and cried about the two of us going nowhere. When I said, 'take it, Phil,' and Ivory sang on, Camille looked at us in disgust.

'You guys are *sick*,' she announced.

But by Tryon, she was singing and laughing like one of the gang. She had a great ear for harmony, too.